The Story of
Jo

First published in 2018 by Sinful Press.
www.sinfulpress.co.uk
Copyright © 2018 Justine Elyot
Cover design by Studioenp

A CIP catalogue record for this book is available from the British Library

ISBN-13: 978-1-910908-30-3

The Story of
Jo

Justine Elyot

SINFUL PRESS

Contents

Part One: Un Coup de Foudre

Chapter One	9
Chapter Two	16
Chapter Three	26
Chapter Four	45
Chapter Five	63

Part Two: Ensemble

Chapter Six	69
Chapter Seven	85
Chapter Eight	97
Chapter Nine	102
Chapter Ten	121

Part Three: L'Étranger

Chapter Eleven	131
Chapter Twelve	139
Chapter Thirteen	151
Chapter Fourteen	168
Chapter Fifteen	184

Part Four: Rapprochement

Chapter Sixteen	191
Chapter Seventeen	196
Chapter Eighteen	199
Chapter Nineteen	217
Chapter Twenty	224
Chapter Twenty One	245

Part Five: Menagerie

Chapter Twenty Two   255
Chapter Twenty Three   268
Chapter Twenty Four   284
Chapter Twenty Five   298

About the Author

Un Coup de Foudre

Chapter One

What does the J stand for?"

"I'm sorry?"

"Emmett J Marlow." I stabbed my forefinger at the name on his lanyard. "What's the J?"

He twisted the laminated card until he could read it for himself.

"No idea," he said. "I don't have a middle name. Clerical error, I guess."

"Oh. Well, it adds a certain gravitas, I suppose. Or maybe a Hollywood vibe."

God, I hated icebreakers. And conferences. And workshops. And group assignments. All of it, it was all hateful, but icebreakers were the absolute worst. What was wrong with ice anyway? Gin and tonics would be nasty without it, and it kept the sea levels down. Why did it have to be broken?

"Mm," he said. "If we're going to pursue the name theme, what's Jo short for, then? Joanne? Jolene? Johannesburg?"

"Actually," I said with my usual reluctance, "it's Josephine."

He smirked.

"Not tonight, Josephine?" he said.

"Believe me, you are *not* the first."

"No, I bet." He had a nice smile, though, and my tight-screwed nerves loosened a bit under its influence. When we'd first turned to each other, at the instruction to form pairs, I hadn't been confident of my choice. First of all, I'd have preferred a woman, and second of all, he looked like a pale, red-haired Genghis Khan about to give the order to slaughter. I'd always been intimidated by high cheekbones, my own being somewhere down near my jaw, but his were like cliff edges with a lightly freckled chalk face sheering down beneath them.

This smiling was a good development, though, and I showed my approval by mirroring it.

Crack! There went that ice.

"Imagine me at school," I said. "Surrounded by Sophies and Katies and Emilys and other ees, and there's me, Josephine. Ugh. It's an elderly auntie name."

"There are plenty of elderly aunt Sophies and Katies," he said. "And besides, you've no room to moan. My name's *Emmett*."

I laughed, not at his name, but at his disgusted intonation.

"Emmett's nice, though," I said. "It's cool."

"Cool, is it? Everyone always thought I must be American. I was so jealous of all the Bens and Joshes. Who all called me Emma."

"Ah, no, we've only gone and bonded. I always try my best not to, just to piss off the course director."

"*Just* to piss off the course director?" His eyes gleamed. Green. Lovely green eyes. "Your name should be Mary. Mary,

Mary, quite contrary."

"I'm a crap gardener, though. No silver bells or cockle shells on my patch." God, why did I have this compulsion to make lame jokes about everything? I was going to alienate this alien-looking man.

"Why do you feel the need to sabotage the course director's work?" The gentle rebuke in the words undid me, and I was left speechless. This wasn't what you did at an icebreaker. You huddled together and bitched about how much you hated this kind of thing. It was obligatory. You didn't...this was wrong. This wasn't fair!

"Oh, I don't mean...it isn't personal, of course, but you know. *Icebreakers.*"

The look I gave him might have been a plea. *Take me back to safer ground. Say something about the bad coffee or what productive things you could be doing if you weren't here.*

"They aren't inherently evil," he said. "They're only intended to put you at your ease." His smile was different now, and I felt he was disappointed in me. I wanted to cry. God. Why? This was crazy.

"You're..." My hands were shaking. I felt like a five-year-old unjustly accused of fighting in the playground. I was too scared and outraged to get the words out. "Right," I finished. "No, they aren't evil. No. You're right."

A bell sounded from the front desk and we all turned our chairs back to face the course director.

One by one, each course participant trotted out the three things they'd learned about their partner. *Jim goes sailing in his spare time. Sandra has three grandchildren. Mick once met David Bowie at an Esso garage.*

It wasn't until the spotlight shone on me that I realised I'd learned bugger all about Emmett.

"Er, he doesn't have a middle name. And…" I glanced at his lanyard, desperate for more clues. "He works for PlayCorp." Very poor, everyone already knew that. "And…" Fuck it, I was going to have to make something up. "And he lives on a houseboat."

A murmur of interest rippled through the horseshoe-shaped group, a kind of polite Mexican wave. I kept my eyes severely away from Emmett, but in my peripheral vision I saw that his knuckles were white on the desk.

"Thank you," said the course director. "And what can you tell us about Jo, Emmett?"

"Jo hates it when people deviate from the script," he said, and I gasped, staring at the freakishly insightful bastard. "She likes to think of herself as rebellious and iconoclastic, but actually she is very rule-bound and respectful of authority. Her comfort zone is quite small, and she's never learned to operate outside it."

"Jesus!" I exclaimed.

"That's not what the J stands for," he said, winking at me.

I looked sharply away, burning from the crown of my head down.

"Okayyy," said the course director, only slightly less uncomfortable than I was. "And turning now to…Mohammed. Can you tell us three interesting facts about Laura?"

At lunch, the woman in the queue behind me—Aisha, I think—commiserated with me on my choice of partner.

"What he said was very rude," she said, confidentially low, as we both looked daggers at an oblivious Emmett, lurking by the coffee dispenser. "It was too personal. Mike only asked for interesting facts, not psychoanalysis."

"Right," I said, almost tearfully grateful for her support. I'd felt absolutely shattered ever since; the course materials had flown way over my head all morning.

"Come with me and Shirley and Laura for the group session this afternoon," she offered. "We'll look after you. And don't take what he said to heart. He was just showing off."

I smiled properly, liking her explanation. Showing off. If my inner five-year-old was an incoherent ball of rage, his was a needy little teacher's pet. Ha.

I was successful in avoiding him for the duration of lunch and the afternoon session, but after the plenary, we were all herded into the hotel bar for 'group feedback', more popularly known as coffee and biscuits.

I was trying to decide between a custard cream or a non-chocolate hobnob when he squeezed in beside me at the long buffet table, rattling the ranks of ugly green coffee cups.

"I only eat jaffa cakes," he said. He reached for a coffee with ridiculously long fingers.

"What, ever?" I said, cursing myself for responding before the words were even out.

"No, at these things. Jaffa cakes or nothing."

"Custard creams are beneath you, are they?" I said, taking a defiant bite of one. I instantly regretted it. Now I'd have crumbs in my mouth, which would inhibit any devastating comeback I might want to make.

"Exactly," he said. "They don't meet my exacting standards."

I struggled with my unwanted mouthful of custard cream, my face heating as I became aware that he was watching me chomp with detached interest.

"Look how long they take to get down, for one thing," he remarked as I swallowed. "A jaffa cake would be gone by now."

"Yeah, well…thanks for the biscuit chat," I said, casting desperately about the room for an escape route. Where the hell was Aisha? "But…"

"I'm sorry for what I said about you in there," he said. "I seem to have upset you."

"Well, what do you expect?" In my outrage, I slopped a bit of coffee into the saucer.

"I'd like to make it up to you," he said.

"Have a packet of jaffa cakes sent over to my office," I said, spotting Aisha at last and preparing for a hundred-yard dash with an almost full coffee cup and a half-eaten custard cream.

"Oh, no, that won't do," he said, and I turned back to him, something in me snagged by his strangely steely tone. He saw the snagging and smiled gently. I'd never seen a more sinister expression in my life. "I was thinking more of taking you out for dinner."

Here it was, on a plate: the perfect revenge. All I had to do was say no. I didn't even need to add a cutting remark. A simple negative would provide ample compensation for the red ears and churning stomach I'd suffered at his hands.

I drew myself up to my full height, which was still a lot less than his, fixed him with my iciest glare and said, "Yeah, why not?"

His lip curled. Lovely lips, so full and curvy.

"Excellent," he said. "Well, I don't particularly want to sit here talking about creative leadership. Shall we leave?"

"What—now?"

"Yes. Seize the moment. There's quite a good sushi place

down the road."

"It's early for dinner."

"Do you care? That lunch was pathetic; hardly enough for six, let alone twenty-six."

He had a point.

I laughed and put down my undrunk coffee.

"OK," I said. "But no more of that Sherlock Holmes bullshit. Promise me."

"I promise."

Chapter Two

O ut on the high street, with the wide open space and the shifting soundscape, I felt giddily free, as if Emmett had sprung me from jail. I almost wanted to spread my arms and spin around. The illicit joy of sloping off from a tedious work obligation was not one I was particularly familiar with. Emmett was right about that. In fact, everything he'd said about me had been right, but I didn't want to admit it just yet.

"So," I said, once we were hidden away in our restaurant booth, waiting for sake and salmon rolls. "Why would you want to spend time with someone you were so scathing about?"

He sighed. "Was that scathing? It wasn't scathing. At least, it wasn't intended to be. Nothing I said about you was derogatory."

"Yes it was! You implied that I was...some petty loser."

"I did nothing of the kind." He raised his eyebrows at me, and it made a kind of shivery tingle run down my back.

"Well...didn't you?" Almost everything he said and did

seemed to score a direct hit on my capacity for articulate speech. He was draining the fight out of me, lip twitch by eyebrow hitch. I couldn't seem to defend myself against whatever it was he was using as a weapon.

"No, Josephine," he said. God, I hated my name, but when he said it… "None of those qualities were negative per se. You prefer a script rather than improvising—that's fine. It's not a flaw. People tend to be either spontaneous or planners, and you're a planner. Did I say that was a bad thing?"

"Well, I *am* a planner, but people always seem to prefer spontaneous types somehow. I wish I was one. I wish I could just do the first thing that came into my head…but I can't. I suppose spontaneity is associated with fun and sparkle; planners are plodders. It's not viewed as sexy."

"Spontaneous types, as you call them, often come a cropper. Their un-thought-out ideas result in a big mess for other people to clean up. That's not sexy at all."

"No." I smiled at him. I could get to like him, perhaps, with about a thousand caveats. But he wasn't forgiven yet. "Which are you?"

"I'm both," he said.

"Oh, that's not fair. You can't be both. You must be spontaneous," I said.

"Why do you say that?"

"Because…" I gestured at the restaurant around us. A waitress came to the table with sake.

"Because I've brought you here? Spontaneous sushi?"

"Oh, you know what I mean." The waitress poured the sake into glasses and left. "Leaving the course like that, before it was officially over. With a person you barely know."

"You did that too," he pointed out.

"But—it's not like me. It was your idea. I only did it because…"

"Why did you do it? Why did you come with me?"

His gentle, smiling gaze was like a snare. I found myself needing to backtrack, to run away from the quicksand that loomed so suddenly before me.

"I don't know," I said. It was an honest answer.

"You really don't?" he said, half-question, half-statement.

I shook my head.

"OK," he said softly, taking a sip of his drink.

His calmness flustered me. There was something so compelling in it; something I'd never experienced before.

"I mean, it's like you said. I never break the rules."

"You like rules," he said. "You like to know where you are, and they provide a map."

"Yeah, maybe. How did you get that, anyway? From what I said back there?"

"You had rules within rules for the icebreaker. Ways in which people were supposed to behave. They were supposed to be a little bit disaffected. When I wasn't, you were disproportionately upset. It ties in with the script thing, really."

"Rules are good, though," I said. "I mean, a civilised society needs them. I know it's uncool to think so. I know creative people are supposed to hate them and live like rebels, but I *am* creative. I just don't want to live in a squat or smoke weed. That's all right, isn't it? It doesn't make me some small-minded twat."

Another beautiful Emmett smile warmed me, or was that the alcohol?

"Not in the least," he said. "I would never describe you as small-minded. Or a twat. Obviously."

How would you describe me?

I almost fell into the trap. After all, it was his psychic-style intuitions of my character that had got me here in the first place. But I managed to swallow the question.

"Thanks," I said instead. "That's good to know."

But why was it good to know? Why did I care what he thought of me? Just under an hour ago I'd thought he was a complete bastard.

"Your rebellion consists of rejecting stereotypical beliefs about what makes people interesting," said Emmett. "I admire that."

Ugh, go away, warm squishy glow in the pit of my stomach. I don't need this man's approval. I don't need anyone's approval. Except I really do.

Something about Emmett was really hitting me where it hurt best. My inner people-pleaser was dying to impress him. *Give me an A*, sir*, it begged.

"It's like the whole introvert extrovert thing," I said eagerly. "Everyone's supposed to be extrovert because that's what society wants you to be, but Jesus Christ, the world would be intolerable if everyone was extrovert."

Emmett laughed. "Spoken like a passionate introvert," he said. "Which is a rather lovely thing to find."

I had no idea where to look, but it was important that Emmett didn't see how his words sent my heart into a flutterstorm. My face was on fire, though, which was surely a dead giveaway.

"Well, yes, definitely an introvert," I said. "And, er…" He was going to have to infer the rest. There was no way I was talking passion with this man. He'd have my favourite Kama Sutra position sussed by the end of the sentence. "Yeah.

Definitely."

"I agree with you on the necessity for rules," he said. "But only good ones. I mean, you don't subscribe to all those dating rules, do you? No holding hands until you've been up and down the canal bank three times while the moon is waxing gibbous and all that?"

"Waxing gibbous." I sighed happily. If I hadn't been before, I was now definitely romantically interested in Emmett 'J' Marlow.

"Yes," he said. "You know. Phases of the moon."

"I do. Sorry, no. Dating rules. No. Don't think you can apply them to all situations and all people. I don't like one size fits all models of thinking. That leads to bad rules, stupid rules. I mean, I'm not talking about the law, obviously, everyone has to not murder and that kind of thing, but…"

He rescued me from my verbal diarrhoea.

"I'm very glad to hear it. Not that you think murder should be universally frowned upon, but that you don't play games in your personal relationships. Neither do I."

"Don't…you?" The words leaked out. I could no longer tell whether I was exhilarated or scared or turned on. Was this how bungee-jumpers felt before taking the fateful step? Not that I'd ever, *ever* bungee-jump.

"No. If I like someone, I show it. No waiting three days to send a text. No strategic thinking. No half-measures. If I'm in, I'm in. What about you?"

I swallowed. "Don't you know?" I said, aiming to sound lightly teasing. It came out on the verge of tears.

"Well, I think I can guess," he said, putting his head to one side. He'd gone from strange-looking ginger bloke to the most attractive man in the world in the space of a few hours. It was

20

unfathomable. "But I want you to tell me."

"OK. Well, I'm the same. I hate that whole 'play or be played' mindset. I think people should just be honest."

He stretched his fingers across the tablecloth until their tips just touched mine. The surge that went through me could have powered the national grid.

"Yes, they should," he said. "What about open?"

I was shivering too much inside to answer the question.

"Open?"

"Yes. I sense that you're quite a private person. Quite secretive. A little clamshell. I want to open you."

There. It was on the table. Literally. His fingertips meshed with mine, the gentlest and sweetest of gestures, but a statement of intent nonetheless. Me joined with him. Togetherness. The thing I had feared for so long.

"Do you really?" I was helplessly at sea. "After all you said… making me sound so pathetic…"

"You're far from pathetic," he said sternly. "You're fascinating to me. There's a duality about you—the girl who craves control, yet craves also to give it up. I need to explore that. I need to explore *you*."

I let him twist and twine his fingers with mine, which trembled too much to resist anyway.

"That last thing you said," I whispered, my last-ditch attempt to derail this unstoppable train. "About not being able to operate outside my comfort zone."

"I'm not going to take you out of your comfort zone, Josephine," he said. "I'm just going to make it bigger."

Neither of us had much appetite for our sushi rolls when they came. Eating seemed such a prosaic activity when all I wanted to ingest was Emmett and his Emmettness.

We left them half-eaten and walked, without making a conscious decision to do so, down the street to the park. It was an early Friday evening in June, and the gates were open late. Runners pounded past us; knots of teenagers ate take-out burgers on the benches, their backpacks clinking with illicit bottles.

Emmett's light-coloured chinos and open-necked French blue shirt were made for the season, while I regretted my tight officey skirt and jacket, wishing I'd worn something fresh and floaty instead. But how could I have known that the dull course would end like this? My big bead necklace felt tight around my throat; I wanted to put a hand to it and pluck it off, sending the beads skittering across the path to entertain the squirrels.

"I was pulling your pigtails, you know," he said, putting an arm through mine and leading me off the path, over a rolling ridge of lawn that sloped down to the boating lake. "When I said all that stuff."

"Pulling my pigtails?" I put a hand up to my gradually disintegrating chignon.

"Yes, you know. Trying to get your attention." He turned and smiled broadly at my bemusement. "Because I fancied you."

"Oh! Did you?"

"From the moment our eyes met over an agenda and a name card," he said. "Except you didn't really notice me."

Had I really not noticed him? It seemed incredible now, looking at him through these rose-tinted eyes. He was blatantly perfect; tall and elegant with his striking hair and his fascinating face. How could *anyone* not be stricken with insatiable desire at first glance? What was wrong with me?

"So I sat next to you and hoped we'd be paired up for something," he continued. "Which we were."

"So in the time it took to get through the welcome and the course introduction, you'd decided you liked me?"

"I liked the way you were absent and present at the same time," he said. "You were saying hello and having those tedious little 'where do you work, what do you do' conversations, but your eyes were all over the place, anywhere but in the room. You were looking for an escape. You reminded me of a sad mermaid a long way from the sea."

"Did I?" I was astonished by all this. I'd had no idea my body language or the tiny things I let slip could give him such a detailed picture of me. "Excuse me, but where did you learn all this intense observational stuff? Are you some kind of, I don't know, forensic behaviour expert or something?"

He laughed. "You know I'm not. You know I work at PlayCorp."

"I'm hazy about what that actually entails," I said. "I mean, I know it's all internetty stuff, but…"

"Yes, internetty stuff," he said. "I make webby things happen. It's very interesting if you like that kind of thing, but if you don't…" He shrugged, spreading his palms. "It would bore you to death."

"So why were you on that course?" I asked. "Creative leadership? You must have a team to manage."

"Yeah," he said with the hint of a sigh. "I do. My boss thinks my interpersonal skills need some work. You'd probably agree with him."

I laughed.

"Probably."

We were at the edge of the lake now, on the side that had been turned into a concrete 'beach', sloping down into the murky water. On the other side, the pedaloes were being secured for the evening, their plastic swan necks bobbing up and down. Glinting ripples covered the surface of the lake, catching the low evening sun.

"Come on, mermaid," said Emmett, unlinking from me and bending to remove his shoes and socks. "Come into your element with me."

"Oh my God, are you serious?" I said, half-laughing as he took a step down towards the water's edge, tiny wavelets lapping against the fading yellow-painted shore.

"Come on," he repeated, in the water now, turning around to gesture me forwards. "It's not cold."

I dithered for a moment, but I was committed now, and still aching for Emmett's approval, so I kicked off my high-heeled courts and basked in the pleasure of their loss, standing on the sun-warmed concrete slope and stretching out my toes.

Emmett had rolled his trousers up to the knee and was wading through the dark waters, throwing back his head to get the last good rays of the sun on to his sun-starved face.

I pattered down the hill after him, wincing and squealing as the water washed around my feet.

"You bloody liar! It's freezing!"

He laughed and held out his hands.

"I'll keep you warm," he offered.

The temptation to run straight back out and shiver on the bank would ordinarily have won this battle, but Emmett's force was stronger and I found myself impelled towards him, the water climbing ticklishly up my ankles and beyond while I cut a path through draggling pondweed and floating cigarette butts.

"Why did you say it wasn't cold?"

"Why did you say I lived on a houseboat?"

I drew near enough for him to seize my hands and pull me

in close. Our shirt buttons clashed and cotton met cotton, the warmth and promise inside pressing tight.

"I don't know. It just popped into my head."

"Your first thought was about where I lived, and you placed me in your own element—water." He bent and whispered the words in my ear. "You wanted me, little mermaid. Don't try and tell me otherwise."

"I…"

He hushed my mouth with a kiss, sending the words back down inside me. I stood in the tight clasp of his arms and did what I never did. I opened up to him. I parted my lips and let him inside.

Hazily I wondered *Is this me?* Josephine Price, so hesitant, so reticent, standing here in a strange man's arms, knee deep in brackish boating lake water, kissing down the sun.

We stood there, lip to lip, tongue against tongue, hands sliding under jackets in heated exploration, until a gust of chill rippled the water around our legs. My cheeks and chin were sticky and sore with stubble burn; my lips were swollen and chapping. But I still wanted more.

"Actually," he said, pressing his forehead to mine, "I do live on a houseboat."

"Oh, you don't," I gasped.

"Well, I might and I might not," he said. "Do you want to find out?"

Chapter Three

He had an apartment in a gated complex; all sharp-angled balconies and tinted glass. There were tall vases of red roses in all the common areas; when you looked through the windows, everything was washed in a strange grey-green.

The carpets were thick and the tiles shone; the hushed air was heavy with wealth.

I wanted to mention it, but I knew it would be unspeakably gauche, so I didn't. I didn't want to reveal myself as a woman who dried her tights on a hanging thing over the bath and fought a constant battle with the mouldy corner in the bedroom. I was pretty sure Emmett didn't spend a lot of time spraying white vinegar on his walls.

His apartment was blindingly white and utterly anonymous. It could have been the show flat, with its understated dark furniture and its bland aesthetic touches—pebbles in a bowl on the breakfast bar, an abstract print over the fireplace.

"How long have you lived here?" I asked, as he pounced on my shoulders to remove my jacket.

"Not long," he said vaguely. "It's not mine. It belongs to the company."

"Oh." That explained the soullessness of it. "Don't you have your own place?"

"They pay for me to live here," he said. "Why would I want my own place?"

"I…don't know."

He bent and unstuck a strip of pondweed from my calf.

"We need a bath," he said, dangling it in front of my face. "Come on."

He went to turn on the taps, then came back to retrieve a bottle of wine and two glasses. I watched his back and shoulders as he uncorked the bottle, suddenly queasy with misgiving.

This was a bad idea, wasn't it? This strange apartment, this barely-known man, so seductive yet so weirdly other-worldly. I needed him to do something stupid; to put a foot wrong. It would comfort me to know that he was fallible.

When he turned back to me, holding up the glasses, I tried to wipe the doubt from my face, but he had seen it.

"What's wrong?" he asked.

I shook my head. "I've got nothing to wear."

"You don't need to wear anything in the bath," he said. "Or anywhere, for that matter. In fact, best that you don't."

I swallowed. "You're very, er, upfront."

"Haven't we agreed? Honesty. No games. Be honest with me, now. You're nervous, aren't you?"

He came closer, but slowly, carefully, as if he knew I was on the verge of bolting.

"Yes," I admitted. "This place…it's weird. It's not lived-in.

It gives me the creeps."

He handed me a glass.

"Come and see the bedroom," he said, smiling at my flinch. "No, not like that. It's the one room I really use. You won't think it's not been lived in."

I followed him around the corner of the kitchen area, into a large square room. The curtains were drawn over dual aspect floor-to-ceiling windows. In the gloom, I saw an unmade bed, shelves heaving with books and papers, some of which were strewn across the floor, a selection of laptops and computer equipment, and a snaking trip hazard of wires everywhere.

"You see," he said, taking a sip of his wine. "Lived in."

"Definitely," I said, laughing with relief. Emmett wasn't perfect after all.

He took my glass, put it down on a chest of drawers and hooked me against him for more kissing. Slowly I loosened, pulled back in by his warmth and his scent and the way we fitted into each other, like two pieces of a puzzle.

"Better see to that bath before we flood the place," he murmured.

In the bathroom, my coyness rose again, along with the steam.

Emmett, sleeves rolled up, swished his hand in the water to assess the temperature. He had lovely forearms. Some of his hair escaped from its product-stiffened subjugation, loose red tresses flopping over his beaded brow.

"Nice and warm," he said, turning to me and unbuttoning his shirt from the neck down. "Are you coming in?"

I chewed my lip, backing into the heated towel rail.

"You're shy," he said. "How sweet. Do you want me to undress you?"

"I've never done this before," I said.

"What? Undressed?"

"No. I mean, had a bath. With a man."

I didn't know how to make him understand. He was acting as though this was all perfectly routine when for me it was anything but. It was new and fragile; it was special. But perhaps he didn't feel the same. In fact, he probably just wanted a one night stand.

Yes. Why hadn't I considered this? It was obvious. I was just an easy pick-up; I'd be back in my mouldy bedroom tomorrow night, with slightly aching thighs, an incipient case of thrush and a notch for the bedpost.

I felt sick.

"I thought you'd like to," he said, his hand frozen halfway to the cabinet where a bottle of bath oil lay in wait. "Was I wrong?"

"No," I said. "But…I don't know. This all feels…upside down. Like, having a bath with someone should come after… oh, don't listen to me, I'm not making sense. Perhaps this is a mistake."

"No, no, no," he said, reaching for my elbow and pulling me towards him. "I've deviated from the script again, haven't I? Tell me what you want me to do. I thought the bath would continue the mermaid theme nicely, but I was probably overthinking it… Talk to me."

This wasn't the manner of a man who wanted to use me and discard me, was it? Or was I deluding myself?

"I want you…to…tell me how it's going to be. And if it has to end, tell me how and when. Otherwise I just can't…"

"I don't want to talk about endings." He stared at me, aghast. The cold feeling at my extremities began to thaw. "I don't have any kind of ending in mind." He held me close for a moment; my heart bumped against his chest. "You really are terribly insecure, aren't you?"

I nodded miserably. I hated myself. Why was I such a stupid killjoy? Couldn't I have gone along with things and just let go for once? Was I so afraid of simple enjoyment?

He held me at arm's length again, his eyes narrow and determined.

"All right then, Josephine Price. Here's the deal. I give you what you want, and you do the same for me. We do this for an indefinite period of time, but I have a minimum of six months in mind. It's a little early in the day for contracts, but if you want to make a more substantial commitment at the end of that time period, we can renegotiate then. Do those terms suit you?"

I nodded. I still felt like an idiot, but a warm idiot who wasn't about to throw up on Emmett's feet.

"There's a caveat," he said, after a pause during which vapours swirled between us like the visible harbingers of our mutual desire. "I don't think you'll object, unless I've read you completely wrong. But that's a possibility, faint as it is, so perhaps I should get it out into the open before you're fully invested."

"What is it?" I asked. There were beads of moisture on his face and neck. I wanted to kiss them off.

"I want complete control of you in the bedroom," he said.

The words shocked me to the core, and when I say 'core' I mean the area between my legs.

"Complete…control," I repeated breathily.

"Within limits," he amended. "Nothing that will damage or traumatise you, obviously. It's for your pleasure as much as mine." He laughed softly and ran a fingertip along my lips.

"The look on your face…I'd like to photograph it."

"Are you talking about, y'know, kinky stuff?"

"That's exactly what I'm talking about. You look shocked. Are you shocked?"

Was I?

"No," I said. "I mean…no."

"So you are that way inclined?" He raised an eyebrow.

"In theory," I said. "I've read…things. But never done… things."

"But you'd like to do…things?"

Could I admit that I'd dreamed of a man like Emmett, who would come and take possession of my body and my sexuality, relieving me of the irksome responsibility? I'd dreamed of a man who would be dominant yet sensitive, cruel but loving, with a resolutely filthy imagination.

Did he actually exist?

And did I have the courage to find out?

He pulled me in close again.

"Do you want me to take you in hand?" he asked, his voice low and sticky in my ear.

"God, yes," I shivered.

"Mmm," his appreciative response turned into a kiss, one of those long, slow, trembly types that only end when your legs start to give way. One hand slid slowly down my spine, moulding itself to the curve of my bottom and squeezing.

"You're still dressed," he accused, his mouth still close enough for his hot breath to whisper over my skin. Red wine, spearmint, salmon, a bitter coffee note further back.

"Sorry."

He quieted me with another kiss, then set his fingers to work on my shirt. With each unbuttoning came a kiss and fingertip-light exploration of what was uncovered. He peppered my skin with lip prints, his tongue darting out to lick the most succulent portions, his hands firm on my hips. When I tried to suck in my stomach, he shook his head and shot up a stern look from his semi-crouching position.

"No you don't," he said. "There's nothing to hide, and you can't hide anything from me anyway."

He stood straight again and slid my shirt down my arms, leaving me in skirt and bra on his bathmat. More kissing ensued, with more skin on skin now. I squashed my breasts into his freckled milky chest, sending my palms behind to explore his back, his spine, his shoulder blades. He reached down for my skirt zipper and edged it lower, tutting when he realised there was a hook and eye at the waistband too.

"Bloody Fort Knox down there," he muttered into the side of my neck. "But I'll get it off you if it kills me."

The hooks and eyes capitulated; the skirt lay in crumpled defeat around my ankles. I pressed my bare legs into the soft linen of his trousers. A hard lump forced itself against my pubic bone, indenting my lower stomach. I undulated gently around it, wondering if the two layers of fabric in between me and it would irritate or enhance the sensation for him.

He grabbed two rough handfuls of me, one on my arse and one at the scruff of my neck, and pushed his tongue hard into my willing throat. I clung on to his shoulders for dear life.

"Come on then," he panted, releasing my mouth. "Show me what's mine."

He didn't wait for me to unclip my bra, sliding his fingers inside the cups before I could reach round. He ran his palms over my nipples, which tightened and swelled against them until it hurt. Then he batted my fumbling hand away from the clips and did it himself, bending to suck each bud as it was exposed to his view.

While he sucked and flicked with the tip of his tongue, a hand plunged down the front of my knickers. My juices sluiced through his hot fingers as he found and took command of my clit. He had a touch that was both delicate and firm, and I felt myself growing beneath it until my whole being was centred between my thighs, turning me into nothing more than one giant pulsing mess of need.

He got to his knees, kissing a line down from my breasts, over my stomach, to my pubic bone. He pulled my knickers down until they settled at mid-thigh and pushed his tongue in there to join his hand. His breath steamed over my clit while he probed inside me with two, then three long fingers.

My legs trembled too much to continue this for much longer. I bent over him, my helpless fingers in his hair, wobbling and gasping.

"All right, get on your back," he whispered, retreating from my pussy to lay me down on the bathmat.

My legs appreciated their respite. He tugged my knickers all the way off and knelt over me, still almost fully dressed, save for his unbuttoned shirt, drinking in the sight of me.

I found his scrutiny difficult; my instinct was to hide myself, and I tried to angle myself into a more modest position, but he ordered me back into full exposure with an admonitory pat on my hip. As if to reinforce the lesson, he took my thighs and spread them as wide as they could go, opening everything to his greedy view.

"You can't keep any of this from me," he said, crouching between my legs and putting his face up so close to my pussy that every word circulated steamy air across my clit. "It belongs to me now. I can look at it whenever I want, for as long as I want. Clear?"

His words hit me deep and strong in the pit of my stomach. I was getting wetter and wetter, and he was watching it happen, watching me grow fat and glossy with shameful excitement. He was right; I couldn't hide from him now. He had X-ray vision into my private, perverse self.

"OK," I whispered.

"No, not OK," he said, pushing his thumbs into the tender skin at the very top of my thighs. "Yes, sir."

"Yes, sir," I parroted, squirming as he fanned a slow stream of warm breath between my underlips.

"This is mine now," he said. "I'm in charge of it. I'll decide when it needs to be used. Your job is to keep it tight and wet and ready for me. Can you do that?"

I arched my back with rapturous embarrassment.

"Yes, sir."

"It's certainly wet enough now." He rubbed a thumb around my soaking clit. I tried to shuffle forwards, to meet his touch, to show him I craved it. "Be patient." He speared two fingers inside me. "You'll get this stretched and filled soon, just the way you want. But I need to examine you first. Mm, nice and tight. Turn over."

I obeyed, but a little grudgingly. I wanted more of his fingers and tongue first. On the other hand, doing as I was told was getting me giddy, making the sensations keener. The mere act of obeying him made me throb with excitement.

And then there was his talent for dirty talk. I'd never known a man hit the spot so perfectly before. Others had been silent, or self-conscious, or aggressive, or used words that threw me out of the zone. Not Emmett. He seemed fine-tuned to my wavelength; filthy, but elegantly so.

He patted my pussy. "Up on your knees now," he said, so gently, and yet it was unquestionably a command. I drew my knees up under my chest and pushed my bottom into the air. He parted my cheeks and let a finger run through the cleft, making my heart thunder when he stopped at my rear entrance.

"Ever been taken back here?" he whispered.

I shook my head, holding everything tense and tight while his finger hovered in the danger area.

"You will be."

"Oh God," I mewed.

"When you're ready," he added, enabling me to breathe out. "I'll be the first. I like that."

He laid a light smack on one of my cheeks, then rubbed the sparking heat in. I sighed with pleasure.

"Saw you, wanted you, got you," he said, bracing himself above me and nuzzling the back of my neck. "This is my best day's work in ages." He pushed himself down on me, forcing me flat on to the mat. His clothed body enveloped me, weighing me down, demonstrating his possession of me. "I can't quite believe my luck."

His stubbly face manoeuvred me into a kissing position. I lay underneath him in eager surrender, opening my mouth to his tongue. I had found something I hadn't even been looking for. I had found my master.

The bath had almost overflowed before we remembered that the taps were still running.

Emmett leapt off me to prevent the flood, then removed the plug to lower the water level. Turning, he shucked off his shirt and got to work on his belt buckle, gazing down at me, still prone on the bathmat.

"Jump in then, little mermaid," he said.

I tried a longing look. I didn't want to get into the bath. I wanted him to come back down and finish what he'd started.

He raised his eyebrows.

It was enough.

I hauled myself up and into the bath. I really did need one; my feet were slimy with old pond residue and my too-heavy workwear had rendered me sweaty and lank. The oil-swirled, fragrant waters closed over me and I was reborn. Jo the awkward office drone became Emmett's mermaid, a creature of weightless, effortless sensuality.

I lay with my hair fanning around me in fronds, watching Emmett take off his trousers. I'd expected his cock to be tall and slender, like him, but, while I'd correctly profiled the length, the thickness was an unexpected bonus. At least it still had a nest of red-gold hair at its base. No surprises there.

It stood upright and ready. I had caused that. I shut my eyes in silent triumph.

He stepped into the water, long and pearly-white and freckled, sliding in behind me.

"You're lovely," I said, dreaming out the words.

"Thank you. So are you."

"I mean, you're much lovelier than I thought, at first. I didn't look at you properly. But you're just…" Ahhh. "Lovely."

"It works," he said, clasping his arms around me, jostling my bum between his thighs.

"What does?"

"The water. You're a different creature in it than out."

I craned my neck to question him to his face.

"What do you mean?"

"Even your voice softens. You stop being scared of saying

what's on your mind. I don't think you'd have remarked on my loveliness if we were still on the bathmat."

"Don't you? Wouldn't I?" It sounded preposterous, but at heart I felt he was right.

"You hold back, on dry land," he said. "Am I going to have to move into a water park?"

I wriggled against him, enjoying the gliding together of our wet skin.

"I don't mean to hold back," I said.

"It's fear," he said. "You overthink too much. I want to get at what you're hiding."

I shivered. I knew even at this early stage that he would poke his clever fingers into every secret corner of me. I stood no chance against him. It was terrifying, but I wanted it to happen anyway.

"I'm not hiding anything," I said. "I've told you more than I've told anyone already."

"Have you?" He liked that. He pushed his face into my neck and kissed droplets off my skin. His hands cupped my breasts, sending little currents of water dancing around them.

"I've told you my dark secret," I sighed, arching back into him, showing him how open I was. "Nobody else knows about that."

"How you want to submit to me?" he murmured into my ear. "You know, submission is about more than just doing what you're told in bed. You have to give yourself to me on every level. You have to belong to me, body and soul."

"This is quite intense for a first date, isn't it?" I said nervously.

"Would you rather we pussyfooted around each other?" He fed a finger into my mouth. I sucked at it, finding the joints with my tongue tip. "Would you rather be sitting in a crowded pub talking about favourite movies, wondering all the time if you'll get a snog at the end of the night?"

He pulled his finger out with a pop and pressed his lips to my face, all over my cheeks, my jawbone, my neck, my shoulders.

"Nooo," I admitted. "I'd rather be here. I'd rather be yours."

"It'll be uncomfortable for you at first," he warned. "I'll prise you open, and I'll keep you open. I'll insist on your being honest at all times. If you aren't, you'll be punished for it. A dynamic like this stands or falls on its clear lines of communication. If you trust me, we can fly. If you don't, we'll crash and burn."

"Trust doesn't happen just like that," I said. "Does it? Although I feel like I *can* trust you. Weirdly. Because I hardly ever trust anyone."

"You feel a connection with me," he said, pouring some oil into his hands and rubbing them together. "I've forced it. So it's accelerated. Which makes it all the more important that you keep telling me how you feel and what you want."

"I never talk about how I feel or what I want."

"I know. So it'll be hard for you. Hard but worthwhile. A steep learning curve. But I'll keep your nose to the grindstone, don't you worry."

"Oh God," I said.

"What? Second thoughts?"

"It's just that, the more you try and frighten me off, the more turned on I get. There. That was honest, wasn't it?"

"I'm proud of you," he said, slathering the oil over my breasts, concentrating on my bullet-hard nipples. "And I knew you'd be a natural anyway."

He fixed his lips to the most sensitive part of my neck, teeth gently indenting the soft skin, and sucked like a demon. My eyes rolled back in my head at the ravishing sexiness of it, even as I worried about visible marking. But at the same time, I wanted him to mark me. I wanted his stamp of ownership on me.

"So when we get out of this bath," he said, resting his hands on my belly so his fingertips fanned out around my pubis, "you're going to keep on being my little mermaid. You're going to stay open and willing and accepting of everything I give you, and if anything's too much or too fast, you're going to tell me. Is that understood?"

I trembled in his arms, deliriously unnerved by the infinite possibilities unfolding before me.

"Though I won't be emptying the toy drawer tonight," he mused. "First things first. Tonight's about learning our way around each other."

I thought he already had the map of me printed and folded, but I didn't say so. I was too busy trying to visualise the contents of his toy drawer.

He made me turn around so I knelt between his thighs, facing him.

"What do you think?" he said. "I keep talking and you look as if you're listening, but I need to know that you've heard me."

"I think...I want to do that. What you say." My eye was level with his neck, and I looked down at his strawberry-pink nipples, wondering if they were as sensitive as mine.

"No, look up at me, Jo, and tell me what you actually think," he said, and there was a sharp edge to his voice that dragged my gaze guiltily upwards.

"I'm a bit scared," I admitted.

He caressed my jaw so that suds ran down my neck from his hand.

"Good," he whispered. "You should be. But you want this?"

I nodded.

He kissed me. Such a kiss, as warm and fragrant as the water than surrounded us, starting off luscious and sweet, turning forceful, showing me what was in store. I put my palm to his chest, but he removed it, holding my wrist tightly.

"No, sweetness, you don't touch me without permission," he said. He took both my hands and placed them gently behind my back. "Now keep them there."

With my hands out of the picture, the sense of my own vulnerability penetrated to my core. I knelt in helpless thrall to him, my breasts pushed out by my new stance, offered to him.

Resuming the kiss, he accepted my offering, weighing my water-heavy breasts in his hands as his tongue flickered deeper into my mouth. I flexed my hips towards him, wanting him to know how he churned me up. I didn't care if he broke me into a million pieces and reformed them in the image that pleased him the most. I was his, if he would have me.

One hand reached around behind me and grabbed my bottom, squeezing it hard. He forced me to kneel up, instead of squatting in the water as I had been, exposing all of me above the knee to the air. Still kissing with ravenous intensity, he slipped his hand between my thighs, rubbing the side of it along my slit, teasing my lips slowly apart. He dragged curls of pubic hair back and forth with his hand, breaking off the kiss to tell me it would have to go.

I gasped.

"Does it *have* to?"

In response, I got a smart slap to each inner thigh in turn.

"The correct response to that was 'yes, sir'," he told me.

Oh God, this was difficult already. I'd eschewed the fashion for denuding oneself of all bodily hair, thinking it un-feminist and a bit creepy. Why would you want to look pre-pubescent?

I didn't want to argue with him, but on the other hand, he had demanded honesty. He couldn't have it both ways.

"I'm not sure I'm comfortable with it, though," I said.

He cupped my face in his hands, looking at me, or right into me—it was hard to tell which.

"Well done for telling me," he said. "Now, explain."

I wasn't sure I could, without accusing him of something unsavoury. I needed to choose my words carefully.

"I would feel like a child," I said haltingly. "And...you know...that would be...weird for me."

"OK," he said, after thinking about this for a moment. "I can understand that. But we both know you're an adult woman. Shaving down there doesn't change that, any more than wearing pigtails or eating a lollipop would. And I'm not going to ask you to do either of those things, before you ask."

Well, thank God for that. I let the first stirrings of relief trickle down from the top of my chest.

"Good," I said. "So...why this one?"

"Because I like to see exactly what belongs to me. Because I don't like getting hairs trapped in the back of my throat. Because it means I can write my name on your mound of venus."

I bit back a squeal. "You would do that?"

"I would. Now, are you going to let me shave you, or do I have to wait for you to get your head round it first?"

"You would wait for that?"

"Of course. Everything is negotiable, sweetness, while we're finding our feet." He paused. "I should warn you, that changes once the contract is drawn up and signed." His hand closed around my sex, a gesture of ownership that made me shiver. "This is going to be mine," he said. "And that means I have final say in all decisions regarding it, including how it looks. So you can shave it now, or you can wait six months. Either way, it's going to happen."

I was glad I was wet from the bathwater down there, otherwise he'd know how much he was turning me on. Why was it a bad thing for him to know that? I wasn't sure. But he seemed to have an awful lot of power over me already, and perhaps that made me nervous enough to want to put the brakes on him acquiring much more.

"OK," I said, working hard not to grind myself on to his hand.

"OK what?"

"OK. You can shave me," I whispered.

His smile was a beam of pure light.

"Good girl," he said, kissing the tip of my nose. "I'm trying not to be an optimistic fool, but I do think you might be what I've been looking for at last."

"I hope so," I said, wondering vaguely if I'd been looking for him. I hadn't. I hadn't known I was looking for anything or anyone. But now he was here…

He let one finger part my underlips and trace a lazy circle around my clit. I shut my eyes, conscious of how fat and swollen it was, and the message he would derive from that.

He took one nipple, then the other, into his mouth, sucking on them, running his tongue lavishly around their hardening tips. I bucked into his hand, begging for the stimulation to continue. He smacked both bottom cheeks with a loud, wet smack, then rubbed the sore spots, still fingering my clit and sucking on my breasts.

I moaned, longing to take my hands from behind my back and push myself on to him, but I knew I should be obedient.

"Mm, you get very wet very quickly," he said, pushing a finger inside me. "That's good."

Was it good? Or was it shameful and embarrassing? My hope that the bathwater might fool him had been in vain.

He added a second finger, then a third, twisting and stretching, assessing me.

"Nice and tight," he said. "And ready. It didn't take much. Why is that?"

He expected an answer from me?

"I...don't know," I said, and he used his free hand to smack my bottom again.

"Yes you do," he said firmly. "Why are you so wet and ready for me, Jo? Tell me."

"Because...oh..." I moaned as he thrust his fingers in and out of me, using his thumb to keep my clit in the game. My thighs trembled and I hoped I would be able to stay upright. "Because you...you do something to me...oh God."

"I do something to you? What?"

"You make me...ahhhh..." This was crazy; I was already bumper-to-bumper with my orgasm. How had this happened so fast? "You make me...I'm going to..."

"No you aren't." He took his fingers out of me and spanked me harder than before, three or four stinging ones. I almost fell forward into him, on the verge of weeping with frustration. "You'll learn to ask my permission before you come," he said.

"Because you're so cruel," I blurted. "And so fucking sexy. I can't stand it."

He chuckled with triumph.

"It turns you on when I'm cruel to you?" he said, capturing my mouth for a sloppy, lip-biting kiss. "Well, that's music to my ears. Mm. And that sweet little pussy of yours will be wet and ready for me as soon as I look at it from now on, won't it?"

"Yes, sir," I moaned, halfway to delirium. I just wanted his fingers back inside me. It didn't even have to be his fingers. Anything, everything.

"First things first, though," he said, reaching out of the bath for a towel. "Let's get you properly prepared."

He pulled me up to stand with a hand under my elbow and wrapped the towel around me.

"Out you get, and make your way to the living room," he commanded.

Chapter Four

I hoped that nobody could see me through the floor-to-ceiling windows as I followed his instruction and dripped a path into the main room, although nothing overlooked us. Hiding behind a sofa, I began to dry myself off, patting my pubis with special care, looking down at my bush with some trepidation. Had I really agreed to shave it off?

When Emmett strode into the room in silky pyjama pants and nothing else, razor in hand, my question was answered. He removed a towel from around his neck and laid it out on his black leather couch, over the arm and beyond.

He patted the arm, one eyebrow raised at me.

"Come and lie down here," he said, helping me into position until I lay with my upper body on the sofa and my bottom up on the arm, pubic triangle uppermost, while my legs dangled over the side. It felt precarious and very vulnerable, to be offering my most sensitive part to his razor, and I think he saw the fear in my eyes.

"Wait a moment," he said. "I need to fetch a few things. And be calm. It won't take long and I have a very steady hand."

He disappeared for a few minutes and I wondered if he was giving me the chance to escape. It certainly seemed like the sane thing to do. I could grab my clothes and be out of the door in seconds. It might mean getting dressed in the lift, but that had to be better than being murdered by a complete stranger, didn't it?

And yet I didn't move a muscle. I lay there, my towel bunched around my stomach and breasts while my lower half was bare and exposed, ready to be shaved clean and put to use.

Did this mean I'd put my trust in this strange and somewhat frightening man I'd met for the first time earlier in the day? Why was I doing it? Why did this all feel so inevitable?

I didn't believe in fate, but there was a Disney glisten in the air. Perhaps that was what fixed me to the sofa, waiting patiently while Emmett stood somewhere nearby, waiting for me to leave. My prince had come. He just happened to be a pervert.

When he reappeared, with a basin of soapy water and some foams and lotions, my heart gave a painful jump.

"Oh, you're a brave girl," he said, putting down his armful and standing at the end of the sofa, looming over me. "Very brave. I'm proud of you already."

Without further ado, he picked up a can and squirted foam all over my triangle, rubbing it generously into my curls and down over my lips until the area was covered.

"In the future," he said softly, picking up the razor and running a frictionless line down the centre of the zone, "you will get this regularly waxed—a Hollywood wax, as they call it, going all the way up between your arse cheeks. Is that clear?"

I pulled a face. I'd tried leg and bikini waxing once before a holiday, and never again.

"Waxing? Can't I just shave?"

"No, I want you to go into a salon, once a month, and get yourself the full Hollywood. I'll pay for it, if that's an issue."

"No, it isn't, it's just…"

"Just?"

I was conscious of keeping myself very, very still. I didn't want to take his mind off the job.

"Nothing. Tell you later," I said, biting down on my lip as his razor moved lower.

I held my breath until he tapped the razor on the side of the basin and put it down, patting any residual foam off with the corner of the towel.

"What were you saying?" he asked, squirting some kind of clearish gel into his palm. What was that for? "This is just to soothe your skin, prevent any irritation," he said, reading my mind. Again.

"Getting a Hollywood wax," I said. "In a salon. Embarrassing. Can't, I mean, can't I do a home wax or something?"

He ran gel-tipped fingers over my newly-bare skin, rubbing it in in slow circles.

"Ah, well, the embarrassment is kind of the point, sweetness," he said. "It pleases me to think of your toes curling and your face bright red at the salon counter. And of you cringing and trying your hardest to pretend you're somewhere else when the beautician rips the solid wax off those areas only I get to see otherwise. Because that's part of the deal, incidentally. Exclusivity. Nobody else is touching you but me. Yes?"

"Yes," I whispered, fighting a losing battle against the arousal his gel-fingered massage triggered. I had been wanting to come for a long time now, and I almost felt he'd only have to breathe on my clit to do the trick.

"Good. Besides, I don't think a home Hollywood is even possible. I could do it, I suppose, but I'm not a professional. I'd be afraid of hurting you." His fingers reached my labia, pushing into them vigorously, causing them to part and reveal their soaking contents to him. "Ironically."

I let out a helpless little whimper of need.

"Now let's have a good look at you," he said, wiping off his fingers on the towel and getting tight between my dangling legs. "Oh yes, that's much better." He prised my lips apart with his thumbs and bent his head low over my pussy, letting the breath I had imagined drift over my clit. I tried to picture how it must look to him, so swollen and congested with all the blood that had rushed there, glistening with the gush of my juices. He must see that I was his for the taking.

He speared one finger inside me and swivelled it about. I felt the early tremors of approaching orgasm, and he felt them too.

"What's the hurry?" he asked, pulling his finger out. "I'm going to spend all night on you. I'd try not to peak too soon, if I were you."

"Oh but…can't last much longer," I pleaded raggedly, my lips still held wide by his thumbs. I tried to wiggle myself closer to his mouth. *Why* wouldn't he let me come? Was he going to ration my climaxes?

"Not yet," he said. "But you'll learn. You'll learn to hold yourself back, and you'll learn to come on my command. I'm going to train you, Jo. When I'm finished, you'll have forgotten you ever thought your sexual response belonged to you. It'll be mine to use and control, mine to spark up and mine to damp down."

This was all technically frightening stuff, but in reality it made me even wilder for him. I was so close to begging, and I'd never begged a man for anything before.

"Please let me…" The words rush out in a fever. "Please, sir, please."

"You really need it, don't you?" he teased. "Poor little mermaid. You'd sell your soul to have me inside you now, wouldn't you?"

"Yes, yes, yes."

He stood up.

"Over," he said briskly, slapping my hip and helping me roll 180 degrees so that my bum was raised inelegantly high by the sofa arm while my face was pressed into the cushions. He stood with one hand planted heavily in the small of my back while the other travelled lazily over my vulnerable bottom and thighs.

He dug his fingers into my crack, making me yelp.

"Your beautician is going to spread these cheeks good and wide when she waxes you," he said. "I might get them red hot first. Send you in there with a well-spanked arse; that would get her attention, wouldn't it?"

Oh my God. I kicked my legs and pushed my bottom higher. *Anything* to make him touch me now.

"Yes, a good spanking followed by anal sex," he mused. "Let her put you on the waxing bed all sore and obviously used. And if she made any comment on it, you'd have to tell her the truth about what I do to you. You'd have to tell her you have a master you're not allowed to disobey, and you're there on his orders. I wonder what she'd say to that?"

"I've never done…that," I mumbled into the upholstery.

"What? Anal sex?"

"Um hmm."

"Not yet," he corrected. "Oh, I wish you could see your thighs. They're absolutely dripping."

I moaned and twisted, but he took his fingers out of my crease and resumed his maddeningly light caresses over my rear cheeks. How had he done this to me? How had he got inside my head and yanked out my guiltiest, most deviant fantasies? Not that there weren't plenty more where this one came from. But the idea of being sexually humiliated was right up there, and his little beautician story played right into it. As for anal sex, I'd been afraid to broach the subject with other lovers, but my curiosity had grown regardless.

It struck me then, with pussy-clenching force, that my fantasies weren't going to be fantasies any more. I was going to get to live them out, each and every one of them, and a few more of Emmett's beside.

This was going to change me. Was I ready to change?

Emmett's palm fell, weighty and loud, on my right bottom cheek. I cried out at the sting, but I was strangely grateful to have this distraction from my desperate pussy. I was also grateful to be living out an experience that had been looping around and around in my head for years.

Emmett was spanking me, and I hadn't even had to ask, or hint, or try to bring up the subject without being too obvious about it, or put on a DVD and be all like, "Oh, *Secretary*, I heard that was a bit kinky, but let's give it a go, shall we?"

"Did that hurt?" he asked me.

"Not…really. A bit."

He laughed.

"That's code for 'do it again', isn't it?"

"No," I said, but it was.

"So you don't want me to do it again?"

"I don't know…look, you aren't supposed to…I mean…"

"I know what you mean," said Emmett. "You want to sustain the fantasy of having things done to you against your will. Having to admit that you enjoy it, or are curious at the very least, spoils it for you."

God damn this man and his uncanny accuracy.

"Maybe," I muttered.

"And I understand that, of course I do," he said. "I like that fantasy too. But this is your first time, and we barely know each other, so please indulge me and tell me unequivocally that you give your consent to this."

"I'm sorry," I said, regretting my unfair reticence. "I do consent to it."

"To what? Let's be clear."

Oh, now he was just tormenting me, the bastard.

"To…what you just did."

"Ha, nice try. Not good enough. Speak to me, little mermaid. Say, 'Yes, Emmett, I would love you to…'."

I kicked my legs angrily. "Spank me," I growled. "All right? Happy now?"

He patted my bottom, on the spot that was still warm from its forceful connection with his hand.

"Almost," he said. "We need a safeword first, though."

"Do we?" I said nervously. How far was he intending to go with this? I had agreed to a spanking, not a full-on whips and chains scenario.

"We do. That way you can pretend you're being cruelly treated to your heart's content, but if you really need to stop, you use the safeword."

"Oh, right." I'd always wondered about safewords and why 'no' wasn't good enough.

"Of course, whining and squirming is fine while you're learning," he said. "But it won't be tolerated further along the line. Anyway, safeword. Any ideas?"

"I can't think," I said, because I couldn't. All I could do was feel; I was one huge jumble of feelings.

"Ariel," he said. "Repeat after me…"

"Ariel," I said.

"Don't forget it. Right. Push that bottom up for me now."

I moaned helplessly, but I did as I was told, thrusting it out until the backs of my thighs trembled.

"I'll go easy on you this first time," he promised.

He made two palm prints on my stretched skin and I sighed into the tingle. It felt good. It felt *really* good. I could take this all day long.

Except I couldn't. Those first smacks gave no indication of just how hard his hand could get.

A half dozen more had me purring with satisfaction, but the next six were harder, knocking little breaths of discomfort out of me. Soon after that, I was sucking in air through my teeth and jiggling my hips.

"Getting warmer?" he asked, moving down to the crease where bottom met thigh.

"Yes," I gasped. "Very warm."

He spanked all over my cheeks and down almost to the backs of my knees then back up again. I managed to hold my position and keep my cries to a moderate volume, but when he sped up and launched into a volley of loud, stinging smacks all over the first still-hot layer, I began to struggle.

"Oh, no, that really hurts," I panted, trying to swivel my bum out of harm's way, but he held one fist firmly in the small of my back and kept me under his palm.

"Yes, it's supposed to," he said calmly, spanking on like a machine. What had he done to his hand? Had he injected it with lead or something?

"Ah-ah-ah-no-no-no," I wailed, now twisting furiously, but futilely.

I could say the word. Why didn't I say the word?

Because he'd called me brave earlier, and I was still glowing from it, and I wanted to prove myself.

I gritted my teeth and kicked a bit, but I didn't use the safeword, even when I began to think my bum must resemble the surface of Mars.

Eventually, he laid on a volley that made me yell and convulse. Even then, I didn't use the safeword, but he stopped anyway.

"What have you forgotten to do, Jo?" he asked, panting with exertion and sounding very stern indeed.

"Er…" I was too busy luxuriating in the absence of a hard hand on my arse to form words. My bottom vibrated with heat. It was going to be sore for quite some time.

"Jo? Why didn't you safeword?"

"What?"

He pulled me up from the sofa and stood me opposite him, tilting my chin up in a none-too-gentle hand.

"Hmm?" He frowned at me. "Why didn't you say Ariel?"

"Oh, I don't know. I just wanted to…you said I was brave and…"

He sighed, tapping my cheek with admonitory fingers.

"I should have known." He put his hands on my shoulders. "Listen, sweetness. I really hope you weren't trying to impress me by taking a harder spanking than you really wanted to. Were you doing that? Honestly, now."

I nodded ruefully, rubbing a hand over my tight, burning buns.

"Well, you mustn't. Not at this stage. BDSM is one of those things where you really do need to be able to walk before you can run. If I take you over your limits before you're ready, you'll be damaged and I'll be angry with myself. And we don't want that, do we?"

I shook my head. I felt ridiculously pathetic and little-girlish, but wonderfully safe and cherished at the same time. I had never felt such an intense complex of emotions, and this was just the beginning.

He pulled me into an embrace, kissing the soft skin around my ear and my neck while I clung to his shoulders, trembling with the headiness of it all.

"OK," he whispered, nuzzling my face out of its hiding place so he could give my lips a long, hungry kiss. "Back over the sofa arm now."

"Back?" I pouted.

"Don't question me," he growled. "Or you'll get another spanking, ready or not."

That meant I wasn't getting one now. I drew a breath and placed myself as directed, bottom up and legs spread.

He took the bottle of aloe gel again and applied it to his fingertips before rubbing it all over my tender cheeks, soothing the burn but doing nothing to lower my sky-high arousal level.

"Is that better?" he asked, prising them apart to get the gel into crevices that hadn't actually suffered from the spanking. I tensed my muscles, fearing invasion, but he didn't go any further.

"Lovely, thanks," I sighed.

"We have to keep this in peak condition," he said, patting

my arse proprietorially. "We don't want the skin getting tough or slow to redden. I'll need you to moisturise thoroughly several times a day. Will you do that for me?"

"Moisturise my bum?"

"Several times a day," he repeated. "I need it soft and easily marked. There's no fun in spanking old shoe leather."

"What moisturiser do you recommend?" I asked, with a little snort of amusement.

"A good one," he said firmly, giving me a light smack. "I'll leave that to you."

"Any other stipulations?" I asked, feeling daring now that the spanking was over.

"Actually, yes," he said. "I'll email you my list. Just general things, mostly, like keeping yourself healthy and in good condition, which I'm sure you already do. The waxing, as mentioned. Certain specific exercises that you might need equipment for."

"Equipment?"

"Pelvic floor strengthening, that kind of thing," he said blithely. "And, of course, you won't be allowed to masturbate."

"Not allowed to…" I said faintly. His gelled-up fingertips were working on my inner thighs now, keeping just close enough to my pussy lips to make me want to beg him to move higher.

"Absolutely not," he said. "This is mine now." He ran a fingertip along my slit, over the swollen bump of my clit and into my vagina, making me gasp. "Nobody touches it but me and your gynaecologist."

"I don't have a gynaecologist. I'm National Health."

"Nobody but me then," he said, his finger gyrating inside me. "Am I going to be able to trust you?"

I thought with sad regret about my vibrator back in my bedside drawer. Was it really doomed to early retirement?

"That's going to be hard," I admitted.

"Not really," he said. "I'm planning to give you plenty of attention. You probably won't miss it."

He pulled out his finger and put his mouth to my spread lips, running his tongue lavishly up the centre. I squirmed and squeaked. He held me by my inner thighs and made me take a slow, lazy licking, smacking me into stillness when I jiggled too much and put him off his stroke.

"Aah, oh God," I moaned. "That's too much, I can't..."

He pushed two fingers inside and continued his oral ministrations, pushing his digits up and down with an obscene sucking sound as he feasted ravenously on my helpless pussy.

"Oh God, I can't stop, I can't, oh God," I flapped, bucking into him as my climax rushed up on me.

A low, throaty sound vibrated on to my clit as he ate me through it, holding my thigh against the sofa to stop me kicking. I bit down on a cushion and cried out, the orgasm powering through me in strong waves that seemed to go on and on, eventually settling into smaller aftershocks.

He gave my spent pussy a luscious last kiss before bending himself over me and finding my mouth, to kiss my juices back on to my tongue.

"I think you felt that," he whispered, smiling tenderly, his eyes both proud and amused. "Didn't you?"

"Oh God," I answered, nothing else seeming to express my thoughts on the matter.

He kissed me again, nuzzling his face against mine. I felt prickly stubble against damp, sensitive skin.

"Isn't that better than anything your rabbit can give you?"

I nodded slowly, my senses in a swirl.

"I think you're going to be a natural," he said, then he laughed at my exhaustion. "Oh dear. You'll need to work on your stamina, though. I'm nowhere *near* finished with you."

He peeled himself off me and helped me up from my crushed, sweaty heap.

"Let's get you into bed," he suggested, guiding me into his curtained lair with a hand on my shoulder.

I fell on to the mattress, lying still while the remnants of my post-orgasmic fuzzy head cleared.

Emmett darted about putting various things away and shoving the tangle of wires under the bed before removing his pyjama pants and joining me. I turned to him instinctively and twined my arms and legs around his sleek, pale body. So many freckles. I wanted to kiss each and every one.

"I promise I'll tidy this place up a bit next time," he said.

"It's OK."

"It's not OK. I want things to be perfect for us."

"Perfectionist."

"Yes, I am," he said. "I'm not ashamed of it either. I'll make this into a pleasure palace for you."

I laughed. "A pleasure palace, wow."

"A place where all your wildest dreams can come true," he promised, kissing the tip of my nose and snuggling in closer. "My God, you feel amazing, all naked and caught up in my clutches."

"You feel gorgeous too," I said.

"Really? I'm not exactly Mr Eight Pack."

"I hate that kind of thing," I assured him, surprised at this first hint of a hairline crack in his confident carapace.

"Just as well. But what do you think of this kind of thing?"

He nudged me on to my back and bent over my breasts, taking each one in his hand and kissing them in turn.

"Mmm," I replied, hoping it was unambiguous enough.

The tip of his tongue circled each nipple until they stood tall and stiff, at which point he sealed his lips around the nearest one and sucked enthusiastically. My pussy, so recently licked into oversensitised exhaustion, buzzed back to life.

As if he read this, he plunged a hand between my thighs and began to delve between my lips, massaging the area into renewed wetness.

"You're ready again so quickly," he marvelled, looking down at his busy hand, inspecting its shining fingers. "Aren't you?" He fed those fingers into my mouth, smiling as I licked my juices from them. He put them back inside me, rubbing his thumb steadily and rhythmically over my clit. "Are you ready to be fucked, Jo?"

I twitched around his fingers, arching my back into their purposeful thrusts.

"Are you?" he persisted, refusing to let me off the humiliating admission. "Tell me you're ready for a good fucking, sweetness, or you won't get one."

"I'm ready," I half-sobbed.

"You missed something out," he said, removing his fingers and patting my hip encouragingly. "What did you forget, sweetness?"

"I…" I just wanted him in me, now. "Please?"

"Are you being deliberately obtuse?" he asked, frowning. "Do I have to spank it out of you? Try again, Jo. Tell me you're ready for a good fucking, as respectfully as you possibly can."

Oh God, this game was cruel, but it was making me even more desperate for him.

"Please, sir, I'm ready for you to fuck me," I whimpered.

Bingo. He beamed down at me and kissed me hard.

"Perfect," he said, preparing to mount. "Get those legs nice and wide for me."

I spread them as far as I could, bending at the knees and lifting my bum half off the mattress to meet his angle. When I tried to get hold of his shoulders, he tutted at me and ordered me to clasp my hands at the back of my head and keep them there.

"I want full control," he said. "In the future, I'll tie them out of the way, but we'll work up to that."

Almost everything he said drove me deeper into insatiable need for him. If he didn't fuck me soon I was going to scream.

He could read it in me, and he teased me more, stroking the tip of his cock up and down and over my clit, bathing it slowly in my juices until it glistened.

I tried to jostle him down, but he held up a finger.

"What have we forgotten?" he said, and I genuinely didn't know or care. "Oh yes. Condom."

He had turned me into something so stupid with lust that the most basic precautions had fled from my mind. I waited, rigid with need, while he opened and shut bedside drawers, then snapped the thing on.

"You need it so badly that you're prepared to let me knock you up?" he said.

"No, I'm on the pill," I ground out.

"Ah. Oh well. All the same, flattering," he said.

And now, at last, he meant business.

He lifted my legs so that my ankles rested on his shoulders and eased the tip of his cock into me, keeping it there in the shallows, taunting me with it, bringing it out to swipe across my clit again once or twice.

"Mm, I can tell you're going to be tight," he predicted.

I wanted to unclasp my hands and claw at him, wrench him down until he was properly inside me, all the way up.

"Don't move your hands," he warned, reading me again. Damn, how did he do that? "All good things come to those who wait."

"I can't wait any longer," I moaned.

"You'll wait as long as I see fit," he said. "Won't you?"

"Yes, sir," I sighed.

"Good girl." He chuckled. "Ah, I'm a bastard. I've tortured you long enough. I'm sorry. OK then, get ready."

He bent forward, grabbed me by my hips and pushed himself fully inside me, inch by glorious inch. Oh God, it felt wonderful, filling me up and stretching me wide.

"Jesus, but you're tight," he hissed, stretching out above me as he packed every last little speck of hard erection into my grateful sheath. "How's that?"

"Good," I raved. "So good. Sir."

"Mm, you're learning," he said. "Take it, now. Take the whole length."

He began to thrust, slowly at first, getting me used to having his thick cock in me. I was so slippery wet, though, that he encountered little resistance and was soon able to increase his pace.

"This," he panted, sawing back and forth, beads of sweat gathering on his pale, freckled brow, "makes you mine. You're going to be getting a lot of this, sweetness, get used to it. Get used to having your pussy filled…right…up…" He lost the power of speech at this point, swept up and away by the rhythm and the gorgeous friction of the fuck.

I felt my arm muscles creak and stretch as I worked hard to keep my hands from breaking free and clutching at his hair. I wanted to so badly, but I wanted to please him even more, so I maintained my half-helpless position and let him thrust into me, dominating me in the way he wanted.

He put his hands under my bottom for purchase and found an angle that struck devastatingly against my sweetest spot with each move forward. Pulling my cheeks apart, he held me utterly open, using this perfect angle to work me up higher and higher. He could see me falling apart at the seams, he knew it was coming, and his eyes glowed with wicked satisfaction.

"Are you going to ask permission?" he goaded, just at the point where my climax became unstoppable.

"Awowoo," I cried, and it was going to have to be good enough until I was able to organise my mouth into a chanted whisper of, "Please, sir, please, sir, please, sir." All too late, because it was happening, but I kept it up until every last ounce of orgasm was drained out of me.

"I'll train you up," he said, and apparently the thought of it took him over the edge, because he pounded into me, his face contorting in ecstatic shock, then held himself in at full hilt until he collapsed on top of me with an exhausted sigh.

My ears roared and my heart thundered for a while, black floaters passing across my eyes. I wondered if I'd been close to losing consciousness; it felt like it. No man had ever dredged up a response like this from me. I hadn't even known it could be done.

I lay with his weight on top of me, loving its crushing solidity. I wanted to worship and adore him. It was frightening. Tears gathered in the corners of my eyes. The safety of home— of everything I'd thought my life was—felt an awfully long way away.

"Well," he said at length, rolling off me and flopping on to his back. "Jesus."

He opened one eye and peered at me sideways.

"Oh, hey, sweetness," he whispered, propping himself up to kiss the tears that were spilling down the side of my face. "Don't cry, little mermaid."

I sniffed and nuzzled into the crook of his shoulder.

"Little mermaid's out of her depth," I said.

"Little mermaid shall be taught to swim," he replied, holding me tighter.

Chapter Five

Twelve hours passed in a haze of sex, sleep, wine, talk, more sex, more sleep, even more sex and a late breakfast. I suppose you'd have to call it brunch.

Sitting up in bed with coffee and a croissant, I felt like a balloon that had been cut loose and flown way up into an unfamiliar sky. I was with Emmett, and that was all I wanted now. He had taken possession of me and my soul was no longer my own.

I ached inside and out, but the sting was so sweet I wanted to keep it. I wanted this weakness in my legs and this soreness between them to last until Emmett came back to renew it.

But for now, we both had commitments for the rest of the day, and we would have to part.

"Do I have time for a shower?" I yawned.

He put down his phone and kissed my forehead.

"You can't have a shower," he said.

I paused mid-sip of coffee. "Why not? Aren't you going to

have one?"

"Yes, I'm going to have one. But you can't."

My look of consternation made him laugh and kiss me again, on the mouth this time.

"I want the cab driver who takes you home to smell me on you," he crooned, his lips still touching mine. "And when you get home, I want your flatmates to see you, wrecked and unwashed, and know exactly what you've been up to. And if they ask, I want you to tell them about me."

"Tell them about you?" I said, my heart skipping beats all over the place. I'd still worried, deep in the deepest pockets of my soul, that he would wave me off this morning with a cheerful final farewell. No phone number, no real address.

"Yes. Tell them you met a man called Emmett and now you belong to him."

"All right."

He sent me on my way in one of his T-shirts instead of the icky work shirt I didn't want to put back on. Before I dressed, he'd pinned me down and written 'Property of Emmett J Marlow' on my mound of Venus with a laundry marker, as promised.

"What does the J stand for?" I asked.

He just laughed and dialled the cab company.

When I got home, my flatmates were out. I rushed to the bathroom and looked at myself in the mirror. My skin was dotted with tiny bruises and love bites, and I laid my fingertip against each one, pushing into it with a kind of masochistic rapture. I was disappointed to see that my bottom was no longer red. I wondered how long it would be before I was bent over for Emmett's punishment again. *Please don't let it be long,* I prayed.

I didn't shower, but went to lie on my bed, breathing in the scent of him still upon me, feeling his traces on my body. I slept for most of the day, slipping in and out of consciousness, waking up to a different sense memory each time. I kept my hand on my mound of Venus, absorbing its thick-nibbed message into my blood.

Real life, in the shape of my flatmates, barged back in during the early evening. I pulled the covers quickly up to my chin, concealing the worst of the evidence.

"We thought you were dead," said Rachel.

"Where the hell were you last…oh my God, is that a love bite? It *is*!" Luana clapped her hands. "Tell us, then?"

Rachel put down the tea tray.

"I met a man called Emmett," I said dreamily. "And now I belong to him."

"What?" They exchanged slightly concerned glances.

I smiled and sipped my tea.

The heavenly bliss lasted another day, and then I started to worry. He had told me to wait for him to contact me. He was going to contact me, wasn't he? I had his T-shirt. He'd written 'Property of Emmett J Marlow' on my fanny. Those weren't the actions of a one-night-stand merchant. Were they?

By Monday morning I'd decided it was all over.

I sat at my desk, banging out a report on the course, trying to ignore the constant barbs that lodged in my heart every time I thought of that day and the other-worldly night that had followed. A constant lump had settled in my throat and I felt as if I had dust behind my eyes. I had to keep blinking away tears. And I had to wear a horrible itchy scarf to hide the love bites.

My phone bleeped, and I picked it up.

"There's a package for you in reception," said the flat voice of the duty receptionist.

I tried not to get my hopes up, but by the time I made it to the ground floor, I was shaking with anticipation. Nobody ever sent me packages. I wasn't expecting anything at all.

The receptionist handed me a Jiffy bag, which I tore open so savagely that the contents fell out on to the floor.

I sobbed with laughter. A pack of Jaffa cakes. And a note.

Meet me in the park at 1.00. EJM.

Ensemble

Chapter Six

I looked at Emmett, then back down at the tickets he had just slapped down on the table. Behind us the baristas clattered and steamed, and people wove around our table with laden trays.

"Seriously?" I said. "They don't mind?"

"I've told you. People do it all the time. As long as I pay for the flight, there's nothing to stop you coming with me." He cocked his head on one side, his eyes sharply questioning. "So? Do you think you can get the time off work?"

"I…yes. I don't see why not." I allowed myself to believe it. "Wow. Barcelona."

"Let's drink these and I'll take you holiday shopping," he offered.

"But it's only for three days."

"You'll still need things," he said. "Sunglasses. Bikini." He leant forward, lowering his voice. "Ben wa balls."

"Oh my God, shut up!" I flicked my eyes guiltily around the coffee shop, mortified at the thought that we might have been overheard. Apparently not, but the burning stain across my cheeks must have been evident from yards away.

"That wasn't a very clever thing to say to me, Josephine, was it?" Emmett sat back, raising an eyebrow. I could tell he was delighted to have this opportunity to castigate me, much as he feigned disapproval, and I pouted back at him.

"This is a public place," I hissed, picking up my comically huge cappuccino cup to hide some of my blushes.

"We're still entitled to have a private conversation in it," he said. "About anything we like. Including sex."

The sibilant nature of the word, and his emphasis on it, drew a few curious glances from the students at the next table. I knew he'd done this on purpose and I tried not to react, but my skin was virtually peeling itself off my face in scorched shame now.

"I'd better check my passport's still in date," I said loudly, picking up the ticket wallet and fidgeting with it.

He smirked.

"You better had," he said, matching me for volume, aware of the earwigging students. "Or somebody will be getting a spanking."

"Oh my God," I muttered under my breath. Clearly the best plan was to finish the coffee in silence. I drained it without raising my eyes from its steaming surface. "Can we go now?"

The Saturday crowds were out in force, clogging up the wide white pavements of the shopping centre.

"Well, that was mortally embarrassing," I said heartily, as he took my hand and laced his fingers with mine.

"It was meant to be," he said, with a sideways grin. "I wanted to see you blush. You're still blushing now, you know. It's sweet."

"You're evil," I muttered.

"But you like it," he countered. "Didn't you find it a little bit exciting?"

"No," I said, but I wasn't being honest, with him or myself. The truth was that I had felt a tremor pass through me, and a certain familiar tension between my thighs.

"You don't like the idea of people knowing what I do to you? What about the girls at the waxing salon? They all know."

"Yes, but they're…I don't know…professionals. They don't seem to turn a hair, so to speak. Even the time I turned up with a bruised bottom, they didn't say a word about it."

"Didn't they?" Emmett seemed disappointed. "I thought they might ask you *something*."

"Yes, but you chose them because they're kink-friendly," I pointed out. "So I guess they don't need to ask."

"True." We walked on in silence for a little while, avoiding a large crowd that had gathered around a street performer. "I want people to know," he said suddenly, halting outside a department store. "I want people to look at us and wonder. I want them to speculate. I want them to *know*."

I had long inferred this, from the kick he seemed to get out of the waxing thing—he always asked me about it afterwards—but we had never really talked about it.

"Why?" I asked.

"Because it makes you more mine…if that makes sense. Probably not." He ran a hand through his hair. "It means other memories than ours are stamped with the knowledge of our dynamic. It makes it *real*. Realer," he amended. "I'm sorry, I'm not explaining this very well."

"No," I said, "I know what you're saying. But we are real—whether anyone else knows it or not. That's what matters, isn't it?"

He slid an arm around my waist and pulled me in for a long kiss in front of the mannequins staring out of the plate glass window.

"Always," he said. "But the idea of other people knowing *turns me on*."

"Oh, well, why didn't you just say so?" I batted his cheek playfully. He grabbed my wrist and drew me into the department store.

Browsing the bikinis and sarongs with me, he said, "I was serious about the ben wa balls, by the way."

"Do we have to talk about this now?" I said through gritted teeth.

He held up the briefest of bikini briefs, coupled with a dangerously low-cut top.

"What about these?"

"A few bits of string would be cheaper and offer more coverage," I said.

"I'll buy them then."

"But will I wear them?" I pondered. "When the Barcelona beach will be packed with bronzed babes. I don't think anyone wants to see my wobbly white flesh."

He frowned at me. "You know I hate it when you put yourself down," he scolded. "That's a fast track route over my knee."

"Sorry," I said hastily. "But...I can't see myself in that."

"You will," he vowed, picking up a similar style in a different colour and heading towards the counter.

Once he had paid, he stood behind me on the escalator with his arms clasped under my breasts and bent to talk into my ear.

I could see other people on their way up looking over at us, indulgently or with mild disgust, and I wondered if Emmett was finding it exciting.

"Guess where I'm taking you next?" he said, his breath hot on my skin.

"Tiffany's?" I suggested.

"Close. Just around the corner."

I clenched my pelvic floor. I knew the place he meant. He had made me go and buy a ton of erotic lingerie in there a few weeks ago, telling me I had to ask the assistant for her opinion on everything. I hadn't really wanted to seek her views on the strappy, shiny body harness, or anything else on the list, but Emmett had made it very clear that he wanted all the details, so she'd given them.

"Amazing for more intense play," she'd said. "The O-rings can clip on to lots of different accessories. And it only needs a wipe down with a mild soap afterwards."

"Right, thanks, I'll take it. And, er, all the other stuff too."

I turned to Emmett.

"You don't mean Cherie Amour?"

"Got it in one."

"Oh God."

He laughed.

"I've always wanted to go in there with you," he said. "And you did so well, getting all that slutty underwear the other day. They'll be like old friends to you now."

That was what I was afraid of.

"This will be a little obedience test for you," he said. "Can you remain submissive under pressure? I'll be interested to see the results."

I huddled in close to him, holding his hand tight as we walked in from the street. It wasn't a tawdry kind of place; in fact it was decidedly chic, but there was no escaping the fact that it was a sex shop that sold sex accessories, and you had no business in there unless you had a lot of interesting sex planned.

Behind the desk, to my consternation, was the assistant whose acquaintance I had made during my earlier spree.

Please don't recognise me, I prayed, but she looked up from the rack of basques she was sorting through and smiled charmingly.

"Hello again," she said.

I tried a casual nod that came out more like a tic, and pretended to look mightily interested in the nearest display. Oh God, bondage gear. The one next to it then. Oh God, vibrators.

My eyes skittered around the place like pinballs until Emmett directed my attention to a wall full of floggers.

"What do you think of these, sweetness?" he asked, without lowering his voice to the required whisper, like any decent human being would.

"I don't know," I mouthed, giving him a desperate look.

He twinkled back, then called over to the assistant.

"Could I ask your advice a moment?"

"Sure," she said, coming up behind us while I tried to put my expressive body language into some kind of order.

"Do you recommend leather or suede?" he asked, reaching out to remove a purple suede number from its hook. He let the tassels shred through his fingers as the assistant gave her reply.

"They both have a lot of great points," she said. "This kind of flogger is perfect for beginners, and for sensation play. With the leather, you can get a bit more sting, but a lot of people think the suede is more sensual."

"Sensation play," repeated Emmett. "So it's good for teasing?"

"Oh yes, it's great for a tie and tease scene," enthused the assistant. "You can really tickle with it. Plus it's soft enough to be nice to use on other parts of the body—breasts or inner thighs or whatever you feel up to."

"Mm, I like to tie and tease," mused Emmett. "I think I might have to buy one of these. What do you think, sweetness? Leather or suede?"

"Whichever," I said tightly, my eyes on the floor.

"Oh come on, don't be rude," he said, with unmistakable steel behind the light tone. "This lady is giving her professional opinion." He put a hand on the back of my neck, and I instantly felt my awkwardness give way to submission.

"I'm sorry," I said, looking quickly at the assistant. "I think I prefer the leather."

She smiled broadly at me. She knew exactly what was going on here. She probably saw it every day.

"So do I," said Emmett. "What you said about sting. Sting is good, especially when you know somebody who benefits from a lot of it."

Oh *God*, he was evil, but I felt a surge between my thighs, flooding my knickers.

"We love sting," agreed the assistant coquettishly. "I guess you've got paddles? Straps?"

"I have plenty of those," affirmed Emmett. "Don't I, sweetness?"

I made an incoherent sound, meant to convey confirmation.

"Although," he continued, apparently spurred on by my open embarrassment, "I've been thinking lately about investing in a good cane. Rattan, maybe. Do you have any?"

"We certainly do," she trilled. "Would you like me to show you?"

"Actually," he said, dropping his voice, as another customer had come in, "could I try this one out first?"

"Oh, sure, take it into our changing room if you like," she said. "It's just behind that mirror there."

It felt like a dream; the racks of fetish paraphernalia, the curious sidelong glance of the other customer, the open beam of the assistant, and most of all Emmett's long fingers twining around mine, leading me to another new frontier. In the three months we'd been together, I'd already crossed so many, and yet every week I found myself hard up against another.

"I'm not sure about this," I muttered, slipping past the mirror into a small cubicle.

"About what?" he asked pleasantly, twisting thin leather strands around his fingers.

"Whatever…you're going to do."

I made the mistake of the pleading look. I should have known by now that the pleading look was absolute catnip to him.

He draped the flogger over my neck, dragging its knotted ends slowly across my bare skin. I shuddered with fearful excitement.

"What do you think I'm going to do?"

"Use that thing…on me," I whispered.

He winked and looked up at the corners of the ceiling.

"I'm not sure there's enough space to swing it," he said. "But let's give it a go anyway."

"Emmett…"

"Ssh. The assistant said it was all right, didn't she?"

"But she's only a few feet away…and the other customer…"

"It's all right," he said, putting his free hand on my cheek. "Nobody minds. This isn't Primark, sweetness, it's a fetish boutique. Nobody thinks people are buying riding crops for their horses around here."

"I know but…"

He tugged me closer by the waistband of my little denim skirt and put his hand on my hip, patting it gently.

"You're usually more adventurous than this," he said softly. "Are you telling me you aren't turned on by the thought of being whipped in a public place?"

The spasm between my thighs gave me away, but I wasn't ready to admit it yet.

"I'm a private kind of person," I said. "And I've never done anything like it…"

Emmett's hand crept lower, inside my skirt, on to my trembling thigh.

"But you'll do it for me," he said, kissing my ear and the soft skin beneath it. "Won't you?"

"I…don't know…" My breath shortened as his hand travelled higher.

"Such modesty," he mouthed, "from one so wet." His fingers found my slick lips and explored each fold and crevice. Today, as always in Emmett's company, I was forbidden to wear knickers.

Words gave way to gasps. He held me around my waist, the handle of the flogger pressed into my back while its strands dangled down over my bottom and legs, using his free hand to massage me into dumb acquiescence. Two fingers invaded me, twisting and probing. I clung to his shirt in a bid to keep upright.

"What if I made you come, really hard, right here?" he wondered, his voice deep and hoarse in my ear. "Would that be better or worse than flogging you?"

"Ah," was all I could say in a desperate staccato.

"You don't seem to have any objections to that," he continued. "So why won't you let me whip you? Hmm? Do you think anyone in here is fooled by your innocent maiden act? Don't you know they're all waiting for you to get what you deserve?" His thumb swept over my clit and I couldn't prevent a broken cry. "You want it really, don't you?" He pumped his fingers back and forth, slowly, while I quivered all around him. "Don't you, Josephine?"

"Yes, yes, yes," I hissed.

"Good," he said briskly, popping his fingers out and putting them to my lips for me to lick clean. "Hands on the chair, then."

There was a straight-backed wooden chair in the corner of the cubicle, for putting clothes on I presumed. My inhibitions banished, I spun around and bent over it, placing my palms flat on the seat. Emmett rucked the heavy fabric of my skirt up my thighs and over my hips with some difficulty until my bottom was bare.

"Can't I keep it on?" I whispered, in a last-ditch attempt to preserve some form of dignity.

"Of course not," he said.

A dozen feathery wisps tickled my offered cheeks until I wriggled, and he dragged the soft leather up my thighs. It felt divine and I sighed quietly, absorbing the tremor as the fronds stroked my slit.

No more than six feet away, on the other side of the mirror, the assistant chattered cheerily with the other customer. I wasn't sure what they were discussing, but the assistant said it was one of their most popular lines. The bell over the door jingled mid-conversation. More customers. Oh hell.

Emmett stopped stroking and laid a stroke. It made a soft shushing sound as it landed painlessly but very sensually on my bottom.

"Sweet," he said. "Does it feel nice?"

"Yes, sir," I said.

He proceeded to whisk it gently all over my bum and thighs, occasionally flicking it inside my legs and over my labia. He handled it quickly and deftly, covering me in seconds then starting all over again. At some point, he began hitting harder, and little prickles of sting added to the growing warmth of my skin.

I was still able to avoid making a sound, but the conversation in the other room was becoming a jumble of noise as I concentrated hard on what was being done to me. I was being whipped on my bare bottom, in a public place while people stood by, able to hear the flickety-swish of the flogger through the feeble barrier that concealed us from view. The thought was still embarrassing and shameful, but somehow the embarrassment and shame added to the erotic urgency of it all.

"Try before you buy, eh?" said a loud voice from the main shop, and there was some slightly awkward laughter.

"…very good customers," said the salesgirl. She was talking about us. She was probably winking, and pointing out some of our previous purchases to the browsers.

I imagined them raising their eyebrows as they saw what Emmett had bought to use on me. *That* vibrator and *that* bondage rope and *those* nipple clamps…oh my!

Emmett drew back his arm and let the flogger fall hard on my now glowing skin.

I let out a grunt of surprised pain. This really could hurt.

He flogged me with all his might until I couldn't hold back

any more and I began to whimper and rock back and forth on the chair.

"Well done," he whispered, kneeling down to kiss my hot bottom and thighs, and give me one long lascivious lick along the split of my lips. I pushed out, begging for another, but he laughed, straightening himself and giving my bum one last loud smack before pulling the scratchy denim back over my tender flesh.

"Very nice, we'll take it," he said, leading me back out to the main shop and slapping the flogger down on the counter. I kept my eyes fixed on his sleeve, avoiding all contact with the other people in the shop.

"I'm so pleased you liked it," said the assistant, breaking off her conversation and coming over to make the transaction. "It's got so many good reviews on the website. And now we've got another satisfied customer. Well, two satisfied customers." She tittered.

Emmett ran his hand over my tightly-skirted rear, doing nothing to relieve the heat underneath.

"Was I right about the sting?" she asked.

"I think you'll need to ask Jo here," said Emmett. I wanted to elbow him in the ribs, but I knew better than that now.

"Yes," I said. "It stings."

"Speak up," prompted Emmett. "And look at the lady when she's talking to you."

I raised my eyes reluctantly, taking in the other customers peripherally—a hipsterish man in his late thirties and a lesbian couple with lots of piercings. All three of them were leaning in slightly, enjoying the exchange.

"It's OK to start with, but after a while it stings," I said, enunciating clearly and looking just aslant of the assistant's eyes.

"Great," she said. "That's what I've always heard. Haven't tried it myself yet, but I'll get there one day. Can I get you anything else? That cane you mentioned, sir?"

She said 'sir' very flirtatiously, fluttering her lashes. I felt a sudden stab of realisation. She was submissive too, and she admired Emmett's unabashed public topping.

"Perhaps next time," he said. "But I would like some ben wa balls and a set of silicone butt plugs, please."

I wanted to sink into the ground, but at the same time I wanted Emmett to know that he was with the right submissive, so I didn't let out a trace of the protest rocking my insides.

"When you say a set," said the assistant, "do you mean different sizes?"

"Yes. Small to large. Just the basic beginner's kit. We can move on to the pretty ones later."

"Oh, some of them are sooo pretty," she sighed. "Beautiful silver ones with crystal bases. And my favourite—the ponytail. I'd love to show you sometime."

"Better get some lube with that too," he said as she laid a pack of three graduated plugs on the counter. I couldn't look at them. Emmett had spent weeks tormenting me with the idea of preparing me for anal sex, but he enjoyed my reaction so much that I had begun to think he actually preferred talking about it to doing it.

Wrong.

"OK," said the assistant, laying everything out in front of us before keying it into the till. "We've got one leather flogger... one set of ben wa balls...one beginner level plug set...one tube of Astroglide. Sounds like a recipe for a great night in." She sighed slightly, fluttering the lashes again.

"I can't wait," I said, wondering where *that* had come from.

So brazen and lewd! It was quite unlike me.

Emmett was grinning like the Cheshire cat as he entered his PIN into the reader.

"I bet you can't," he said. "But you'll need to let that bum of yours cool off first."

He winked at the assistant, who looked quite devastated with envy, and picked up the fancy monogrammed bag.

"Come on, pet," he said, taking my hand and leading me out of this strange little enclave. "Suddenly I'm in an awful hurry to get home."

He made me suck him off in the car before we drove back to his apartment; the sex shop adventure had got him good and hard, and there was plenty to swallow down.

He wouldn't let me get my own release, though. Instead, he handed me the bag from the sex shop.

"Take out the ben wa balls," he ordered, "and put them inside you."

"What, here?"

"Yes, here," he said with measured calm.

I took a covert look around us. I'd been lucky that nobody had come back to the cars either side while I'd been giving the blow-job, but what if they returned now and caught sight of me?

"It'll be good practice for the flight," he said, as I took the little embroidered box out of the bag and opened it up. Two medium-sized silver balls nestled in black velvet. When I moved the box, they chimed prettily.

"For the flight?" I stared at him.

"Yes. You'll be wearing them all the way to Barcelona, baby." He smiled and patted my knee. "They're excellent for your pelvic floor."

"Really?" I picked one out and held it in my palm. It

weighed more than I'd expected.

"You want to stay nice and tight for me, don't you?"

I couldn't answer. He reduced me to a state of awkward incoherence several times a day; I really ought to be used to it by now.

"Put it in then."

I shot him one last mute plea, but was met only by the set, firm expression I knew so well.

I spread my knees a little and let my hand disappear under my skirt. The ball jingle-jangled as I pressed it to my opening.

"Do you need lube?" he asked, more gently. "Help yourself, if you do."

I shook my head, glimpsing my scarlet cheeks in the wing mirror. I was more than wet enough.

"I'm never going shopping with you again," I muttered, feeling my vagina yield to the cold, round pressure.

He chuckled and ruffled the hair on the back of my neck.

"Yes you are," he said.

The ball travelled up inside me, its mellow chime set off occasionally by my over-anxious fingers. I wasn't sure how far I should push it—what if it ended up in my womb and I could never get it out again?—so I didn't let it go the whole length of my finger and left it about halfway up.

"Now the other one," he prompted.

I repeated the process with the second ball, pushing it in until it knocked against the first.

"How does that feel?" he asked.

"I don't know…a bit strange."

"You're aware of them?"

"Oh yes. I don't think I'd forget they were there."

"Good. And in order for them to stay, you need to exercise

those pelvic floor muscles—the same ones you use to milk my cock when I'm fucking you. It's very important that you keep them tight and strong, sweetness, because your cunt belongs to me and I intend to keep it in peak condition. Do you understand me?"

"Yes, sir," I said, a mite sulkily, feeling both hectored and patronised.

"Do you?" he said, drawing out the agony as punishment for my less-than-enthusiastic response. "Tell me."

"Oh God," I muttered under my breath, then with a bright, forced smile. "I need to keep my vagina in tip top condition for you, because you own it, sir."

"Once more, without the manic smile and with more respect."

I wanted to kick the footwell, but I knew he could keep this up indefinitely—I had learned this the hard way—so I banished my pettishness and gave him the version he wanted with maximum humility.

"Much better," he said. "If you behave yourself until we get home, I might even let you come."

Chapter Seven

It was one thing wearing the stupid things in the car with only Emmett for company; quite another to hurry to our airport gate with them jingling away inside me. I'd had to remove them to get through security, and then go straight to the bathroom to replace them once we were flight side. I'd sat in a coffee bar with my thighs clamped tight, scared to move in case my muscles gave out on me and they dropped out.

And they weren't my only problem.

We had been waiting for the taxi in Emmett's apartment, our bags packed and ready by the door, when he called me over from the window.

"I like your holiday outfit," he said, referring to the short flippy printed skirt and criss-cross strappy vest top I was wearing. No knickers, no bra. Flips flops and a wide-brimmed straw hat. "But it's missing something. Come here over my lap."

"What?"

I looked back to the window. The taxi was due any minute. This was no time to start fooling around.

"Didn't you hear me, Josephine?"

That tone worked on me every time. Meekly, I positioned myself as if for a spanking, although surely that wasn't what he had in mind. The ben wa balls shifted inside me, dinging faintly.

He pushed my skirt up over my bottom.

"Why are you...?"

"This won't take a minute. Keep still and don't fidget."

He reached down and got something out of his flight bag. Seconds later, he had wrenched apart my bum cheeks and was dripping something cold and gelatinous directly on to my anal pucker.

"Oh God, what are you doing?" I gasped, kicking a bit.

He smacked each cheek briskly, then moved his fingers down to spread the lube evenly around the area, massaging my ring with firm intent.

"I've waited a long time for you to be ready for this," he said, "and now I think you are. It's time to start preparing you in earnest. By the time we leave Barcelona, this particular virginity will have been well and truly taken."

I moaned a bit, then grunted as he pressed his finger down, almost breaking through the tight barrier.

"You've always known it would happen," he reminded me. "Are you going to make me proud of you today?"

I squirmed again, then tried to relax. I didn't want to fight him. I wanted him to be master of me. I wanted to show that I could do this.

"I'll try, sir," I whispered.

He stroked my hair.

"Such a good little mermaid," he crooned. "Now then..."

He removed his finger, then introduced something slick and

smooth with a tapered end between my quivering cheeks. I knew it must be the smallest of the butt plugs he'd bought in Cherie Amour, which had been mysteriously unmentioned since. He'd been waiting to surprise me with it, I realised.

And I was definitely surprised.

I let out an 'ah' of pained discomfort as he began to twist the tapered end this way and that, skewering it slowly but inexorably through my anxious sphincter and into my bum.

"Keep nice and open for me," he murmured. "Don't try and push back. You know you need this."

I didn't know anything of the kind, but I didn't argue with him.

"It's good for girls like you to have their bottoms plugged," he said, seating the first inch and moving ever forwards. "It keeps them focused. Reminds them who owns that tight little passage, and who has the right to use it. I'll see that you won't be forgetting that from now on—not for one moment."

"Girls like me," I echoed, trying very, very hard not to repel his advance. It felt so counter to everything natural that I couldn't help jerking a little and pulling my muscles in, much as I wanted to show my submission.

"Girls like you," he said softly. "Most girls don't need this, but you do. I saw it in you the moment we first crossed paths. I saw you were the sort of girl who needs frequent and regular discipline, plenty of sex, and a very firm hand. Was I right?"

"Yes, sir," I gasped. It had to be halfway in now. I was struggling more than ever, feeling a painful burn that suggested I'd been stretched too far.

My woes were multiplied by the sudden buzz of the intercom. I jolted over Emmett's lap, panicking. He shushed me, gave me a light smack and shouted across to the receiver.

"Give us five minutes, yeah?"

"OK."

"We'll be late," I mewled, hoping this would cause Emmett to remove the invader in my bottom and make a dash for the door.

No such luck.

"No we won't," he said, screwing it further in. The burn receded and it settled itself inside me, the flanged end resting comfortably between my cheeks. "There. You are firmly plugged, my love. How does that feel?" He patted it, causing a mild tremor within.

"Weird," I panted. "Full."

"You'll get used to it. And this is only the smallest one. We have two more to try yet."

"The plane trip's going to be so uncomfortable," I complained, but already I was feeling the erotic potential and wondering how I would make it to Barcelona without melting into a pool of sweaty need.

"For me too," said Emmett, "knowing what I know. I'll be harder than granite until we get to the hotel. Spare a thought, eh?"

I snorted.

"Poor baby."

"OK, just a very quick pre-flight spanking, and then we can go."

"What? Emmett! We have to go now!"

But my protests were drowned by the energetic slap-slap-slap of his hand on my rear. Being spanked with a plug in was a very interesting sensation; it swayed and prodded as my bottom warmed, whilst the balls jogged against each other with musical results.

Once Emmett was satisfied I was properly prepared, he let me stand. My skirt draped over my hot, tingling bottom, hiding the plug from view. But I couldn't forget about it for a minute, all the way to the airport, shifting now and again against the leather seats. Emmett had to put his flight bag on his lap to conceal his very obvious arousal.

"You can take out the balls before we go through security," he said, leaning over to whisper into my ear as we huddled in the back seat. "But you have to leave the plug in."

"What if I have to be body-searched?" I whispered back, the thought plunging me into all kinds of consternation.

"They only pat down the sides," he said. "I just like the idea of them finding it. They won't though."

"They'd better not!"

They didn't. I made it through security with no issues, thank God, but the look on Emmett's face as he watched me come through the arch was pure avid lust.

Sitting in the departure lounge waiting to be called on to the plane, he leant over and muttered into my ear again.

"Do you think any of these people know?"

I felt my cheeks catch fire. They had been mildly warm throughout, thanks to my predicament, but this was a higher order of heat.

"Don't," I pleaded.

"I mean, they all know you aren't wearing a bra. That's obvious. Wish I'd put some clamps on you now."

Pavlovianly, my nipples hardened into bullet points.

"So they can probably extrapolate that you aren't wearing knickers either. They can probably tell by the way you're keeping your knees so tightly together."

He slid his arm around my waist and kissed my shoulder,

moving up to the curve of my neck.

I shut my eyes. I didn't want to face these people who were so apparently well-informed about what was underneath my clothes. If I couldn't see them, perhaps they wouldn't see me.

"I think they all know that you're my bitch," he whispered, nipping at my earlobe. "I think they all know you're in heat for me right now." He manoeuvred me into a long, passionate kiss, pushing his tongue all the way in. I felt myself grow slippery wet around the balls while the plug moved inside me as I rocked a little on my seat. I was perilously, tremblingly close to embarrassing myself.

"They know how desperate you are to come," he whispered, pressing his lips to my earhole, sliding his hand down to my thigh, grabbing a handful of my skirt hem. Oh God, was he going to lift it? "I bet some of them even know what you've got inside you." He moved it up, just an inch. I whimpered and tried to push at his chest.

The bored amplified tones of the flight attendant calling us on to the plane saved me.

We broke apart and stood up, moving with the rest of the passengers in a gormless mass to the desk. He put his hand on my bottom, stroking it, occasionally pushing a knuckle against the flange of the plug. I hid my face in the crook of his arm and willed us to make it to the plane without any kind of public loss of control.

I was lightheaded and sticky with longing by the time I slid into my window seat. The cool pressurised air freshened me up a bit. I pressed my thighs together and breathed deeply a few times. All the same, I knew the hour and a half flight was going to be challenging. I was dripping wet and dry-mouthed, my bottom spasming around the plug with increasing frequency.

Emmett took hold of my hand.

"Are you still nervous about flying?" he asked.

I looked at him in wonder. I'd forgotten all about that.

"Was this all part of a plan?" I asked.

He grinned. "In a way. After the umpteenth time you said something fretful about the flight, I decided to do something to take your mind off it. With moderate success, it seems."

"We're not in the air yet," I reminded him.

"No. So I want you to lift your skirt behind so that your bare bum is on the seat and keep your legs nice and wide for me."

I stared at him, consternated. All around us, people were ambling about, putting things into the overhead lockers, swapping seats to be near the window.

"I can't," I whispered.

"Of course you can. Nobody's looking at us. They're all busy with their own concerns."

I waited for the burly middle-aged man in the row opposite to settle down with his book, then I performed a slow bum-shuffle in my seat, pulling the back of my skirt up bit by bit until I was able to reach behind and bunch it above the flange of the plug, which had twisted inside me as I moved. Now there was nothing between my skin and the slightly fuzzy plane seat. The rubber plug settled itself into position, more comfortable now but still unforgettably present at all times.

Under Emmett's approving but stern gaze, I edged my knees apart until their backs rested against each front corner of the seat. The seat wasn't wide, so it wasn't too much of a stretch, but it certainly looked strange. The stewards would notice it when they came past on their rounds.

I would just have to have the tray down as soon as I possibly could, with a big newspaper over my lap to conceal it.

Unfortunately, the tray had to remain upright until we reached cruising altitude, so for now, I was stuck with the weird 'womanspreading' stance. At least nobody had taken the seat on Emmett's other side.

"Good," said Emmett, bending to retrieve something from his hand luggage. He handed me what looked like a pink rubber butterfly, attached to a bundle of elastic straps. "Now go to the toilet and put this on."

"What? What is it?"

"Don't play the innocent with me, sweetness," he said, baring his teeth. "It's a clitoral vibrator. Go and put it on. I'm sure you can figure it out. Quick, before the sign goes on to stay in your seat."

I closed my hand around it and did as I was told, hoping nobody would know what the pinkness protruding from between my fingers was. It looked for all the world like a child's toy, after all.

I locked myself into the tiny cubicle and began to wrestle with the elastic straps. Eventually I was able to fix the vibrator between my labia with the butterfly's 'nose' resting comfortably on my clit. The elastic straps held it in place, wrapped snugly around my thighs and hips. I had no chance to practise walking with it in situ, so I just had to hope I would make it back to my seat without incident. What with this, the balls in my vagina and the plug up my bum, I had a very busy lower region indeed.

I let my skirt fall down to mid thigh and emerged from the toilet to find the stewards preparing for the safety talk. I scurried, very carefully, back to my seat, keeping everything tensed and my thighs awkwardly wide. I was never so grateful to sit down as I was when I slipped past Emmett and collapsed, bare bum on upholstery and knees spread, beside him.

"You managed it then," he said quietly, as the safety vid rolled above our heads.

"It feels like Piccadilly Circus down there," I muttered. "Are you sure you've brought enough toys for the journey?"

"Don't tempt me," he replied. "I'm sure I've got a pair of nipple clamps somewhere."

A steward stuck her head around the seat backs, checking that we were both strapped in. I wanted to clamp my knees together, but Emmett kept a hand on the one nearest him, prepared for this eventuality. I was paranoid that the steward would see that the back of my skirt was rucked up, or catch a glimpse of pink elastic strap, but she seemed oblivious, and Emmett probably blocked out any of that kind of view anyway.

After another few minutes, the plane began its slow build-up to the runway. This was the point at which my stomach always turned to liquid. I grabbed at Emmett's hand, crushing his fingers.

He responded by taking a slim remote control unit from his inner breast pocket and flicking the switch.

Straightaway, the rubber butterfly between my thighs began to vibrate, on a teasingly gentle setting. It might have been weak, but it was enough to concentrate my mind on my nether regions. Within half a minute, the plane, the passengers and all their doings became irrelevant. All I could think about was the maddening, not-quite-hard-enough buzzing on my clit, combining with my stuffed passages to make me gush with juices.

"Oh God," I whispered. "You can't do that..."

"Mm hmm," he said, taking it up a notch.

"Emmett!" I squirmed helplessly, wanting to claw the thing

out from between my lips, but not daring to in full view of whomever chose to turn their head in my direction. The butt plug nestled snugly, moving in sync with my restless bottom. The balls gave a tremulous little jingle.

I froze in position, waiting for somebody to look round.

Nobody did. I let out a breath.

The plane was taxiing now, twisting and turning as it headed for the queue. Everybody was preoccupied with their own concerns: parents pacifying children, nervous fliers shutting their eyes and holding their partners' hands, blasé old-timers reading their books. Nobody knew that I was sitting on a butt plug, doing my damnedest to keep my ben wa balls still and quiet, while a rubber butterfly pulsated maddeningly against my clit.

The plane stopped, ready to commence take-off. I squeezed Emmett's hand harder.

As soon as we moved again, he turned the vibe up another notch. I could really feel it now, and the continuous erotic torment of the last few hours meant that I stood very little chance of warding off its inevitable effect.

The engines roared, drowning out the increasing butterfly buzz. I gripped Emmett's fingers in mine and let the sweat and tears pour out as an orgasm powered through me.

We had lift off.

He leant across and kissed me hard until we reached cruising altitude. The people in the row opposite must have thought we had a plane take-off fetish.

Once the seatbelt sign went off, he extracted his tongue from my throat and whispered a 'well done' in my ear. The butterfly was placed in retirement until we were over the Pyrenees and ready to make our descent.

He gave me some gum to chew, then switched the perishing thing on again.

"Emmett," I pleaded, having spent the last hour recovering and trying to ignore the various pressures on different points of my nether regions.

"Are you trying to tell me that you own your body?" he asked, tapping the remote control against his thigh. "I thought you knew better than that, Josephine. Remind me again, who owns you?"

"You do, sir," I said faintly, dying at the thought that the people in front or behind us might hear, although they were all talking loudly about being able to see the sea.

"Who is in charge of your body?"

"You are, sir."

"Correct. And that includes full control of your sexual response, doesn't it? Didn't we agree that? Was I dreaming?"

"No, sir, we agreed it," I said, bucking slightly as the buzzing became more intense. I was dripping on to the seat, rolling my hips as subtly as I could.

"So if I want you to come, you will come. Yes?"

"Yes, sir."

"If I decide to have you come fifty times in a row, that's what will happen. Understood?"

"Understood, sssir, ohhh."

"That well-used little clit that's getting so much attention just now belongs to me," he murmured, rubbing my thigh beneath my skirt. "And I like it swollen and overstimulated and *just* this side of painful," he continued. "So that's how it's going to be."

"Yeeeesssss, ssssssirrrrrrr." I let my head drop to my knees, panting hard as another orgasm rocked through me.

I got a few funny looks at the baggage claim, but I didn't care too much, as Emmett and I were busy snogging the faces off each other.

Chapter Eight

At the hotel we made straight for the bed and didn't come out of it until evening fell and we were expected at a drinks reception in the bar.

There wasn't a dress code for it, but we dolled ourselves up anyway: Emmett in his trademark light linen suit and me in a floaty slip of a thing with strappy gold heels. I was bare underneath, but free now of plugs, balls and all other accoutrements. After the day I'd had, sex was the last thing on my mind.

I was very curious to meet some of Emmett's work colleagues. Although we were months into our relationship, he rarely talked about work. The only name he'd mentioned was that of a former boss and mentor who had since moved on, a man called Charles something. It was clear that this individual had earned Emmett's heartfelt admiration and respect, something he didn't give lightly. This Charles was not going to be at the conference, however, so I had no steer on the identity of anyone in the room until Emmett introduced us.

"Emmett!" A rumpled-looking guy in jeans and Converse hauled himself out of a bucket chair. "Over here, dude."

Dude. I turned to Emmett, squashing a smile, but his cheeks were pink and he didn't seem to want to share a joke.

The rumpled guy was sitting with a dark-haired woman in her thirties and an older man. The older man was wearing a fleece, which made me instantly turn away from him. I didn't want to think about why a man would bring a fleece to Barcelona in the height of summer.

"Ray, this is the one I was telling you about," said Converse dude enthusiastically. "Our resident genius, Mr Emmett J Marlow."

That J again.

"Pleased to meet you, Ray," said Emmett, putting out an elegantly formal hand. Fleece guy half-rose from his chair to shake it. "Calum, Alex, this is Jo."

I offered self-conscious 'hi's to the interested faces all around me.

"Cool to meet you, Jo," said Calum. "So you're, like…" He waved his hand in the space between us. "Seeing each other?"

Emmett pulled up a chair for me from another table and I tried to sit elegantly, without my skirt riding up to an indecent degree.

"Yes," he said, taking his place beside me.

"You're a dark horse, Emmett," said the woman, Alex. "You should have brought her to the curry night last week."

"Oh, last week was difficult," he said vaguely, though it hadn't been. "Anyway, you're all here for the grand unveiling now."

Calum chuckled around the neck of his Estrella Damm bottle, then belched unexpectedly.

"Grand unveiling," he said. "He's such a man of mystery. Is he like this with you, Jo?"

"All the time," I said, smiling.

A waiter came over to take our order. Once he was out of range again, Alex spoke up.

"Guess where Ray works," she said.

Emmett shook his head. "You'll have to enlighten me," he said.

"I'll give you a clue," said Ray. "It's in Switzerland."

"Head office?" said Emmett, leaning forward. "Do you know…?"

"Charles Fox? Oh yes. We were just talking about him before you came down."

Emmett hesitated, taking refuge in the return of the waiter with his glass of rioja and mine of cava.

"How…is he?" he asked, after swallowing a sip.

"I thought you guys had kept in touch," said Alex, but Ray spoke over her.

"Good. I mean, as far as you can tell. You know Charles."

"Yes," said Emmett.

"Not easy to read," finished Ray.

"Right," said Emmett.

I wondered what the little cloud of unease over the group was about, but it soon became clear when Calum and Alex fell to teasing Emmett over his former protégé status. It was clear that Charles Fox had had a very high opinion of him, and had made it crystal clear to everyone in the workplace.

"Do you remember those rumours, Alex?" Calum elbowed her.

Emmett's brow darkened. My stomach did a little flip. Calum was very lucky not to be in a D/s relationship with

Emmett, that was all I could say.

"Oh God. They were so stupid. I don't really see the need to bring that up." She gave Calum a beady look.

"It was like being back at school," said Emmett. "Beyond puerile."

"People used to say that Fox and Emmett were, y'know," Calum said to me, apparently in the spirit of helpfulness. He lowered his voice to a whisper. "*Involved.*"

"We were involved," said Emmett, with such lightness of tone that it took the company a few beats to react. He smiled acidly at their little gasps and o-shaped mouths. "Professionally and personally. Mutual respect led to a very fruitful friendship, which still continues."

"Ah."

"Oh."

"Hahaha, yes, right, friendship, yeah."

"I heard you were involved in the Trubshaw project," said Ray, moving the conversation on before it could get any more excruciating.

I sat, trying to smile and nod at the right places, while the discussion flew wildly over my head. After an hour and a half of this, Emmett sensed that I'd glazed over, and made our excuses.

"Sorry," he said, wrapping his arms around me from behind as the lift ascended. "That must have been deathly dull for you."

"Well, I couldn't really follow much of it," I said. "It was interesting to meet some of your colleagues though. Fancy Ray working with Charles Fox."

I felt his grip stiffen a little.

"Yes," he said.

"It's a shame he isn't here at the conference. I'd love to meet him. He's obviously a man of taste and discernment."

"Oh, you think so?"

I twisted my neck to smile up at him. His expression was wary, watchful.

"A great talent spotter," I said.

He bent and pecked me on the lips. "Takes one to know one," he said.

The lift door opened.

"Come on," he whispered, sticking a hand up my skirt and squeezing the back of my thigh. "Let's get you to bed."

Chapter Nine

I was left alone after breakfast the next day while Emmett went downstairs to confer, or whatever you're meant to do at a conference.

I put the used breakfast tray outside the door and wrapped myself up in the sheets until the lure of the Barcelona streetlife became too tempting.

Showered and dressed in a strappy cotton top and denim cut-offs, I headed out into the city to take a look at the Gothic Quarter. Wandering through the narrow old streets, looking for places to eat that evening, I felt the absence of Emmett. We should be doing this together; I ached to spend some time with Emmett that didn't revolve around kinky sex, and so far, there hadn't been too much of that. I just wanted to walk hand-in-hand with him, laugh at a street performer, eat churros at a pavement café, all the corny stuff he'd probably turn up his nose at.

Or would he? After all, how well did I know him?

I knew him so intimately as a lover, yet as a person, he remained infuriatingly out of reach. He refused to be drawn on his family or his past, insisting that he had no interest in anything but the present, and how its careful handling might make different futures possible. But then, he didn't really want to talk about his plans for those futures either.

My contractual period was coming up for renewal. Would he want to renew it?

I sat down heavily on the cathedral steps. Little groups of young people and older tourists surrounded me, taking selfies, eating ice-cream, talking and laughing. One young guy strummed at a guitar, but the music swirled around my head, never getting far enough inside me to touch.

What if this was it? What if this was one last debauch before the end?

Stop it, I chided myself, *he hates it when you're insecure.* When I'd asked a few weeks ago where he thought we were heading, he'd said, 'Further along the same wonderful road. Why, do you want to turn back?' 'Of course not.' 'Good.'

Further along the same road had sounded good at the time. But now I wanted to know how long the road was, and what was at the end of it.

He was in the lobby, amidst a group of fellow conferencers, when I returned to the hotel.

"You've been out," he said, claiming me as soon as he laid eyes on me. I felt better for that.

"Just thought I'd do the tourist thing," I said.

"I was going to show you around myself," he said with mild reproach.

"Oh, were you?" The hand-in-hand stuff with churros might actually happen! "I'm sorry, I just assumed you'd be busy most of the time…"

"We'll go out tonight," he said. "It's different after dark. I'll dress you up and show you off."

My heart beat faster and I saw Alex, who had been within earshot, turn suddenly away.

"Show me off?" I whispered.

"Mmm, yes. I think so. There's a bar I know of." His eyes glittered. My dreams of a touristy soft-focus kind of evening faded. He was thinking kink.

"A bar? But we'll get something to eat too, won't we?"

"Oh, sure," he said, but he wasn't really listening. "Why don't you go up to the room, and I'll see you in a little while. Just need to sort something out first."

Alex joined me in the lift.

"Hi," she said.

"Hi."

Awkward silence.

"Good day at the conference?" I asked politely.

"Pretty good." She cleared her throat. "Emmett seems really happy these days."

"Does he?"

"Oh yes. You can actually have a conversation with him that doesn't end in some kind of sarcastic remark now."

"Is that what he does?"

"He was famous for it. He doesn't suffer fools, that's for sure."

So does that mean I'm not a fool? Good to know.

"I mean, it must be difficult for him," she continued. "Being so brilliant and having to deal with us lesser mortals and our screw-ups. But he didn't need to be so… Anyway, he's a lot better now. So if you're the one we have to thank for it, thank you."

"Oh, I shouldn't think it's anything to do with me."

"Don't be so modest. He was really hit hard by Fox leaving for Switzerland, but it's as if a cloud has lifted now. And here you are! Can't be a coincidence."

She winked.

"Aw, that's nice to hear," I said, wanting to ask more about Fox, but seeing that we were nearly at our floor.

"Whatever you're doing, keep it up," she said, stepping out of the lift.

"I will."

I was light-headed by the time I lay down on the bed. I beamed up at the ceiling fan. I made him happy. People noticed a difference in him. They wanted things to work out for us.

I felt that the universe was in tune with my desires. Surely this was something too precious to spoil.

I was in the bath when he came back. Through the open door, I saw him dump bags on the bed.

"You've been shopping?" I called.

"Ah, might've known you'd be in here, little mermaid," he said, finding me. "Come on, out of there. I need to work on you."

"Work on me?" I stood, bubbles sliding down my bare wet skin, and took the hands he held out to me.

"You are a blank canvas," he said, looking me up and down as I stepped out onto the marble tiles. "Albeit a lot sexier than anything you'd find in an art supplies shop."

"You aren't going to paint on me?" I said, although the idea of him laying brushstrokes all over my naked body was perversely appealing in its way. Perhaps that was something to keep in mind for a bohemian afternoon.

"No," he said, wrapping a towel around me and leading me into the bedroom. "I'm going to prepare you. Come on, dry yourself off and let's get started."

Once I was dried and moisturised, he had me sit naked in the dressing table chair while he unpacked his shopping bags.

"Here," he said, handing me a suspender belt and a pair of stockings. "These go on first."

"Knickers?" I said dubiously, standing to clip the belt around my hips. "Bra?"

"You know the rules," he said, and I looked up at him to see if he was joking.

He wasn't.

"Is this going to be like the plane trip all over again?"

He shook his head. "Not quite. No toys involved tonight."

I rolled the delicate stockings up my legs and snapped them on to the belt. It always felt weird to be bare above them. My chest fluttered, wondering what he had in store for me.

"All right," he said, after taking a moment to look me up and down. "I want to get you on the bed right now, but tonight is all about deferred gratification. So here you are."

The dress was a wraparound, short and silky with a deep V-neck. No matter how tightly I secured the waist ties, it was still obvious that I wasn't wearing a bra. The thin material delineated my stiffening nipples, and I would have to be careful how I moved and sat in case the skirt fell open.

"I can't go out in this," I said, tugging and adjusting it to try and make it less hazardous, without success. If I wrapped the skirt around enough to ensure it stayed shut, a breast popped out. If I replaced the breast, the skirt returned to the danger zone.

"There were much sluttier dresses I could have gone for,"

said Emmett. "That one's conservative in comparison."

"I guess I can't ask you to exchange it then?"

"Not unless you want to go out in scarlet latex."

"Christ!" I winced at myself in the mirror, still fighting to find some way of making the dress respectable.

"Leave it, I want it like that," said Emmett, putting his hands over my upper arms.

"But what if it falls open?"

"It won't. Not unless you want it to. It's a clever design— you're quite safe, as long as you're confident and stop fiddling with it."

"I'm not confident though. I won't be able to think about anything except trying to keep my private parts private."

"Well, that's good too." Emmett's smile was lascivious. "I want your near-nakedness to be on your mind all the time. It'll keep you on your toes."

"Are you sure 'on my toes' is where you want me?" I asked, poking my tongue out at his mirror reflection.

"For now," he said, moving in close behind me so I could feel how hard he was inside those roomy linen trousers. He slid a hand down my thigh and rubbed the telltale bulge of a suspender snap, kissing the back of my neck. "I want every man in Barcelona to have a good long look at you…and I want every man in Barcelona to know that you are mine. I want those men straining at the leash to get near you. I want them to think about you as they get themselves off tonight. I want them to wish they were me."

I released a heavy breath. Emmett leant over my shoulder to get to my make-up bag.

"Do your face," he said. "Lots of make-up."

"What if one of those men snaps the leash and gets too close

107

to me?" I asked nervously, uncapping a mascara.

"That won't happen," said Emmett. "I'll make sure of it. Nobody touches you but me. Looking, though…that's different."

"I hope you're right."

"Trust me."

Half an hour later, I was tottering in stripper heels across the Ramblas on Emmett's arm. Among the early evening crowds, there were many who found me more interesting than the human statues or the street hawkers or the ice-cream stands. I tried to keep my eyes trained severely forward, but I caught their glances, the men sidelong and shifty, the women gawping and nudging each other.

Look at her. She must be a prostitute. Isn't the red light district further down the street?

When we reached the upmarket piano bar Emmett was aiming for, he told me I was imagining their reactions.

"They were just admiring you," he said. "You look extraordinarily sexy, but in a classy way. Not many people can pull that off."

"Classy, with my nipples like bullets and my stocking tops on display?" I snipped. "I don't think so."

"OK," he conceded. "You are dressed for sex and it's pretty hard to think otherwise. But I still think they're jealous."

"But do you think they think you've paid for me?" I said, biting my tongue as a waiter appeared with our drinks.

"What? That you're a hooker?"

The waiter set our drinks down without flinching. I guess he didn't speak English, or was just used to this kind of conversation.

"Emmett," I hissed. "For God's sake."

"What?"

I waited for the waiter to disappear.

"Did you have to?"

"What?" Emmett chuckled. "Your face. You didn't need to put blusher on."

"You'll get us thrown out."

"Why? This is Barcelona—they're pretty relaxed about sex here."

"But I'm *not* a prostitute."

"Well, that's all right then." He sipped at his cocktail. "Do you ever wonder what it would be like?"

"What? Prostitution? I should think it's pretty grim."

"In real life, perhaps. But let's talk about it as a fantasy, where all the clients are clean and you're not rattling for your next fix. Would the idea of being for sale turn you on?"

"As a fantasy…maybe. A little bit."

"Think of it," said Emmett, his voice down low, his hand on my knee. "Displaying yourself on a street corner while men size you up, deciding whether they want to give you a ride or not. You have to solicit them—beg them to give you a go."

I tried not to be aroused by his words, but they were working on me, slowly but inexorably. I shouldn't be turned on by this, I shouldn't…

"Maybe you'll pull your dress just a little to the side, give them a flash of nipple," he continued softly. "Or lift the hem of your skirt so they see your suspender strap. Some of them pass by, but others are interested. Seeing that you might have a customer, you beg again, promise they can do whatever they want with you. The others watch while one man says he'll hire you if you let him feel you up on the street. You need the business, so you agree. Right there on your street corner, you let him touch your breasts and put his hand between your legs. He fingers you for a little while, until you're soaking wet. That's what he wants—a whore who's genuinely wet for him. He turns to the others and recommends they try you out, tells them how wet you are. You take him up to your little room and let him have you every way he wants, while outside, a queue forms on the stairs. You won't be short of money tonight."

"Jesus." I breathed again, and clamped my thighs together.

Emmett patted my knee.

"I knew it," he said. "Knew you'd go for that one."

"It's the way you tell it, that's all," I told him, annoyed at myself for letting him get me so hot and bothered.

Exquisite music played in the background; glasses clinked and well-dressed, fragrant people conversed in murmurs. It was no place for a hooker fantasy. Or perhaps it was exactly the place.

He kissed my ear.

"I don't want you to sell yourself anyway," he said. "I'd take it rather hard if you did."

"Good."

"But I don't mind people thinking I've bought you for the night. I don't mind people trying to imagine what kind of services you'll be rendering me. I wonder if anyone's imagining it right now?"

"That waiter, probably."

"Yes, standing behind the bar trying to get rid of his hard on while he imagines you on your knees, giving me head."

"Don't!"

"He wishes he could watch. Even more than that, he wishes he could join in. In his fantasies, I call him up for room service, and he comes in to find you naked on all fours while I take you

110

from behind. He mumbles an apology, but I tell him not to be silly. Get over here and feed his dick into your mouth, since you aren't doing anything else with it. It's OK, he won't be charged. I've paid a flat rate for the full night, and I've told you to expect company."

"You're evil."

"I wish. I'd be rich."

"Well, you're not badly off though, are you?"

He sighed, looking a little chagrined to be steered off the kinky sex path.

"Of course not. But if I had no principles, I'd be in the private jet and megayacht league by now."

"Well, I'd rather have you with your principles than without. Principles are sexy."

"Is that principles in the ethical sense, or the school headteacher sense? I bet you have a thing for authority figures."

He was clearly unwilling to stray from pervy territory tonight. My tourist dream wasn't going to come true yet.

"I have a thing," I said, unable to look at him as I spoke, "for you. Just you."

He put down his drink and took hold of my hands, waiting for me to raise my eyes to his.

"That thing is mutual," he said. "You know it is. Something's wrong. What's up?"

I held his gaze for a moment, then shook my head.

"No, I'm sorry. Nothing's wrong."

He tapped my wrist, very lightly, but there was a definite hint of warning in it.

"You aren't being straight with me, Josephine. You know how I feel about that."

"I don't know," I said, panicking inside. "There are

questions I want to ask, but I'm afraid of the answers I might get, so…"

"Go on. Ask them."

"I wish I hadn't said anything now."

He tapped his fingers restlessly against my wrist. "Do you want me to spank it out of you?" he said. "Come on. We owe each other honesty, remember."

"I wouldn't mind that, actually," I said, with an irresistible upward curve of lip.

"No, I bet you wouldn't. But even I don't have the cojones to do it here in this bar. So you're just going to have to tell me what's on your mind. Although I think I know."

"You think so? So what do you think it is?"

"Ah, no, you don't get away with it that easily, pet."

"OK." I took a deep breath. "We're in a beautiful, exciting city. The weather is warm, the surroundings are interesting, the culture is vibrant, and…and…oh God, I don't know."

"You think it should be more romantic than this?" Emmett translated, as accurately as ever.

"Well…"

"We should be walking hand-in-hand along the shore to the Olympic Port, where we'll share a seafood fideuà and drink champagne and dance cheek to cheek while fireworks go off behind us?"

"Well, maybe not *exactly* that, but…"

"Yes, exactly that. Because that's what I've got planned for tomorrow night." He took a sip of wine, observing my reaction with amused detachment.

"Oh! Oh God, really?"

"Really. Does that answer your question?"

"Yes, it does. I'm sorry. I feel like a fool, but there's

something about being here, in a strange place, that's thrown me off balance and made me…well, made me *yearn*, I suppose. For some kind of emotional security or comfort."

"I understand, and I apologise too. It must have looked as if I was making this whole trip about sex, and that wasn't my intention. Perhaps I should have ordered things the other way around. Candlelight first, red lights second."

"Well, maybe."

"I forget sometimes how insecure you can be."

"I wish I wasn't."

"Don't worry about it. It's hardly a dealbreaker."

"So…what would be? What are your dealbreakers?" I held my breath, waiting for his answer. He speared an olive and chewed it ruminatively.

"Dishonesty, mainly," he said. "Of all kinds. Not just straight out lying to me, but avoiding issues, letting me think things are fine when they're not, that sort of thing. I have to know that what I see is what I get. It's so important to me, you can't know how important."

"Have people been dishonest with you in the past?" I asked gently.

A twisted smile was my answer, and the spearing of another olive.

"I still feel I know so little about you," I pursued.

"There were a lot of secrets in my family," he said after a pause. "Secrets that I didn't find out about until it was too late."

"That sounds rough on you."

"It was. Very." Another tight smile. "I don't want you to think that I don't trust you enough to tell you…but it's all very bloody and not really what I had in mind for tonight…"

"It's OK," I said quickly. "You don't have to tell me now."

He shut his eyes.

"Thanks," he whispered.

For that moment, there was a rare vulnerability about him. I wanted to hold him against me, stroke his hair, whisper reassurances. Until his eyes opened again, and he was the Emmett I recognised, fully in control and seething with perverse ideas.

"Besides, you're hardly in a position to make demands," he said. "In that dress. And those stockings."

"Where did you even get them from?" I asked, reminded so sharply of my scanty state that I felt my stocking tops digging into my thighs.

"Oh, I know a place," he said. "You'd be surprised what you can find at the bottom end of the Ramblas."

"Cherie Amour in Spanish?" I suggested. "What would that be? Cariña amor?"

"Something like that. I just wanted something that would make you feel exposed. And easily accessible."

He put a hand on my thigh, stroking the silky material against the elastic lace of my stocking top. It kept catching and snagging, a dangerous little crackling sensation.

"What are you going to do?" I asked, my breath catching. I felt the situation slipping rapidly out of my control; it was heady, scary and exhilarating.

"I'll do whatever I want with you," he said into my ear, watching the waiters. "That's how we work, isn't it?"

"Emmett…"

He pulled my hem just above my stocking top, so a white strip of thigh was visible between them. At least, it was visible to anyone who thought to look under our table—hopefully everyone would be too absorbed in their own business to bother.

Emmett's hand slipped between my upper thighs, his fingertips moving lightly around the tender skin and under my suspender elastics.

My mouth was too dry to let sound escape. Was he going to touch me, here, in front of all these people?

"Have you ever done anything like this before, Jo?" he asked, teasing his fingers ever closer to the very tops of my thighs. "Anything in public?"

I shook my head, my heart pounding. My eyes flickered all over the place, desperate to make sure we weren't observed.

"Let's start slowly," he breathed, pulling me in for a deep kiss. His hand rested under my skirt, on my bare thigh, as he worked on my mouth. I knew kissing in public wasn't any kind of offence, but this felt weirdly obscene, especially when his tongue slid inside.

It took no time at all—mere seconds—for my anxieties about being watched to melt in the blast-furnace of my desire for him. I surrendered to the kiss, opening myself up, feeling the turmoil in my lower belly that would soon translate to wetness.

The hand that wasn't on my thigh crept around to nudge the side of my breast, stroking it with his knuckles. My nipples were soon hard and swollen; I thought they must look huge under the thin silk that barely covered them.

Before long, I felt my clit follow suit, blossoming between my lower lips as if begging for attention. Emmett's hand felt heavier on my thigh. It was hot and damp, or was that me? I couldn't tell any more.

He began to knead my flesh with his fingertips, every pressing motion causing my lips to spread slightly, teasing my needy clit until I squirmed in my seat.

He moved his lips to my ear.

"Do you want me to touch you?" he murmured, moving down to kiss and nip at my neck.

My eyes were rolling around inside their lids, crazy pinballs of desire. I could hardly keep back the tide of little animal noises that threatened to pour out of me. I needed him to stop them up with his mouth again.

"Uhhhh," I confirmed, seeking out his lips and tongue.

Carefully, slowly, he moved his hand further up my thigh—with some difficulty, as they had begun to feel glued together. He slipped his little finger into my cleft and brushed against my clit. Such a light touch shouldn't have set off such incredible sparks, but it did. I whimpered and clenched my buttocks against the force of it.

And now something else was happening. I was coming out of my cocoon of pure sensation and becoming aware of the people around me—and instead of panicking about being seen, I was positively relishing the idea.

Look at me, I begged silently. *See what he's doing to me, right here in front of you all.*

The voices nearest to us all spoke in Spanish, but I tried to imagine their conversation, as Emmett grew bolder and introduced more fingers into my soaked slit.

She's hot for it. Look at her, opening her legs for him right in front of us.

And check out the size of those nipples.

He's got his tongue right down as far as he can get it. Bet he'll be doing the same with his cock soon enough.

I bet he could bend her over right now and she'd be up for it.

She isn't wearing anything under that dress—you can practically see her pussy.

You can definitely smell *her pussy. I've never seen such a slut in my whole life, even in the red light district.*

She'd make a great whore, that's for sure. I fancy having a go on her myself.

I couldn't take it any more. I was burning up. There was a roaring in my ears and the conversation faded into confused gabble as a sudden, shocking climax ripped through me.

I trembled against Emmett's hands and tongue, my breath ragged in his mouth. He felt the tremor and sighed with delight, keeping his fingertips firmly pressed against my clit until my orgasm was ridden out.

"Oh, you little beauty," he crooned brokenly, releasing me from the kiss but keeping his face close to mine. "You really bought into that, didn't you? I wasn't sure you would."

"Can we go back to the hotel?" I muttered, suddenly uncomfortably damp and prickly.

"I'm not sure I can stand yet," he cautioned, moving a hand to cover his tented crotch. "Let's finish our drinks first."

As my vision cleared, I tried to decide whether any of the people surrounding us had had an inkling of what was going on. But they were all preoccupied with their own groups—almost too preoccupied. It seemed Emmett's ravenous kissing had done the trick of making them look politely away, giving him a free pass to go further.

Out on the Ramblas, a man juggled with fire. We stood watching for a while in the flaring glow, Emmett with his arms around me from behind. Occasionally, he plucked at my skirt, offering a quick glimpse of my stocking tops to anyone who might be looking. But of course, everyone's attention was on the juggler, so Emmett was free to suckle my neck and cup my breasts to his heart's content.

By the time we reached the hotel, we were drunk with lust

for each other. He shoved me up against one of the pillars that framed the door and kissed me hard, his erection forcing my legs apart. He reached under my skirt and took two handfuls of my bare bum, squeezing and kneading them as the night-time crowd flowed past us, fast clubbers and slow tourists, skateboarding or eating fries, never stopping to see what was going on right under their noses.

"Oh, hey, Emmett...oops."

Calum and Alex emerged through the automated glass doors. They cleared their throats and moved away into the crowd.

"They saw us," I gasped later, on my back with my heels on Emmett's shoulders. He carried on powering into me, his eyes hard with determination.

"I know. Good," he panted. "I wanted them to."

"Do you think they saw...?"

"Your arse?" He let go of one of my legs and smacked the area in question. "I hope so. I don't care who knows what I do to you. I hope they know you're getting it right now, and you'll get it again, several times, before we see them again at breakfast. I'd like to send them an itemised list of what I do to you. I'd like to send them a clip of it. Ah, God."

His words slurred into the alphabet stew of orgasm. I watched him keenly, still floppy from my own two climaxes.

How absurd it was that I hadn't found him particularly attractive at first sight. Every inch of his face was transcendentally beautiful to me now; the perfect configuration of structure and spirit. The handsome celebrities I had admired in the past might as well have been blank cardboard cut-outs for all the effect they had on me now. If it wasn't Emmett, I wasn't interested.

But did he feel anything similar? Or did he still cast an idle eye over other faces, legs, breasts? Why should I even care if he did? Apparently this was a hard-wired male habit. But I'd read that every relationship contained one person who was more invested in it than the other, and since Emmett could hardly surpass me in that regard, that would have to be me.

I'd always tried to be the other person, the one that held the better cards. And now I wasn't, and it felt like trying to cross a high wire without a safety net.

"Emmett," I whispered, my fingers fluttering through his hair. He lay on top of me still, his cheek pressed to my shoulder.

"Mm hmm?"

"I belong to you."

He stretched his neck enough to peer at me. His eyes looked as if they had some kind of soft-focus filter on them; a veil of blue-green.

"You belong to me? Yes, you do."

I smiled, but my eyes were veiled themselves now, with a sheen of tears.

"That's all I want," I continued. "To belong to you."

"Is that your way of saying you love me?"

My assent trembled on a threshold, afraid of crossing it and finding the reception unwelcoming.

"I guess…"

"Because if you're trying to draw it out of me, you don't need to. I don't need to be coaxed or cajoled into telling you I love you. You only had to ask."

"Or you could just…tell me."

"Yes. Is it safe for me to do that?"

His face seemed to mirror my own fears and my heart leapt, all the way to the end of the high wire. I was safe now, on my plinth. Everything was going to be all right.

"Of course it is," I said. "You can tell me anything."

"Then I will," he said. "I love you. If you want to belong to me, I'm honoured and humbled by that. And I'll do everything I can to own you in the way you want, for as long as you want."

"I love you," I told him, smiling as the tears spilled. "So much. So unbelievably much, oh God."

We held each other close, sailing into sleep, both exactly where we wanted to be at last.

Chapter Ten

The next day, I got the hand-in-hand walk along the shore. I didn't get the churros, but only because they would spoil my dinner. Besides, there was always our final Barcelona breakfast for those.

Emmett's conference ended at lunchtime, so we had an afternoon to spend on the Gaudi trail, punctuating each interesting architectural experience with cafés and shops, not to mention kissing. Lots of that. My fantasy of being a 'proper couple' was indulged to the hilt.

We returned to the hotel to go back to bed, then dress for dinner, leaving as the sun began to set over the Mediterranean.

At the waterfront restaurant, Emmett ordered lobster and champagne.

"You don't have to impress me," I said. "I'm already about as impressed as I can be."

"No harm in keeping my credit topped up though, is there?" he said, sighing a little before taking a sip of fizz.

"Of course not. I hope I like lobster, that's all. I've never had it before."

"You'll like it." He looked out over the marina, to the sea beyond.

"You seem a little…pensive," I suggested. "Do you wish you could stay here?"

"No, it's not that," he said, then he turned to me. "I've arrived somewhere I never thought I'd be. I'm on the point of breaking a very solemn promise I made to myself, as a fourteen-year-old."

"Oh, promises you make at fourteen aren't binding, are they?" I said, trying to keep the tone as gentle as possible. "Or I'd still be kissing my poster of Captain Jack Sparrow every night before going to sleep."

His smile was a mere straightening of the lips.

"I told you my family were a secretive bunch, didn't I?" he said.

I nodded, keeping my breath in suspension halfway up my lungs.

"My dad had another wife."

"Bloody hell! A bigamist?"

"Yeah…that's what the charge would've been. If my mother had pursued it, which she didn't."

"Wow. When did you find out?"

"At fourteen," he said, with a faltering wink. "The second Mrs Marlowe turned up on the doorstep one night. I was on my way to a band rehearsal—yes, I was in a band, bass guitar, no, we weren't very good. Anyway, we split up after…had to move away…"

"Christ. What happened?"

"My dad had to go abroad on business trips a lot—about ten a year, mostly to South East Asia. While he was there he met this Thai girl and, well…he did love her, I think, and genuinely wanted to help her. The way he tells it, he married her out of a sense of duty and obligation. He thought it was the right thing to do." Emmett let out a sharp bark of a laugh. "He could justify anything to himself, though. He was never wrong, my dad. Never."

I didn't speak.

"Don't accuse me of taking after him," said Emmett, reading my silence correctly.

"I only meant that you generally *are* right about things," I said. "I don't think you'd do something like that, though. That's not like you at all."

He looked down at his place setting.

"Thanks."

"And I understand why you're so hot on honesty now," I added. "Makes perfect sense."

He narrowed his eyes at me. "You think I'd be a lying cheat if my dad hadn't wrecked our family in that way?" He paused, took a breath. "Sorry, I know you don't think that. And I've no way of knowing if it's nature or life experience that's made me such a stickler for the truth. Either way, it's affected me. Of course it has. Why else do you think I'm so good at reading people?"

I nodded, getting it.

"Nobody's going to fool me with their tricksy body language or things left unsaid again," he vowed savagely. "Nobody. Ever."

I reached out for his hand. He flinched at first, but made himself accept the gesture with a forced smile.

"I won't keep anything from you," I said. "I promise. Small, benign surprises excepted."

123

"To be honest, I'm not one for surprises either," he said.

"You need control."

"I sometimes wish I didn't. But there it is."

His fingers crept over my hand, tightening.

"There it is," I whispered, aching with love for him. "Do you see anything of your dad now?"

"No. He makes overtures from time to time, but I don't need or want him in my life, so…"

"Is your mother OK?"

"Oh, she's just about over it, I think. Remarried a couple of years ago, seems happy enough. Her new husband is nothing at all like dad. I think she deliberately went for his opposite."

"It's good that she's moved on. She deserves happiness. So do you."

The lobster arrived, just before he squeezed my hand into numbness.

After we'd finished eating, and were sipping the last of the champagne under a starlit sky, I asked Emmett if that had been the promise he made at fourteen.

"What?"

"That you'd never be deceived again."

He shook his head.

"I *did* make that promise, but it's not the one I meant."

"Oh, so what *did* you mean?"

I had never seen him look uncertain, or vulnerable, or afraid, but all three emotions passed across his face before he gave his reply.

"I was never going to get in too deep," he said. "I was never going to be in the position my mother was—of having her whole life trashed by somebody she loved."

"Bigamy isn't very common, you know."

I quailed at the look he gave me.

"I know that. I meant that I wasn't ever going to give that much of myself to another person. I'd seen the dangers and it seemed to me that the wise thing was to keep aloof, always hold something back."

"Oh. And is that…?"

"What I've done with you? No, that's the point I'm making. I've always enjoyed my past relationships, knowing I could step back from them as soon as they started to look serious. I've admired, liked, been captivated, been infatuated, even. But I've never…well, you know…"

Say it.

"Oh God, you're going to make me say it, aren't you?"

"I think we need to be absolutely clear here," I muttered, barely able to breathe.

"OK, I've never been in love." His expression was almost angry.

"That's sad," I said gently. "You should try it. I'm finding it pretty nice, personally."

"For Christ's sake, Jo, you *know* what I'm trying to say. Stop torturing me."

"It is a pretty novel role reversal, I admit. Oh, Emmett." Half-laughing, I stroked his cheek. "It's all right. I love you, and all I want is to be with you. You're safe with me."

His gaze softened.

"Yeah. I know. I'm sorry. And thanks for loving me…the way I love you. There. I said it."

I leant over to kiss his ridiculous lips.

"You make me so happy. I've never been this happy."

"And you just let yourself be?" he said, almost wonderingly. "You just accept it and don't worry about losing it?"

125

"Of course I worry about losing it," I said. "I sometimes lie awake at night and wonder what the hell I'd do if we broke up. I'd never, *ever* find another man like you. It would seem pointless even to try looking for one."

"All that worry," he whispered. "Such a waste of energy. Why don't we put an end to it?"

Something stabbed me in the chest, so sharply the scene swam before me, all the candlelight blurring into jagged lines. I hadn't realised emotional pain could feel so viscerally real.

"Put an end?" I whispered.

"Oh shit, no, that's not what I meant. Oh God. No." He was laughing, but his eyes were too bright. The light threatened to spill over. "Jo, I don't mean ending it. I meant putting an end to our doubts and worries. By making a real commitment. The contract to end all contracts."

"Oh!"

"Look, since I don't seem able to express myself tonight, I'll let this do the talking."

He reached inside his jacket and brought out a velvet-covered box.

Everybody knows what these velvet-covered boxes contain; by the time we're at secondary school we've seen a hundred of them in films, on TV, in storybooks. They're not big enough for anything else.

All the same, I couldn't help thinking that perhaps I was mistaken and the box held a single chocolate, or a button, or a rice krispie. Or, knowing Emmett, a nipple clamp.

So when I opened it up and saw the flash of fire that heralded a real diamond set in its circlet of white gold, I let out an ugly shrill of a laugh.

I looked at him, and the laughter died. He was absolutely

serious.

"What do you say?" he whispered.

I didn't have to think twice.

"Yes."

L'Étranger

Chapter Eleven

S o what's it going to be then?"
I tried to flex my wrists free of Emmett's pinion fingers, but without success.

"I've told you, I don't know yet."

"Well, isn't it time you did? The wedding's in three weeks."

I nudged his hip with a knee, needing to escape the pressure of his weight on my body, but he wouldn't budge. A boy at primary school had pinned me down this way in the playground once. I had fought like a tigress, but secretly I'd been thrilled by the feeling of helplessness and thought about it a lot in my bed at night.

"I'm aware of that, thanks."

"Mm, sarcasm? Are you sure that's wise?"

It certainly wasn't wise. My bottom was still sore from a brisk encounter with my hairbrush before landing on my back in bed; I wasn't sure I could take a second round.

"Not sarcasm, just…communication," I said, yelping a little as his mouth dipped to my neck and sucked at leisure. *Oh God,*

I thought, *don't leave a mark. My dress has a sweetheart neckline.*

He withdrew before damage could be done.

"Just a reminder that a lot of my preferred methods of communication are non-verbal," he said with a devilish grin. "As your bottom can attest."

Only too well, I thought, sticking out my lower lip.

"Anyway," he said, his lips so close to mine that I felt his words as little puffs of warmth. "As I was saying. You have something old. You have something new. You have something borrowed. What are you going to have that's blue?"

"I guess I'll just do what everyone does and have a blue garter on one stocking top," I said.

"I have a better idea," said Emmett. There was a glitter in his eye that usually meant trouble.

"Do you?"

"Yes. Something different and…fitting. Expressive of our relationship."

"Oh God," I said, picturing him leading me down the aisle by a baby-blue leash and collar. "Emmett, all my friends and relatives…"

"Yes, yes, don't panic. I don't have any kind of bizarre public spectacle in mind." He paused. "Actually, that's not true."

"*Emmett!*"

He laughed softly and released me from his grip, rolling over to lie on his side, looking down at me.

"OK, I'll tell you what I have in mind. You're under no obligation etcetera etcetera. It's just an idea I had. I wish I'd had it before, but I didn't. Anyway. I bumped into my old friend Mustang the other day."

"Mustang?"

"It's his biker gang name. No idea what his real name is."

"You have a friend in a biker gang?"

"You have a problem with that?"

"Not at all. It's just…you're so not a biker."

"I like a nice bit of leather," he objected.

"Leather, yes. Engine oil, no."

"Well, yeah. You'll be interested to know how we met." He smiled dazzlingly.

"How…did you meet?" I asked.

"On a local fetish noticeboard," he said. "Back in the day, when I was a single deviant exploring that side of myself. We chatted, he gave me advice, talked me through the local scene."

I was always fascinated to hear about Emmett's earlier adventures in BDSM. He had thrown himself into it, involving himself in everything that was going on. He'd dommed dozens of submissives across the region, but he'd quite never made the connection he was looking for. We bumped into one once, on an afternoon walk at a local beauty spot. She'd been with another man and their dog, and had blushed the deepest crimson I had ever seen. We passed each other without an exchange of greetings.

("She was married," Emmett told me. "Her husband had no idea. Neither did I. I finished it when I found out.")

"So he's a kinky biker?"

"That's exactly what he is. Anyway, I bumped into him in Tesco Metro after work last week. We went next door to the Feathers for a swift half and a catch up. Turns out he got married six months ago, to his Old Lady, as they call their girlfriends."

"Old Lady?" I screwed up my nose. "I wouldn't care for that."

"I'm not asking you to. Anyway, he told me about a little ceremony he and Shona had before the official wedding, and I was fascinated. And inspired."

"Another ceremony?" I blinked up at him. This wedding had been more than enough to organise, what with doing it all in three months. "Emmett, I've still got to book a hairdresser and sort out…"

"Shhh. You don't have to organise a thing. You just need to be available for an hour or two on Sunday afternoon."

"This Sunday afternoon? Emmett, what the hell is it? What have you signed us up for?"

"A collaring ceremony," he said. "Kinky version of a wedding, I suppose. But there's a little bit more to it."

I'd been right about the collar and leash! Oh Jesus. How the hell was that going to look in the wedding photos?

"I'm not walking up the aisle in a dog collar!"

"Josephine, I suggest you moderate your tone." He frowned, but I merely glared back at him. "No, your imagination is failing you. Unusually. By 'collaring', I don't mean a literal collar. I want you to have something around your neck at all times, but it can be anything—a necklace is the obvious. A velvet ribbon. Whatever matches the occasion."

"OK," I said, breathing more freely. "So this ceremony—it's just you putting a necklace on me? Like the ring bit of the wedding service?"

"With some vows," he said. "And witnesses—Mustang and Shona, basically."

"I don't know them," I said nervously.

"That doesn't matter," he said. "They know what we are to each other. They won't judge. They'll celebrate it. I feel quite strongly, now I've thought of this, that it's important we have a celebration of that aspect of our relationship we usually have to keep private."

"It's important to you," I said, a little bit sulkily, but I was coming round to his way of thinking. "But hideously embarrassing for me."

"The embarrassment is part of the commitment," he said seriously. "You show me that you will bear the shame and the humiliation as part of your submission to me. You show me just how deep our connection is."

He stroked my cheek. I held my breath.

"And what do you bear, for me?" I asked.

"I take responsibility for you," he said. "I make your happiness my highest aspiration."

"And that's it? You put a necklace on me and we come out with some jargon about being safe, sane and consensual?"

"Weeell…"

"What?" I sat up, pulling the duvet over my chest. "Emmett, you're making me nervous."

"The 'something blue' I had in mind isn't a necklace, or a collar. It's…well…Mustang owns the tattoo parlour on Ridley Road."

"Oh, you have *got* to be fucking kidding me!" I scooted back in alarm, my head hitting the wall behind me.

"Have I?" He held my panicked gaze, using that steady-eyed voodoo to try and still me. Somehow it always worked.

"Yes," I whispered, but already cracks were forming in my resolve. If he decided I was getting one, then I was getting one. This was what I was signing up for. "It's, like, too soon before the wedding for one thing."

"No, it's not," he said. "Not for a little one. It'll have healed, pretty much, by then. Besides, it won't be anywhere visible to the public."

"Oh God." My head was spinning. I had never even considered getting a tattoo. The whole needly, messy, permanent horror of it made me feel weak. "Can't you just draw on me with a Sharpie?"

He laughed and coaxed me back down, into his arms, where he lay stroking my face for a moment or two.

"You're brave enough to marry me," he said softly. "But scared to get a little bit of ink on your skin?"

"Needles," I wailed.

"If it's the pain you're worried about, you don't have to. Where I want to put it, you'll barely feel it. And it'll be over in a few minutes. Honestly, it's tiny."

"Where do you want to put it?"

"I'm surprised you have to ask. It's my favourite bit of you." He reached around and squeezed one bum cheek. "I love it so much I want to put my mark on it. Forever."

Mm, now that was kind of a hot thought, to be fair. I still felt weak, but it was more a kind of between-the-thigh swoon than needle-phobia now.

"What kind of mark?" I asked, highly conscious that I shouldn't be asking this—I should be rejecting the idea out of hand and refusing to discuss it. Why wasn't I doing that? Damn it!

He reached behind him, opening his top drawer and rummaging blindly before producing, of all things, a pub beermat.

"Mustang and I came up with a design," he said. "As we were in the pub at the time and neither of us had a notebook…"

He turned the cardboard square and showed me a very simple little design. At first I thought it was some kind of family crest before I realised that the graphic beneath Emmett's gothic initials was a pair of crossed riding whips.

"Oh," I said with a little gulp of a laugh. "Classy."

"Isn't it?" said Emmett without a trace of irony. "And it'll be tiny—no bigger than this." He indicated a small space between thumb and fingertip. "And completely invisible to anyone you'd prefer to keep it from."

"Everyone, basically," I said.

"Even me?"

"Even *me*! Oh God, I don't know. I've never been attracted to the idea of a tattoo…"

"But this isn't really. Don't think of it as a tattoo. Think of it as my mark, on you."

Again, my heart beat a little faster and my eyes rolled back. *His mark, on me.* Definitely hot.

"Forever," he whispered seductively. "As ineradicable as our love for one another."

"Oh, if you're going to be all romantic about it," I snapped, sensing defeat.

"It is romantic," he insisted. "It's real commitment. Only laser treatment can reverse it. You have to be sure as sure can be about us. That's a very romantic statement to make."

I narrowed my eyes. "Is this some kind of test? Like you think I'm going to stand you up at the altar or something?"

Emmett swallowed and his eyes flicked away for a moment. Had I hit on something?

"You really think that could happen?" I continued. "I thought I was the one who worried about that kind of thing. I've been trying really hard not to think about what I would do if I turned up on our wedding day and you weren't there. I can't even begin to… You don't have any reason to worry about that.

Seriously."

"I don't," he said, "not *really*. Just in my nightmares. And unguarded moments."

We clung to each other like jungle monkeys to a vine.

"Don't get the tattoo if you don't want to," he said, in a high, tight voice. "It's OK. I was just being…"

"No, I will," I said. "I want to. Phone up Mustang and tell him to book me in."

Chapter Twelve

Those brave words came back to bite me in the arse. Literally.

Standing in front of the luridly-fronted tattoo parlour on dismal Ridley Road, I had to lean into Emmett to stop my knees from buckling.

PASSION AND PAIN, read the signboard, with images of dripping knives and flaming roses wound about the lettering. I certainly knew about both of those, and was about to find out some more.

"Are you sure about this?" he murmured into my ear, wrapping an arm tightly about my waist.

I nodded. "Collar me," I whispered back. "Make me yours."

He breathed in sharply, then out in a ragged stream.

"Oh boy," he muttered. He bent and kissed me hard and long while the wind-whipped litter eddied around our feet and the traffic hummed and beeped behind us.

The shop was officially closed, so we had to knock on the door for admission. It was opened by a tiny woman in a black vinyl halterneck dress. Snakes and unicorns cavorted down her arms, whilst her cleavage was an homage to Axl Rose. Only her face, beaming out at us, was free of ink.

"Hello, you must be Emmett and Jo. I'm Shona. Come on in."

We followed her through a dark passageway into a back room.

A bearded giant was in there, pulling some cover sheets tight on a padded therapy couch. There was a chemical tang in the air that froze my blood. It all felt frighteningly medical, despite the walls being plastered with skulls and whatnot.

"Mustang," said Emmett. "Meet Jo."

The bearded giant straightened up and held out a massive hand for me to shake.

"So you're the one that's taken our international playboy off the scene, eh?" he said with a wink. "There'll be subs crying into their coffee all over town."

A nervous laugh was all I could manage.

"You look scared," he observed. "Never been under the needle before?"

I shook my head, pressing my lips together to stop them quivering.

"Well, you can relax. I'm a professional. Been tattooing for thirty years this summer. Right, Shona?"

"That's right," she said. "And just look how many times I've let him loose on me! That's a vote of confidence right there."

"I sometimes tell Shona she should put on a bit of weight— stretch out that skin until there's some extra space for me to work on. We're all out of canvas there. Sho, pour the girl a measure of Jack. Looks like she could do with some Dutch courage."

Shona busied herself at a cabinet while Mustang took a moment to look over his tools.

"All in working order," he said.

I took my measure of Jack Daniels and necked it down in one.

"So you're all set then?" said Mustang. "Might as well get down to business."

Emmett gave my hand a squeeze and whispered, "OK then."

I put my hand up to the top button of my coat, faltering. Could I really do this? Did Mustang and Shona know exactly what I was about to do?

Emmett, seeing my hesitation, nudged me. "Don't be shy," he said, a little more sternly. "Nobody's going to be shocked."

Shona laughed. "Been there myself. Done it, got the T-shirt. Well, the collar, I should say." She put her fingers to a thick black leather choker and tugged at it in illustration.

"It's just feels a bit weird," I muttered, undoing the top button. "With other people…"

"It's meant to," said Mustang, refusing to look away from me, as I'd hoped he might.

I fixed my eyes on the floor—it was clean, I was relieved to note—and loosened button after button. When at last the coat fell open, cool air crept in and goose-bumped my skin.

I hesitated again, my strong sense of shame taking me over until Emmett took the lapels and slid the garment off me.

I stood in front of the three of them—my lover and two total strangers—in a glossy black bondage-inspired underwear set, with criss-crossing straps linking the bra to the knickers and the suspender belt to the stockings. All my most intimate areas were covered, and yet I felt obscenely displayed.

"Very nice," said Mustang softly. "Very nice indeed. Turn

around for us."

I caught Emmett nodding from the corner of my eye and obeyed. At the back, the knickers thinned into a thong, exposing my bare cheeks to view.

"And that's where you want it? On the left hand side?"

"Yes, as we discussed," said Emmett, his voice a little uneven.

"Gotcha. OK, well, are we going to start with the ceremony?"

"Absolutely," he said, more decisively. "On your knees, pet."

I dropped down on the spotless, but very cold, floor.

Shona coughed and offered to get me a kneeling mat, which Emmett thankfully sanctioned. Perhaps it was a plus, having a fellow submissive here. She had a perspective the men lacked. I shifted on to the warmer foam and tried to forget that I was being watched.

Emmett had written and memorised the vows; I had only to respond or repeat, which was just as well, because I could hardly think.

He stood in front of me, so my eyes were roughly level with his crotch. I wasn't going to be allowed to spend the excruciating ceremony staring at that focal point, though. He reached down, gripped my chin between finger and thumb and yanked it up, so I had to look into his face.

I began to tremble. He kept a hold of my chin as he started to speak.

"I am here today to cast off my solitary life and bind another to me. The bond is one of love, which we promise to make strong enough to last our whole lives. Jo will be bound to me, and I will keep the knot tied tight by protecting and caring for her. From this day, she belongs to me, and I accept full responsibility for her safety and happiness. Now I ask Jo to repeat her vows after me."

He loosened his grip a little, allowing me to swallow and prepare to speak.

"I promise that I will be honest in all things. I will not lie to you and I will not hide the truth from you."

I repeated the words, croakily, shakily.

"I promise that I will obey you and accept that your decisions are made for my own benefit."

This was difficult to say, especially with witnesses, but we had discussed it beforehand and agreed that he would never demand anything unreasonable of me. He would only insist if I was putting myself in danger of some kind.

"I promise that I will love and respect you always, as my lover and my master."

Much as I felt like a jerk coming out with all this, at a deeper level I experienced the emotional truth of it, like gold struck far below ground.

I had no more to say, mercifully. Instead, I had only to listen as Emmett recited his own vows—to protect and cherish, to guide and direct, to be always loving and sensitive to my needs.

Mustang handed Emmett a round, flexible necklet—not so much a collar, although it seemed to be made of plaited leather.

Emmett placed it against my throat.

"With this collar, I make you mine," he said softly. Unable to look away, I felt my eyes brim until his face blurred. The collar clicked shut with a magnet. "You belong to me, for as long as you wear it. Tell me you belong to me, Jo."

A tear spilled on to my cheek.

"I belong to you, Emmett."

The shimmering suspension of reality was broken by Mustang and Shona clapping heartily. Shona bent to kiss my cheek, whispering, "Congratulations." Mustang shook Emmett's hand.

"Aren't you going to kiss her?" he asked in jovial rebuke.

Emmett pulled me to my feet and wrapped me in his arms, kissing me long and hard until Mustang and Shona began clearing their throats and talking about their plans for later in the day.

He broke off, still holding me tight to his side, and said, "Right then, where do you want her?"

All my fuzzy feelings sharpened into blades of dread. I'd almost forgotten.

"Up here on the bench, little one," said Mustang, patting the crease-new cotton cover on. "On your front, of course."

I climbed up and lay prone on the wide leather cushion, keeping my eyes down and my face hidden. Mustang adjusted the bench so that my bottom was raised a little higher than the rest of me. It reminded me of being positioned by Emmett for a spanking, and my cheeks flooded with heat.

"This is a beautiful rear end," remarked Shona. "What a canvas, sir."

"What a canvas indeed," agreed Mustang. "Must be a peach to have over your knee, Emmett, huh?"

"Oh yes," said Emmett. I jumped a little as his hand descended on to my curves, stroking them proprietorially. "It reddens up beautifully too."

"I'll bet," said Mustang. "Now, look, I can offer to strap her down if you think it'll help. Special offer, all part of the service for good friends and favoured customers."

"Yes, I think that'd be a good idea," said Emmett.

I gulped as a wide leather strap was passed over the backs of my legs and the small of my back. There would be no escape now.

"How are you feeling?" whispered Emmett, up near my ear after securing the top strap.

"Scared," I whispered back.

He brought a stool around to the top end of the bench and sat on it, taking my hands and holding them tight.

"I'm here, pet," he said, squeezing my fingers. "Just keep holding on to me."

I heard strange sounds from behind me; bottles being collected, ink being loaded.

"Do you like your collar?" asked Emmett, perhaps sensing that I needed some distraction.

"It's lovely. Not what I was expecting."

"What were you expecting?"

"Stiff dog collar type thing…ohh!"

Icy coldness on my left cheek would have made me kick my legs if they hadn't been tethered. It must have been Shona, swabbing me with surgical wipes.

"Easy there," she said. "Just getting you prepped."

The area she rubbed was reassuringly small. I tried to concentrate on my breathing, feeling my breasts rise and fall against the cotton-covered leather.

"OK," said Mustang. "Putting on the transfer now."

He pressed something firmly into my skin, dimpling it for a moment.

"Emmett, come and tell me this is what we agreed. Just in case I've got the wrong one."

Emmett dropped my hands and moved behind me for a moment.

"That's the one," he confirmed, his voice husky with approval. "Perfect placement."

He returned. "It's going to look so good," he said, retrieving my hands. "It just needs to stay on for a minute, then Mustang will be able to start properly."

"Wish I could see," I said.

"You will, in the mirror, when it's all healed. It'll only take a week or so." He raised his voice, addressing Mustang. "I suppose I won't be able to spank her for a while?"

"Not on that spot, no," chuckled Mustang. "Maybe keep it all to the one side."

"Oh God, please don't," I blurted. I hated it when Emmett concentrated all his attention on one spot. Luckily he only did it when he was feeling extra-specially sadistic.

Shona made a sympathetic clucking sound.

"I feel you, babe," she said. "Nothing worse than a one-sided whipping. Will this week feel like a really long time now, Emmett?"

"An eternity," he said grimly.

"I guess it's all still new and fresh to you, and you're up to it all the time, huh?" said Mustang. "I remember those days. Shona could barely sit down the first six months after we met. And I was inking her a new one near enough every few weeks."

"I think this'll be Jo's first and last," said Emmett. "She wasn't keen when I suggested it."

"Well, it's not for everyone," said Shona.

The transfer was ripped suddenly and without warning from my skin. It didn't hurt, but I made a little mew of shock.

I gritted my teeth, ready for the drill, but instead I got a soothing ointment smeared over me with big latex-covered fingers.

"OK," said Mustang. "Now we're ready. You hold on to your man there, keep it calm and relaxed. It'll sting a bit, but you're used to a sore bum, aren't you?"

I didn't answer, too intent on clinging to Emmett for dear life.

"Don't clench," he whispered. "You know better than that by now, surely."

I did, but a tattooist's needle wasn't the same as a leather strap or a wooden paddle wielded by somebody I loved and trusted. My nails dug into Emmett's skin as the drill was fired up, sounding to me like the prelude to a chainsaw massacre.

"Oh God. I hate this. I hate drills. I hate the dentist. Please…"

"Be brave. It hurts much less than the cane."

"You've never given me the cane."

"Hmm, no, I haven't, have I? Must rectify that soon. All right, then, less than the paddle."

I screwed my eyes shut, but I soon found that he was right. Compared to a good blistering with a flat wooden paddle, this tattoo lark was a breeze. The sting was mild and localised, almost perversely enjoyable. The drill buzzed itchily away for about ten minutes, during which I relaxed by increments until, at the turning off, I was almost drowsy.

"There, that wasn't so bad, was it?" Emmett dropped a kiss on to my forehead. "You needn't have worried after all."

"It wasn't painful, really."

"Disappointed?" Mustang's voice held a hint of smirk. "I can do one on the base of your spine if you want something a bit harder to bear."

"No, that's fine."

"All right, just need to wipe away any residue…" Mustang

blotted a tissue around the affected area, then stood back. "What's the verdict, Emmett?"

Emmett dropped my hands and went to inspect Mustang's handiwork.

"That's exactly what I had in mind. My mark, indelible now."

"It's very romantic," gushed Shona. "Jo, would you like a drink of water?"

"Please." I moved to get up, but of course I was strapped down. The sensation of being in bondage, in scanty underwear while three people checked out my arse sent an unwanted message of arousal down between my legs. I tried to ignore it, but I felt sure everyone in the room was aware of it.

I took the glass that Shona gave me and drank it steadily. The strap across my back meant that I had to strain my neck to raise my head, but at least my arms and hands were free.

"I guess that's it, then?" I said, clamping my thighs tight together in the hope that nobody would notice any dewy sheen on their upper portions.

"Hang on," said Mustang. "Just going to..."

He taped a gauze pad on to the tattoo site. His fingers were rough against the smooth skin of my bottom, calluses scraping the curve. "You'll need to keep that there for a week, maybe ten days. Do *not* take it off before, no matter how much it itches, and do *not* try and pick at the scab. Do you understand?"

"Yes."

"Promise me?"

"I promise."

"By the time your wedding day comes around, it'll be in perfect shape. Now...I think Shona and I had something to sort out in the store room, right, Shona? We'll leave you alone for a little while."

They shuffled out through a back door.

"That's weird," I said. "Why are they leaving?"

"Oh, Jo," said Emmett softly, unbuckling the strap that held my legs in place. "Can't you guess?"

He bent and kissed the unsullied side of my bottom. I shivered.

"Not here, surely."

"Why not here? The ceremony is done. The mark is made. All that remains is the consummation. A collaring is no different to a wedding in that respect."

"But Emmett…" I dropped the empty cup and contorted my arms, trying to find the buckle on the strap that still held me, but it was just out of my reach. "They're just next door!"

"They won't come back," he reassured, parting my legs with determined hands and planting more kisses on my exposed inner thighs. "Besides, I think…" He placed his knuckles between my vulnerable lower lips. "You might not be completely averse. Did that turn you on? Getting my initials tattooed on you, like my brand of ownership?" I squirmed as he rocked his knuckles gently across my clit. "Oh, I think it did. Definitely."

I stopped trying to fight and clung instead to the top of the bench. Emmett pulled some kind of lever so that my legs lowered to a steepish slope and I was bent over at the waist. He held my hip with one hand while the other dealt with his belt and trousers. I heard them shush and jingle to his ankles, then he was there where I wanted him.

The sex was fast and furtive. I tried not to make a sound, hearing only the steady creak of the bench as Emmett forced it into unfamiliar motion, and the light slap of his thighs on mine.

He skewered into me, finding little resistance from my wet depths. As he fucked me, one hand caressed the skin around my concealed tattoo.

"You'll have this forever," he grunted, pressing his thumb into the plentiful cushioning.

"Mmm."

"Because this is mine." He parted my cheeks and my heart sped up, picturing him staring into that most intimate of voids. "And this…on our wedding night. At last." He pushed a fingertip against the unviolated pucker, a dark promise.

I came, hard, unable to prevent a sharp little cry that must have carried to the next room.

He continued his implacable thrusting. The cotton cover began to come away from the leather cushion, rumpling around the top of my breasts. I bit down on the leather to stop up the little gasps that came out with each strong jolt forwards.

He grabbed my collar and pulled on it as he emptied noisily into me, careless of listening ears, perhaps glorying in them. More than probably.

"There now," he panted, rubbing between my shoulder blades as he made a slow business of pulling out. I worried about staining the cotton cover, although I imagined they were boil washed at a high temperature, if ever re-used. "The job is done."

"I'm collared," I said faintly, fingering the plaited leather necklet.

"And marked." He gave the dressing a gentle prod, enough to make me suck in a breath. "I guess we can go home."

Chapter Thirteen

As promised, the tattoo was fully healed by the morning of my wedding.

I pulled my white silk knickers over it and got to work on the stockings. A knock on the door made me fumble the clips. I swore under my breath.

"Hang on a minute."

"Aren't you ready for the dress?"

Maria, my oldest school friend and chief bridesmaid, was taking her duties seriously. She was the only one of my social circle able to step into the role at such short notice, but she was doing a sterling job. She'd only flown in from Edinburgh the night before, but she'd taken charge of champagne breakfast, luxury bubble bath, hair, make-up and everything else that needed doing while my parents played host to a random selection of my relatives downstairs.

I clipped at speed, then flung on my bra.

"Ready for my close-up, Mr DeMille," I called.

She came in, the dress draped over her outstretched arms.

"Sorry, I got brown sauce on it while I was doing the bacon sandwiches earlier," she said, then laughed at my frozen face. "Kidding. God, you're gullible. Why would I take it into the kitchen?"

"Just don't. I don't have my normal ninja wits about me today. It's my wedding day! Have pity."

She held the dress up against me. "Gorgeous," she said. "He's a lucky dog."

"I can't wait for you to meet him," I said, stepping into the pool of white and silver.

"I can't believe I haven't either. What was the rush, mate? Are you up the duff?"

"No! And it's not *that* quick."

"Six months from 'hi' to hitched. Come on, that's quite quick. What's this? Oh my God, you've got a tattoo."

"Leave it." I placed a panicking hand over the area. My bloody knicker elastic cut right across it, so the lower left hand portion of it was visible beneath.

"Was that his initials? Oh my God. You've got his initials tattooed on your arse? Seriously?"

"It's private. Just do the dress up, will you?"

"I will if you'll move your bloody hand. Oh wow. It really is his initials. I don't know if that's cute or scary."

"It's none of your biz, is what it is," I grumbled as she began to hook and eye me into my silky streamlined new silhouette.

"Right." She was quiet for a moment, concentrating. "But Jo."

"What?"

"You always said you'd never get a tattoo and nothing could ever persuade you. Remember, when I got the Japanese symbol on my ankle?"

"That was years ago. You weren't even legal."

"Not *that* long ago. I suppose I'm wondering…was it your idea, or was it his?"

"Does it matter?" I squirmed in my dress. It was not uncomfortably tight, but it certainly kept my posture in full *Black Swan* mode. "Whoever's idea it was, we both agreed to have it done."

"His idea then," she said, grimly satisfied. "And the shotgun wedding—was that his idea too?"

"It's not a shotgun wedding. We know what we're doing, all right? Neither of us expected this…it just happened. And we couldn't be happier."

"OK. I'm just…your mum said a few things downstairs. I think she's a bit bamboozled by it all as well. I guess I just need to be sure…"

"Mum likes Emmett," I said, a little stung.

"She said she finds him very charming," corrected Maria. "Not always the same thing. Very charming, and very clever, she said. She made 'clever' sound like an insult."

"Oh, look, I know they worry about every little thing, but I'm a big girl now. I can make my own decisions and I can stick to them."

I admired myself in the mirror, trying to see what Emmett would see. Try as I might, I still couldn't quite accept that I was good enough for him. A Type A overachiever and a slacker, bobbing along, failing to realise her potential.

But he saw the potential in me. He thought I was perfect.

"I need my something new," I remembered, taking the box out of my dresser drawer.

Maria helped me put on the sparkling silver choker, a delicate thing with additional loops nestling between my collar bones. This, we had agreed, would be my 'dress collar' for special occasions.

I put my hand to it, feeling it press into my skin. At all times, I was his.

"It's very pretty," said Maria. "Unusual. He has good taste. Obviously."

She jabbed me in the ribs, and I was able to smile again.

"Please just be happy for me," I said. "We love each other. That's what matters, isn't it?"

"Yeah," she said softly. "In the end."

It was a relief to get the ceremony over.

I felt like laughing all the way through it, or maybe crying—somehow I wasn't sure which—and was highly conscious of having an audience.

Emmett spoke his vows clearly and confidently; for me, it was more a case of muttering and staring at my hands, locked into Emmett's, his warm grip keeping their shaking to a minimum.

Suddenly everything seemed very *big* and very real, in a way it hadn't before. This was a legally binding commitment, after all. Whatever we'd been playing at was now a job at which we had to stick for the rest of our lives.

I tried to imagine what we'd be like in ten, twenty, fifty years. What if one of us died ages before the other? What if one of us needed twenty-four-hour care? What about kids? Would we be able to have any? What if we couldn't?

My spiralling thoughts were halted by the ring part of the service. I watched him slide the gold band on to the relevant finger, then repeated the action on him. It was done. We were married.

There was no cancelling this contract, except through the

courts.

Sitting in the restaurant afterwards, I tried to identify any difference in me. Did I feel married? I had to conclude that I did not, that nothing seemed to have changed in any material sense, until my mother called me 'Mrs Marlow' and I felt a bit sick.

"No, I'm just me. Still me," I murmured, seeking refuge in wine.

Emmett placed his hand on mine.

"My wife," he said, into my ear.

"I hate the word wife," I told him. "It makes me think of medieval women in torn aprons with boiled red hands."

"Oh?" He was amused. "And what about husband? What image does that evoke?"

"That's not so bad. Just a generic man, really. Husband is a strange word, but has a sexy thing going on. There is nothing at all sexy about the word 'wife'."

"So what would you prefer to be?"

"Oh…I don't know. Spouse is horrible too. Makes me think of water spouts."

"The old ball and chain?" he suggested lightly.

"That would suit *you* better," I reminded him. "Can't I just be your beloved?"

"Always. But I'd sound a bit of a dick introducing you as such to strangers and work colleagues."

I sighed. "With nomenclature, as with all things, women get the rough end of the stick."

"I thought you liked the rough end of the stick."

"Ssh. People will hear!"

"Anyway, a historical usage for husband is 'lord and master'. Which implies a wife is 'commoner and servant'. Shall I call you that?"

"Er, no, thanks. Perhaps I'll stick with wife after all."

"Perhaps you should."

A voice from the lobby caused Emmett to prick his ears and stiffen like a hare in gunsights. The voice, indistinct at first but growing clearer as it approached our conservatory room, was low and authoritative.

Its owner, when he appeared in the room, was tall and impeccably suited, in his mid-forties perhaps, with one of those sharp beards that look so good on long-faced men.

Emmett launched himself into space, rising with such haste that the cutlery clattered and my wine almost spilled.

"Charles," he yelped. I had never seen him so disarranged and spontaneous. It was like watching a different man. "My God! You came!"

"Ah, Emmett," he said, smiling with all his teeth. "My profound apologies. I know I said I couldn't come, but I found myself unexpectedly in the area, and wondered if you would mind…"

"Christ, no, of course not, not at all. I'm…" Emmett laughed, and there was a strange shining in his eyes. "I can't believe you're here."

"Well?" The famous Charles beamed his teeth at me. "I presume this is your bride?"

Bride. Now that's a nice word. Couldn't I be a bride forever? Charles had true green eyes, of that high-set, narrow kind that seem to hide much more than they convey.

"Oh, forgive me, I'm all over the place," gushed Emmett. Who *was* this man? Where was my composed, controlled husband? "Charles Fox, this is my wife, Mrs Josephine Marlow. Jo, this is Charles Fox."

"You used to work for him," I prompted myself. "Early in

your career."

"That's right."

"Delighted to meet you, Josephine," said Fox, holding out a signet-ringed hand. I took it, expecting a handshake. What I got was a kiss on the fingertips, very Regency romantic.

Confused, I snatched my hand away, and instantly wished I hadn't. The stern look on Fox's face was nothing compared to the look of disappointment on Emmett's.

"Sorry," I mumbled. "Thought you were going to..." I lapsed into embarrassed silence.

"Well, pull up a chair," said Emmett, covering my shame. "How come you're in England? What's been going on since I last heard from you?"

And that was it. A full hour of my wedding reception lost to this uninvited business bore. By the time the cake was cut, I hated him.

Oh, he tried to include me in the conversation. It wasn't just his dress that was impeccable. Courtesy, graciousness, charm —it was all there. But Emmett wasn't Emmett when he was with Fox, so I had no recourse but to hate him.

After the cake-cutting, Fox had the good manners to melt away into the other guests, attaching himself to some of Emmett's work colleagues at one of the more distant tables.

"Boy, someone has a crush," I said, immediately regretting my cutting tone even more than I'd regretted my reaction to the fingertip kiss.

"Are you jealous?" Emmett's lip curled in a way I rarely saw, an unpleasant, slightly threatening way.

"A bride should never have to be jealous on her wedding day," I said.

"No, especially when she has no reason to."

The first bars of *Someone To Watch Over Me* struck up. It didn't seem the right moment, but there was nothing for it. We had to step down off our top table podium and dance.

In Emmett's arms, feeling the silken inside of his waistcoat slide against his shirt, taking in the warmth and familiar promise inside, my ugly mood melted and I was new again. His forehead tilted to mine, a loose strand of red hair brushing my nose now and again, but not enough to make me break our eye contact.

The chatter from the tables all around became nothing, swallowed up by the yearning melody of the song.

"I love you," I told him.

"I love you too," he replied. "Nothing will ever take me away from you. Nothing."

In the honeymoon suite, we fell, laughing and kissing, on to the king sized circular bed. Somebody—I suspected Maria—had scattered rose petals all over the pillows and quilt, and a bottle of champagne lay in an ice bucket on the nightstand.

"Do you feel married?" asked Emmett, having kissed me as much as one pair of lips could stand.

"I don't know. It's weird. I feel *happy*. Do you think that's the same thing?"

"I hope so."

Emmett popped the champagne cork and poured us a flute each.

"One glass," he said. "To toast ourselves."

We clinked glasses, beaming at each other until Emmett's attention turned to the champagne cork, lying in his palm.

"These champagne corks are funny things, aren't they?" he said.

"Hilarious. Umm, in what way?"

"Well, look at the base of it. It's much bigger in

circumference than the neck of the bottle. You wouldn't think it would fit in there, would you?"

"Doesn't it expand while it's in the bottle or something?" I said vaguely, not particularly in the mood for a physics discussion.

"It absorbs carbon dioxide from the champagne which forces it to expand," said Emmett. "But that's just one example from nature."

"Oh!" I saw what he was driving at now and I clenched my buttocks. "You're talking about…"

"Tonight's the night," he teased. "New frontiers."

"Oh God."

"You can't say you haven't been prepared," he admonished, and it was true. The butt plugs had been growing steadily in size over the preceding few weeks. I knew that I was physically able to accommodate him. But it was still a cringe-inducing thought.

"I know, but somehow I don't *feel* prepared."

"Nervous?"

He kissed my forehead.

"Yeah."

"That's good. I don't want you ever getting blasé about anything I do to you. I want you to have that racing heart, those trembling thighs, those doe eyes. I love all that. Now turn around and I'll unlace that dress."

Obediently I presented my rear aspect to him and he pulled the ribbons out of my eyelets until the corseted top was loose and my lungs were able to expand and contract in the old familiar way again. He reached around, investigating my breasts, which hadn't needed a bra due to the tight embrace of the boned bodice. My dress fell inevitably down to my hips, where it rested a while, waiting for Emmett to have his fill of my hardening nipples.

When he had had enough, he pushed the gown down to my knees and pulled it out from under me, leaving me in my white silk knickers, stockings and suspender belt.

He hooked an arm around me and twisted me into a long, hungry kiss, his free hand wandering all over my body as his tongue possessed my mouth.

"I love you, Jo," he said, coming up for air. "You know that, don't you?"

"I love you, more than anything. I never, ever want to be without you."

"You never have to be."

He grabbed all the pillows from the head of the bed and piled them up in the centre, rose petals fluttering about as he worked.

"All right, darling," he said. "Put yourself over these pillows for me."

He ran a hand down my spine, reassuring me with his touch, and I draped myself across the plump, firm barrier.

His hand on one of my bottom cheeks, he said, "Hmm, maybe a few more," and added some cushions in underneath my stomach, pushing my arse up higher, until my knees barely reached the mattress. "That's better. Are you comfortable?"

"Pretty much."

He patted my silk-clad cheek.

"Pretty much…what?"

"Oh." I huffed with a mix of embarrassment, impatience and frustration with myself. "Pretty much, *sir*."

"Actually, I think we'll change that, just for tonight, in honour of the occasion. Tonight I want you to refer to me as 'my lord and master'. Shall we practise? Are you comfortable, pet?"

I rolled my eyes, grateful that he couldn't see my face, and parroted the phrase as he wished.

"Good." Kneeling behind me, he took hold of my inner thighs and spread them wide apart, twanging my suspender snaps so that I gasped as he did so.

"I bet not many brides get into this position on their wedding night," he said, cupping and squeezing my buttocks, then grazing my sensitive inner thighs with his fingertips. "Most brides get the romantic treatment they deserve. But you're not most brides, are you, pet?" He slapped my bum in illustration.

"No, my lord and master," I moaned, feeling my hips shudder with desire.

"Most brides don't have their groom's initials permanently tattooed on their backside, do they?" He ran a finger under the elastic, across his little coat of arms. "Most brides don't need collars or cuffs or regular spankings. But you do. Don't you, little one?"

"Yes, my lord and master." I swallowed, desperate for him to reach inside my knickers and give my clit some attention.

"I think, as your husband, I'll have to step up the routine," he said, peeling my silky knickers slowly over my outthrust cheeks. "Much more sex, and I'll be aiming to keep this bottom red most of the time. What do you think of that?"

"If that's what you think is best, my lord and master." A plea for him to touch me, finger me, fuck me was on the tip of my tongue.

The knickers were effectively trapped in place by my suspender snaps. I felt them stretched to bursting underneath me, the sides digging into my stocking tops.

With his thumbs, Emmett parted my bare cheeks and

massaged their soft inner skin, holding them open for a good look at the barrier he intended to breach.

Taking pity on me for the briefest of moments, he dipped his fingertips between my legs, swiping my clit.

"You get wet so quickly," he said admiringly. "It's as if you're in permanent heat. How do you do it?"

"You make me do it, my lord and master. Mmm. Ohh God, please…"

He removed his fingers and gave my bottom a good hard smack.

"I'm going to have your arse," he told me, laying on several more. "But not until it's hot enough. You need to be well warmed up first."

His sound, percussive swats bounced off the walls of the room, echoing like pistol cracks. Anybody passing outside could be in no doubt that someone was getting a spanking in here. I wondered how many brides had been bent over and dealt with like this on their wedding night. Was I one of many, or a mere few?

I began to grunt with discomfort after the first dozen, but he kept going. Somewhere in amongst my pathetic whimpers, I heard the clink and thunder of a housekeeping trolley passing the bedroom door.

Oh God, they wouldn't come in here, would they?

But the noise faded, and once again only the crack of Emmett's palm against my bottom and our combined laboured breathing filled our ears.

"OK." The smacks turned to caresses across my well-warmed rear. "That's a gorgeous colour now. I want you to reach behind and spread your cheeks for me."

It didn't surprise me that he wanted to make me complicit

in my own degradation, but it was still difficult to perform the expected task. My spanked skin was warm against my palms as I opened this private passage up to him, and the action made it impossible to clench in the way instinct warned me I should.

I heard him rooting around in his trouser pocket, then the well-known sound of a lubricant bottle being uncapped.

"Oh my God," I exclaimed involuntarily. "You've been carrying that around all day? I mean, you had it in your pocket during the marriage service?"

"Yeah, forgot to pack it, had to grab it at the last minute," he said. I heard the faint glug as he upended it on to his fingers.

"Not like you to forget a thing like that."

"Hmm, well, it might surprise you to learn that I don't have sex on the brain every *minute* of the day. And this morning was more than averagely busy."

"It must have been. Wow."

"You're beginning to sound a little cheeky, madam. I don't think that's a good idea, do you?"

He pressed one fingertip unceremoniously to the target, making me want to let go of my cheeks and rear up, but I managed to keep myself in position without a major flinch somehow.

I knew I could get through this—he had pushed his fingers inside here on numerous occasions, either to ease the passage of a plug or to add an extra dimension while he fucked me — but it felt more ceremonial and momentous, and therefore more nerve-racking.

He rubbed and massaged the tight ring, easing it open with slicked-up fingers while I clung to my cheeks, my fingernails digging into the heated flesh.

"I can't wait to make this all mine," he said, sliding in gently then holding still for a moment before rotating his fingers to ensure I stayed well aware of what he did to me. "I'm not sure how I've waited this long…God, you're going to be so tight…" He pushed forward suddenly, embedding his two fingers to the knuckles. I began to pant as he moved them backwards and forwards, then scissored them outwards, stretching me.

I felt utterly surrendered, being toyed with and used by him in the basest possible way. My pussy was soaked with the excitement of it, longing to be filled, but that wasn't the plan tonight.

He pulled out his fingers and started removing his own clothes, first the waistcoat, then the shirt, then the trousers and underwear. I saw bits of them from the corner of my eye, flying on to the floor, while I worked on keeping my cheeks spread and ready for him.

He took hold of my hips and got himself into position. I screwed my eyes tight shut. This did not feel like a lubed fingertip, nor the friendly narrow rounded end of a butt plug. This felt like something much too broad to take.

"Oh, it's going to tear me," I panicked as he began to push.

"It isn't, darling, it isn't. Hold still. I wouldn't damage you, I promise."

There was nothing left to do but trust. I wriggled uncomfortably as he kept that blunt wide intruder pressing hard at my tiny door, but the lube did its miraculous work and I felt myself stretch and open up to him, just as I had done to his fingers.

It wasn't painless, though. There was a definite smart to the sensation as he inched his way in. It was like the bad part of inserting a butt plug, but constant.

"Ohhhh, this is…" His voice was overloaded with dark

pleasure, as if he'd taken strong narcotics.

"It's…ahh," I added. "Feels…really weird…hurts a bit…"

"Just a bit," he slurred. "Soon be all the way there…then it won't hurt…Jeeeesus, sooo tight."

There was a red flare of strong pain and I let go of my parted cheeks and tried to pull myself free, but Emmett held me tight and surged all the way in, and it turned out he was right.

There was a throb, a residual soreness, but that moment of serious pain was over very quickly. And now I felt fuller than I thought possible, and it was highly, giddily erotic.

"You should see yourself now," whispered Emmett. "You should see what I can see. My cock all the way up your arse. How does it feel?"

"Incredibly weird, but…good. I feel so full. So stretched."

"Is it sore?"

"A little bit…just enough…"

"Good. It should always be a little bit sore. Fuck, I'm too turned on to breathe. How am I going to last?"

"I don't know. You feel so huge up there. And so hard."

"Shut up, that's not helping! OK…beg me."

I wondered if this would be over before it properly began, but I did as I was told anyway.

"Please, my lord and master, will you fuck me hard in my arse?"

"How hard?"

"Really hard."

"You want me to come in it?"

"Yes, yes, I want that. Please come in my arse, sir."

He sighed shudderingly. "Can be arranged," he said, sounding pained.

I clawed at the duvet as he pulled himself back. Now that he was all the way in, apparently my body wanted to keep him there and I tightened reflexively, trying to avoid the withdrawal. But he kept going before thrusting back again. It was nothing like vaginal sex; there seemed to be different instincts at play, and very different sensations, and yet there was definite pleasure in it.

The definite pleasure increased when he slid one hand between us and found my clit. He rubbed it fiercely as his cock sawed to and fro, and very soon I could feel myself building towards an orgasm—but it wasn't going to be any old orgasm. It felt darker, deeper-seated, wider-reaching right from the beginning.

"I can't...last...much longer..." he warned, but it was all right because that was the moment I lost my mind.

My hands slammed repetitively on the mattress as a whitewater torrent of a climax threw me along on its forceful current. I cried out, no longer caring who heard what, until my voice gave out and I collapsed, whimpering helplessly, over my pillows.

I felt Emmett, huge now, pumping inside me, emptying himself out. He waited a long time, until he was more or less flaccid again, before pulling out. It still felt weird and a bit horrible, but it was worth it.

"There, that virginity is well and truly taken," he said brokenly, spreading himself flat on the bed beside me.

I threw the pillows back up towards the headboard and lay carefully on my side. I could feel where he had been, in a way that didn't often happen with the other kind of sex, unless you really went at it hammer and tongs. I liked that physical reminder, and I hoped it would last a few hours at least.

He wrapped his arms around me and held me tight, as if he

thought I might slither away at any moment.

"I can't believe how lucky I am," he said. "I love you so much."

"Same," I said, yawning. "But more so."

Chapter Fourteen

B reakfasting in bed the next morning, Emmett took a call from Reception.

"Oh, is he? Yes, sure. Tell him we'll meet him for lunch in the restaurant—one o'clock? Great, thanks."

"What was that?" I asked, swirling my smoked salmon scrambled eggs around on their toasted muffin with my fork.

"Charles was hoping to see us in the breakfast room."

"Charles…? Oh, that guy you used to work with."

"He's staying here. I wonder how long he's in the country for? Anyway, I said we'd meet him for lunch."

"OK," I said tonelessly.

He caught on to that straight away, cocking his head to one side and regarding me through shrewdly narrowed eyes.

"You don't want to?"

"No, I don't mean… It's just…you know… I thought we'd have this time to ourselves."

Emmett put down his coffee cup and leant over to kiss me.

"We have the rest of our lives," he said softly. "It's just one lunch."

"I know."

"But…?"

"I'm probably being silly, but…something about him makes me nervous."

"About Charles?" Emmett laughed. "You aren't the only one. He makes everyone nervous. That's why they made him the company troubleshooter."

"Ah, that figures," I said, laughing with him. "But there's no trouble to shoot here."

"No, none. So you've nothing to be nervous about. He'll just want to say hello, meet you properly, wish us luck and all that. I haven't seen him in ages, although we still email pretty regularly."

"Ugh, God, I dread to think what you've told him about me." This was getting worse.

"Oh, I bitch about you to him all the time," said Emmett, pinching my cheek. "I tell him what a fucking nightmare you are to be near. He hates you now."

"Shut up! For all I know, you might be telling the truth."

"Oh, for God's sake, Josephine. Put down that muffin and come here. Obviously a certain message hasn't got through to you yet."

By lunchtime, the message was well reinforced.

I had dressed carefully, in a chic white blouse and dark pencil skirt, discreet jewellery, hair in a chignon, high heels and stockings, a cloud of my most expensive perfume. I didn't want Charles thinking Emmett had married beneath him.

"You look sexy as hell," remarked Emmett, coming up behind me as I put on my earrings. "I thought you were trying to impress him, not seduce him."

"The last thing I want to do right now is seduce anyone," I said, feeling the pleasant muscular ache induced by our very active morning. "I feel like a burst balloon."

"Well, you don't look like one." He kissed the back of my neck lingeringly. "Thanks for making the effort, sweetness," he whispered. "I appreciate it."

Charles Fox was waiting for us in the conservatory area of the restaurant. He obviously had Emmett's eye for sharp tailoring—or was it Emmett that had his eye? Either way, his charcoal suit made him look like something from *GQ*, and I worried Emmett might feel underdressed in his open-necked shirt and slim chinos.

He stood up to greet us, once the waiter had escorted us to the table.

"Ah, the newlyweds," he said, smiling and kissing my cheek. His beard was strangely silky against my face. He must use some kind of expensive oil on it, I thought.

We all sat down, and I felt uncomfortably aware of how excited Emmett was. He was positively buzzing beside me.

"I'm still pinching myself," he said.

"That you're married?" asked Charles, raising a glass of mineral water to his lips.

"No, that you made it to the wedding."

"Ah, well, I couldn't have missed it," he said. "Not intending any disrespect to your parents, but you've always felt a bit like a not-quite-young-enough son to me. Or a younger brother, perhaps. Yes, let's go with younger brother, then I can carry on being in denial about my fading youth."

"You wouldn't want my dad," said Emmett, the lightness of his tone failing to cover an undercurrent of bitterness.

"Ah, no, indeed," sympathised Fox.

"I won't make his mistakes, anyway," said Emmett. "One wedding will be enough for me."

"Are you married?" I asked Fox, feeling that a quick reverse out of this conversational alley was in order.

"Oh, no. No." He and Emmett exchange a glance that I couldn't help but think loaded. What the hell was going on here? Had they been lovers? Was that silly rumour true?

"No children of your own?" I continued, feeling that if Fox was so keen to have Emmett for a surrogate son he should go out and father one.

Fox shook his head, smiling secretly into his mineral water.

"Have you looked at the menu?" he asked, handing it to me.

Having ordered, attention turned once more to me.

"So, Josephine," said Fox, leaning towards me. He had a way of looking at me that was like a searchlight. It made me feel naked. "You swept Emmett off his feet, it seems. You met only six months ago?"

"Yes, at a very dull training event at a hotel in town. It still seems like last week to me."

"Tell me about yourself."

Never an easy question to answer, and the quality of Fox's scrutiny made it doubly difficult. I stumbled through an ad hoc potted life story, thinking all the time that his rapt attention must be some kind of ironic pose, for he treated me as if I were the most captivating creature he had ever set eyes upon.

"I hope we'll get to know each other well," he said, once I'd been let off the hook and allowed to concentrate on my lobster bisque.

"Not that easy if you're in Switzerland," I said.

"Ah, well, that's what I wanted to tell you." He beamed at Emmett, who had put down his forkful of goats cheese and gone very still. "I'm coming back to the UK. I've left PlayCorp and I'm in the process of starting up my own consultancy, which will be based in London."

"Are you serious?" Emmett let out a stunned laugh.

"Quite serious. I'm also serious about offering you a job. I'm going to need a talented software designer at my right hand."

I stared at Emmett. Emmett stared at Fox.

"Are you talking about…a salaried position?"

"To begin with, until the business has grown into itself. After that, I'd offer you a partnership. We'll meet in a week or so to talk details, but I'd like to know if you're interested in principle first."

"Can we think about it?" I said.

"Of course I am," said Emmett, across me. "Oh my God, Charles! Of *course* I am!"

He laughed again as both men stood and leaned across to each other for an awkward crushing hug and back pat.

"That's a weight off my mind," said Fox. "I know this is going to take us into a fantastic future—a new level. And you'll have the freedom to work on your own projects alongside the consulting work."

"It's what I've always wanted," said Emmett happily.

Oh, how could I object, after he said that?

"In London, though," I said, touching his hand.

He turned to me, shaking his head.

"So? It's half an hour to Paddington from here. Thousands of people commute already. Besides, we could move into London if we wanted."

"But my job's here."

"You can get a job in London. Christ, you don't even need to work, Jo. I earn more than enough for both of us. You don't even *like* your job!"

It was true. My job was boring and used about ten percent of my available brain cells. But I liked the people I worked with, and I was comfortable there.

"With the money Emmett will be earning, you can start your own little business," suggested Charles. "Do what you've always wanted to do."

I baulked at the 'little', but the prospect was tempting. There were a thousand things I never had time for. Writing, photography, spending all day in research libraries.

"And you can't be bored in London," added Emmett. "You'd be in your element. All that interesting…stuff."

"I guarantee you'd be kept busy," said Fox, and there was something in his tone that made me prickle all over. "And Emmett will keep you happy."

Another of those complicit looks passed between them.

I opted out of further conversation and let them yarn on about techy stuff for the rest of the lunch, but I kept a close eye on the character of their interactions. There was something intimate about it, not quite in the way that Emmett and I were intimate, but as if they were members of the same family. Yet even though they were able to be completely relaxed with each other, I sensed a kind of deference from Emmett that wasn't returned by Fox. Nobody coming to sit with us would be in any doubt about who was the senior man of the pair, and not just because Fox was transparently about fifteen years older.

He absolutely exuded power and authority, in that kind of global way that couldn't be misinterpreted. It contrasted with Emmett's understated self-possession. You could see that they were both master of themselves, but Fox was master of everyone else too.

The waiter returned with dessert menus but Fox waved him away.

"I've taken up too much of your precious honeymoon time," he said, casting me an apologetic glance. "I'm sure you have much better things to do. Emmett, I'll call you in a couple of days."

"Yes, I'll look forward to it," said Emmett.

"Wonderful to meet you, Mrs Marlow," he said, doing that olde-worlde hand kiss again. "I look forward to seeing you again, soon and often."

"Yes, that'll be nice," I said faintly, and rather insincerely.

It occurred to me, as he walked away, that I was afraid of him.

"All my dreams coming true, all at once," said Emmett, watching Fox disappear into the lobby. "I can't believe it."

"You and Fox," I said, pushing my plate away.

"Mm?" His eyes moved to me, as if seeing me for the first time.

"When we were in Barcelona, somebody mentioned a rumour."

He sighed gustily.

"Oh, here it comes. Jesus Christ. No, Fox and I have never been lovers, OK?"

I nodded. "OK. I think you would have told me, anyway."

"Of course I would."

"You would," I said decisively, but questions still hung in the air between us, thickening the atmosphere. I didn't want to ask any of them. I waited for Emmett to speak.

"All right," he said quietly. "There is something I should probably tell you. I didn't, because I didn't want you to feel uncomfortable with him, but I guess there's no reason not to…"

"What? What is it?"

The waiter came to ask if we wanted dessert, saying that 'the gentleman' had already settled the rest of our bill. Emmett gave him a tense wave away.

"Let's go out for a walk in the gardens," he suggested. "This restaurant doesn't really suit confessions."

"Confessions?"

I let him take my hand and lead me through the French doors into the tranquil rose garden beyond, but I was jittery now, the lunch lying heavy on my stomach.

We walked all the way down the lawn, through a green arch of trees down to where a cluster of benches looked over the river valley and the forest on the other side. I'd seen the view from our bedroom window, but it was closer and more striking from this vantage.

I sat down beside him on one of the benches and waited silently, wanting to erase the coming of Charles Fox and any impact it might have on us and our lives together.

"When I started working at PlayCorp," said Emmett, twisting his fingers into mine, "I was a pretty lonely person. Straight out of university, no friends, no girlfriend, living in a shared house with strangers who made me contemplate murder several times a week."

"Sounds familiar," I sighed and he squeezed my fingers.

"I know," he said. "It's not an unusual story. People get through it, make headway, find their pairs or groups eventually. But I've never found it easy to socialise, and I tended to avoid the Friday afternoon pub and the team bonding at the bowling alley and all that kind of thing."

"Yeah, I hate all that too."

"The one saving grace was that I loved my work. I spent a

175

lot of time in the office. I worked late…then later…then very late. The place was open all night, so I got to know the security staff better than I knew my colleagues." He paused. "At that time, I didn't really know Charles. I'd been in a couple of meetings with him, and he'd commented on some of my work —complimenting me. He seemed like a cool guy, but he wasn't really in my orbit. Anyway, it turned out that he was a fellow night owl. A couple of nights a week, he'd be in the building till after midnight too. We met at the coffee machine and got talking, and then we started synchronising coffee breaks and gradually got to like each other, although we mainly talked about work and new projects and that kind of thing. Nothing personal."

He looked into my eyes, as if needing me to believe this.

I nodded.

"OK."

"Well…oh God, here's where it gets… The thing is, back then, I used to take in this memory stick that had some… personal stuff…on it. OK, porn, basically."

He flushed beautifully. I found it fascinating that he thought I would judge him.

"I used to wait till the building was basically empty, then take my laptop into a security camera blind spot and, er, well, you can imagine."

"Not really acceptable office behaviour, Emmett," I said primly.

He put a hand over his face. "I know. I know that. And I was watching some clip one night—I think it was a girl in handcuffs giving a guy a blow job while another girl paddled her behind—when Charles appeared unexpectedly behind me."

"Oh my God!"

"Quite. I'd been *sure* he'd gone home…I'd seen him getting into the lift. But he'd come back to ask me something about some meeting the next day… Well. You can imagine my surprise."

"And his."

"Actually, no. He wasn't surprised at all. He stood behind me, watching the clip with me, for about three minutes before he let me know he was there."

"I thought he looked like a perv."

Emmett raised his eyebrows at me.

"Even though he looks nothing like you?" he said pointedly.

"Fair comment," I said. "So…what happened next? Clearly he didn't get you booted out on your arse."

"No." Emmett put his head in his hands for a moment and chuckled guiltily. "No, he, er… He asked me if I wanted to go back to his place for a drink."

"He *did* try to seduce you!"

"Well, I did wonder at first…but no. That wasn't what he had in mind. He said he thought he could help me out. So we went back to his place, which was this huge fenced-off glass and steel edifice out in the country. I really didn't know what to expect. It was half-past midnight, in the middle of nowhere. I have to admit, I was a bit scared, even though I considered Charles a friend now. But I went up to the front door with him, and he opened it up and…" Emmett laughed.

"What?"

"I thought I was hallucinating, seriously. There was this gorgeous woman, kneeling there, absolutely starkers, on the welcome mat."

"No! You are *kidding* me."

"Absolute cross my heart and hope to die truth. She had her

hands joined behind her neck and she had a collar on, and these metal cuffs, but nothing else."

I gaped.

"Go on."

"Well, for obvious reasons, I was intrigued. She kissed the toes of his shoes, then she kissed *mine*. I was so weirded out. And turned on, to be honest. Anyway, Charles didn't even speak to her, no acknowledgement, nothing. He just walked on down the hall with me, and she crawled after us on her hands and knees. Clearly, we had certain interests in common…and it just kind of went from there."

"Oh, come on, you can't leave it like that," I cried. "What happened next?"

"Well, that night we just talked. I mean, he did offer, uh, services from his submissive, but I just felt too awkward about it that first time. Later on, though…"

"You availed yourself," I said, staring hard.

He coughed.

"It was kind of a dry spell."

"You shared his submissive. Wow. Well, I must admit, that really is another level of friendship. No wonder there were all those rumours."

"She wanted to do it," he said. "Suzette. That was her name. She had a kind of thing about being double topped."

"Double topped. That's the technical term, I take it. So, I mean, you weren't even just sloping off to the bedroom with her and having your way. Fox was actually there, participating."

"Uh huh." He chewed on his lower lip.

I gazed down over the valley. It was such a beautiful day, the kind of rustling, buzzing summer country day that makes you feel world peace can exist. It was hard to focus on the thought of hardcore BDSM scenes in such surroundings.

"Wow," I said at last. "That's blown my mind."

"How do you feel about it?" asked Emmett, side-eyeing me.

"I don't know. I just...don't know. I mean, when you say you weren't lovers, you almost kind of *were*. You were in sexual situations together. Even if you didn't fuck each other, you must have been excited by the idea of doing stuff together. And I'm not saying that's wrong, by the way. I don't have any issue with bisexuality, hell, I've kissed a few girls myself. But this is just...I don't know. It's just so *out there*."

"Threesomes are one of the commonest fantasies there is," pointed out Emmett.

"Yeah, but the conventional thing is that it's a male fantasy of having two women at once."

"Whereas Charles and I were living out Suzette's fantasy. It's feminism in action, Jo."

I burst out laughing.

"You are such a..."

"Seriously, Jo, I don't want this to upset you. It was all a long time before we met. And actually, the Suzette thing only went on for a few months."

"I'm not upset."

He put a hand on my knee. "Look at me and say that."

I looked into his beautiful, beloved face and said it again, with feeling.

Later on, over dinner in the restaurant, I had questions.

"If the Suzette thing only went on for a few months," I said, "why did it end?"

"Oh," he said, frowning at a pepper mill as he ground it. "She left."

"She left? Broke up with Charles Fox?"

"In a manner of speaking."

"Emmett, so evasive. What actually happened?"

"She decided she wanted more than Charles was willing to give. So, well…this was *entirely* her idea, by the way…he auctioned her off."

My fork clanged on to my plate.

"What?"

"An auction. You know, a…slave auction type of thing," said Emmett unhappily. "God, it sounds awful when you say it out loud, but it's all totally consensual. No *actual* slavery. It's all contracts and agreed limits and all that. Everyone's a winner."

"So it wasn't that he got sick of her and palmed her off on some stranger?"

"No. Jo, look. She didn't literally *belong* to him. It's just a game they liked to play. But eventually Suzette decided that she wanted to go more hardcore than Charles was happy with, so she moved on. The auction was kind of a fiction, really, because they'd already agreed in private who her next dom was going to be. But the auction thing made it more dramatic."

"This BDSM scene does seem to love the drama."

"Yes." He smiled. "I like that kind of drama—the set pieces —but the other kind, the internal politics and gossip and rumour-mongering, put me off in the end."

"So you were involved in it?"

"After Suzette moved on, I used to go with Charles to this club he was a member of. It was interesting. He had a lot of private parties, too. He was always trying to set me up with one sub or another."

"But he didn't manage to?"

"I went through a few, but it was always short term. It'd be fun for a while but we'd both realise that it wasn't going to be forever. Back to square one. Wild times, though. Good times, in their way."

"You stopped going to those parties?"

"When Charles moved overseas, they all dried up. I've told you I did a bit of kinky online dating, hung out with Mustang and his crew—that all happened after this. And that brings us up to date."

"I'd love to have been a fly on the wall at one of Charles's parties," I said, trying to picture the scene, then, "Oh!"

Emmett smiled at my village-idiot open-mouthed stare.

"What, sweetness?"

"I just thought. Charles's parties. Do you think he'll…?"

Emmett held my gaze.

"How would you feel about that?"

"I don't know." It was becoming my signature refrain. "God. I can't even imagine…" I gave him a hard look. "Does he know? About us? I mean, about how we, er, relate?"

"He'd be pretty stupid if he didn't," said Emmett softly. "Whether I said anything to him or not. He knows me."

"Christ." The realisation that Charles Fox had been looking at me and seeing my sex life was intensely sobering. "That's… God, I'm glad you didn't tell me all this before I met him. I'd have died on the spot."

"I haven't discussed it with him." Emmett put a hand over mine. "He hasn't asked, and I haven't volunteered the information. But he knows. I know he does."

"Yeah," I said, thinking back to the way Fox looked at me. "I know it too."

In bed that night, I did something I had never done before with Emmett.

I fantasised.

It wasn't that I needed to, or that Emmett was boring me—far from it. The brilliant, life-changing thing about sex with Emmett was how intensely present in the moment it forced me to be. My mind had nowhere to wander to; whatever I desired or dreamed of, Emmett would do it.

But that night I found myself imagining something he hadn't done, couldn't do. I found myself imagining another man with us, another body to rule me, another master to submit to.

When Emmett knelt behind me on the bed, kissing my neck and playing with my nipples, I imagined another man pressing against my belly and hips, his tongue in my mouth, his fingers plying my clit. When Emmett bent me over to take me from behind, I imagined myself sucking another man's cock, matching my pace with Emmett's thrusts until I milked both of them dry simultaneously. When Emmett impaled me on his erection, I lowered my spine, kissed him hard, let my breasts brush his chest, and imagined a man behind me, spreading my cheeks and fitting his own hard length between them. What would that kind of double penetration feel like? What had Suzette felt that I could never feel?

I came guiltily hard, throwing myself down beside Emmett and hiding my face in his neck once his own pleasure had been had.

He flushed me out of my burrow, tilting my face to his for sated kissing.

"I don't know why it's called a honeymoon," he said, yawning. "More like a bunnymoon. At it like rabbits."

"I see what you did there," I yawned back.

I let him spoon me, huddling into him, but I felt as if I'd been unfaithful. Because the man I'd imagined all the way through had not been some vague shadow-creature, some indeterminate collection of dominant tropes.

It had been Charles Fox.

"I love you," I said, suddenly, anxiously.

He squeezed me, but he was half asleep as he murmured the expected rejoinder.

Chapter Fifteen

I couldn't sleep that night, so I got up at dawn and decided to take a walk in the garden.

After throwing on a sundress, cardigan and flip flops, I went out through the French doors of the restaurant, where the staff were groggily setting up for breakfast.

It was colder than I thought it would be and I wrapped the cardigan around myself as I wandered through the dewy grass, watching the flower buds getting ready to unfurl and show themselves to the sun.

I had spent all night trying and failing to order my thoughts, but now, out here in the clean new air of the morning, everything felt simple.

I loved Emmett. I would be with him and be happy. There was nothing more to my life than this.

I walked around a giant yew tree, severely clipped into the shape of a pyramid, and stopped dead in my tracks. Standing on the other side, looking soulfully towards the horizon and smoking a cigarette, was Charles Fox.

"Oh," I said, taking a step back.

He stared at me as if he didn't recognise me for a half a second, then his taut face relaxed into a smile.

"Well, what a surprise," he said, stubbing his cigarette out underfoot. "I'm sorry, you've caught me out in my disgusting habit. I try not to indulge but…"

I shrugged my indifference to it. "Oh, I know kicking it's a killer. Took me five goes, and I was only a smoker for about three years."

"I've never really tried to give up," said Charles. "Just cut down, and cut down, and now I'm as cut down as I'll ever want to be. But congratulations to you. A testament to your strength of will."

"I don't think I'm particularly strong-willed."

"Don't you? I'm sure you must be. Most submissives I've met have been."

His quietly-spoken words were like a shock of cold water in the face.

He watched me hard through those intense green eyes while I tried to compose myself enough to speak.

"Right," I managed.

"I'm sorry," he said, and he did sound genuinely regretful. "That was rude and presumptuous of me. Can we forget I said it?"

Well, could we? I suspected he knew very well that we could not, but I decided to take his words at face value and nodded.

"Have you seen the view from the end of the arbour?" he said, straightening up and indicating the benches Emmett and I had talked on the day before. "Come and watch the sun rise with me."

I was under no obligation to do it, but something compelled

me to follow him beneath the arch of trees and along to the viewing point.

"You know," he said, seating himself beside me, "I'm glad we bumped into each other. I've been hoping we could meet as people, rather than adjuncts of Emmett."

"Have you?" I tried to imply by inflection that I hadn't been hoping for any such thing, but I wasn't sure if it came off. "I don't really see myself as an adjunct of Emmett. I'm sure you don't either."

"You know what I mean. Our relation to him is what links us."

The idea that we were linked made my hair stand on end. I wondered why he had to say it. Was he deliberately putting the idea of chains and bondage and us as a trio into my head? Or was it just a chance turn of phrase, meaning nothing?

"I guess we both have good taste," I said, annoyed with myself for the meaningless remark.

"Indeed we do." Fox smiled at me. "I was very pleased to hear that Emmett had found happiness. As I understand, it was quite the *coup de foudre*."

Aha, I knew his game. Trying to bamboozle me with fancy foreign phrases. But I had plenty of those up my sleeve.

"Yes, it was kind of a *koi no yokan*," I said.

He frowned and I did an internal fist-pump at having succeeded where he had failed.

"Japanese," I said. "Similar kind of thing. You look at a person and know that there will be…"

I trailed off, much too aware that this exchange was making me over-animated and excited. I needed to look away from him, but I couldn't.

He kept looking at me, with this flicker of a smile playing

about his lips. Smug. I wanted to smack it off his face.

"There will be what?" His voice was almost a whisper.

"A thing," I ended lamely. "A thing…between you."

Those strangely slanted eyes held me fast while sick panic built up inside me. What the hell was going on here? I should get up, make an excuse, leave.

"What was it again?" he said. "Koi no…?"

"*Koi no yokan*," I repeated.

"I'll remember that one," he said.

"I'd better…Emmett might wake up and wonder…"

"Oh, don't go just yet. It's still very early, and the sun hasn't quite made it all the way up. Take a deep breath. Go on. A good, deep one."

Somehow I found myself doing it, inhaling the dew-damp freshness of the morning.

"It feels good, doesn't it? New. A whole clean slate on which to make whatever marks we want."

I let out the breath, finally able to tear my gaze from his.

"Yesterday was good enough for me," I said tonelessly.

He said nothing, but I could feel him looking at me, and my cheek burned with it.

"I want the same as you, Jo," he said at last. "I want Emmett to be happy."

"And he is," I said vehemently. "We both are."

"I can see why he was so drawn to you."

"Can you? Well, I really must go now." I stood up, brushing down the back of my sundress where the overnight damp of the bench's struts had clung.

"You're so conflicted," he said. "So afraid of what you want. It's fascinating."

"Do you know what, Charles?" I said, turning to him. "You

think you're such an amateur psychologist but really you know fuck all about me. You need to know one thing. One. Thing. I love Emmett, and I will always love him, and I would never, ever do anything to hurt him. Is that crystal clear?"

One side of his mouth quirked up and he nodded, infuriatingly, as if to say, "*Look at the little spitfire, isn't she thrilling when she's angry?*"

An enormous temptation to slap him across the face took hold of me, but I knew, right at the core of me, that if I did that we'd end up kissing like maniacs, flat out on the bench, so I restrained myself.

Instead I turned my back and marched away.

Behind me, I heard the click of a cigarette lighter being opened, the song of a lark, the deep rustling hush of very early morning.

Rapprochement

Chapter Sixteen

There," said Emmett, placing our wedding portrait at the precise centre of the mantelpiece. "Now it's home. What do you think?"

I sat down on an upturned empty crate and admired our new living room.

"We're Londoners," I said. "Though I'm not sure what that means."

"It means we live in London," said Emmett.

The flat consisted of the basement and ground floors of a converted Victorian house. It was astonishingly small, considering the price we were paying for it, but it had a 'garden' in the form of a patch of decking at the back, a very chic new kitchen, and the area was considered desirable, with parks and a tube station in easy walking distance.

"I'll have to sign up with some agencies tomorrow," I said. "See if I can find some temp work in the City. Hopefully something more interesting than the Thames Valley Borough Council."

"You're getting ahead of yourself," said Emmett, crouching in front of me and taking my hands. "There's important business to take care of before you even think about that."

"Oh?"

He raised my fingers to his lips and kissed them each in turn.

"Come downstairs."

The bedrooms and bathroom were in the basement.

"There isn't any bedding on the bed," I said.

"Pfft. Details. Come on, now, or do I have to order you?"

He pulled me to my feet and I followed him without protest down the stairs. We had chosen to use the back bedroom, with its view on to the 'garden'. It was less dark and more private than the slightly bigger front room.

We had indulged ourselves in a super king size bed and it took up much of the space, our cupboards and drawers lining the walls as if flattened to them at gunpoint. The bed had been chosen for its kink appeal, with four posts and barred head and foot boards, ideal for the easy attachment of bondage paraphernalia.

Today, however, all our bondage paraphernalia was still packed away, so we would have to rely on our natural chemistry —and there was nothing lacking there.

Emmett and I kissed a hectic path to the bed until he pushed me down on to the edge of it, falling on top of me in the process. We lay there, writhing and snogging and plucking at each other's clothes until we were fully on the bare mattress, wrapped around each other, breathing hard.

Emmett released me only to pull off my T-shirt and unclip my bra, then take off his own top. His teeth grazed my neck, then he feasted on my breasts while I fiddled with his belt and jeans.

He waited only until his jeans and underpants were at mid-thigh, and my own denim mini was rucked up around my hips, before pushing my gusset aside and plunging into me. Although it was autumn, rich sunshine flooded through the window, adding to our heat. We sweated and rutted, the constraint of our denim garments somehow adding to the thrill. Emmett's belt buckle clinked with each thrust, the cold metal stroking my thigh in the process.

I could feel him swell inside me as I tightened my pelvic muscles and wrapped my legs around his grinding hips. He clamped his mouth over mine, questing with his tongue, kneading at my breasts.

I swivelled and swerved, trying to ease him into that perfect angle so that he could rub against my g-spot. When I found it, I moaned into his mouth and fluttered my fingers in his hair, hinting to him that I wouldn't be holding out for much longer.

This was a required signal during all sexual encounters now. I had to let him know when I was coming, so he could decide whether I was allowed to or not.

"Yes," he gasped, breaking off the ravaging kiss for a moment. "You may."

I lay back, giving myself to the gathering storm. When it broke, I tried to get free of Emmett's kiss so I could breathe through it, but he wouldn't release me and I had to thrash underneath him and whimper into his throat. This petty act of tyranny strengthened my climax, made it last longer. I was still sobbing out my final throes when he filled me up.

"I'm going to have to scrub this mattress," I said, lying in his arms, still inconveniently caught up in my denim mini. Most of our shared fluids had soaked into the knickers I was still wearing, if I was honest, but I wanted him to feel that guilty satisfaction he seemed to enjoy so much.

"Bang! And the spunk is gone," he said, channelling an old advert.

"I hope so," I said, tittering at his impression. "Need to get this place organised before you start work tomorrow. Oh God. I hate moving house."

"Oh." Emmett's hand on my stomach twitched, his fingers straightening.

"What?"

"I've just remembered. Shit."

"*What?*"

"Sorry, I meant to mention it earlier. I invited Charles round for housewarming drinks later."

"Oh, you're *kidding*." I sat up and stared at him.

"Well, you know, he is giving me a job and a new life and all that. Seemed only polite."

I ran stressed fingers through my wild woman hair.

"What time?"

"About sevenish. Thought I might cook something. Have we got anything?"

"Of course not. We haven't had a chance to get to the shops yet."

"Takeaway then, maybe."

"Oh God. Right. You do something about the state of the place and I'll head up to that supermarket we saw on the way down."

He raised an eyebrow at me, his face still blurred with post-coital exhaustion.

"You giving the orders now?"

"I'm in crisis mode," I told him. "Def con one."

I got up off the bed and went to sit on the edge of the bath and moan silently into a clenched fist.

Chapter Seventeen

I hadn't seen Fox since that unsettling conversation at the hotel, but he had been in my thoughts much too often for comfort.

My choice to take the supermarket run turned out to be a mistake—it forced me to think of him even more. What would he want to eat? To drink? Candles? Scented or plain? The grocery shop took twice as long as it needed to, and I kept finding myself standing in front of a shelf, staring unseeing at tinned goods or fancy cakes while my earlier encounter with Fox unspooled itself inside my head.

There had been something between us that had knocked me off balance, and I needed to steel myself. I would have to be on my guard. Easy on the wine. Where was the superglue aisle? Perhaps I could use it to stick myself to Emmett for the duration.

"What did you get?" asked Emmett, shoving cookware into kitchen cupboards. "You were ages. Did you get lost?"

"This place looks almost habitable," I said, looking round

before dumping the bags on the counter. "No, didn't get lost. Just couldn't decide what to get for dinner. I thought nothing fancy, since we've only just got here. He'll have to take us as he finds us."

I regretted my choice of phrase, which gave rise to an unwanted image.

"Fine, so what, then?"

"Shepherd's pie, and I got a ready-made cheesecake. Three bottles of wine. Don't want to go too mad, though, if you're working tomorrow."

Emmett shut the cupboard and turned to face me, leaning on the counter with his arms folded.

"Good. Happy with that. Are you happy?"

"Am I...? Well...yeah."

"You sound stressed. Tense." He cocked his head, waiting for my confession.

"Well, it was a bit short notice," I fudged.

He nodded.

"And is that all that's bothering you?"

I was silent for a few beats, then I nodded and started putting the shopping away.

"Charles makes you nervous, doesn't he?" continued Emmett, coming to help.

"A bit," I admitted.

"It's OK. He makes everyone nervous. Even me, still, sometimes." He flashed a grin at me, reaching past me to put something on the highest shelf.

"Emmett," I said, the words coming out before I could take them back, "Fox and I...we had this conversation back at the hotel. Early morning, you were still in bed. And it was...I don't know how to describe it."

Emmett put down a packet of cornflour and gave me his full attention.

"He didn't try anything on or anything," I said, rushing to reassure him. "It was nothing like that. There was just...it's his manner. It's kind of..."

"Seductive?" suggested Emmett. "I know. Were you...are you...attracted to him, in any way?"

This was a tough question, but I couldn't lie my way out of it—not to Emmett.

"I don't know if I'd call it 'attracted'," I said slowly. "But kind of...drawn. I suppose. In a way. Not that I have a crush or anything..."

"I know, I know." Emmett reached out and twirled a lock of my hair. "It's OK, pet. Really."

"Really?"

He smiled, and his eyes were loaded with undefinable emotions. None of them seemed to be negative.

"Really really," he whispered. He bent over to kiss my forehead, then my lips. "Right, let's get down to business. Where'd you put the potatoes?"

Chapter Eighteen

Emmett was upstairs, putting cashew nuts into fingerbowls, while I tried to wrestle my hair into something approximating a style.

I grimaced at myself in the mirror. Why was I making all this effort for a casual supper? One guest?

And it wasn't just me. Emmett had come down and fussed about what I should wear, making me change from a favourite shirt dress into a proper cocktail number, all beading and flippy chiffon skirts. He'd even chosen my underwear, and it was the good stuff.

"Are you trying to pimp me out to Fox?" I'd joked, and he'd laughed, but there'd been something behind it.

"I'd never make you do anything you didn't want," he said after a pause, during which he chose the shade of lipstick I should wear. "You know that, don't you?"

It wasn't exactly the reassuring answer I'd been expecting. I wanted to ask him more, but he made some excuse about burning the mince and ran off upstairs.

The hair would have to do. I put on some jewellery, sprayed a bit of perfume over my wrists and temples. The doorbell rang as I was replacing the lid.

I'm not ready for this.

Male voices filtered down the stairs: Emmett's clear and distinct, Fox's coming from a deeper, grittier place. I couldn't make out the words. There was a laugh, the clink of bottles.

For a long moment, I couldn't bring myself to go upstairs. I contemplated feigning an illness, hiding under the duvet until Fox went home.

But Emmett called my name, and I knew I had to respond.

"Just coming," I said, taking it slowly, one step at a time, my body suddenly heavy.

The landing opened into the living room, where Fox and Emmett stood in front of the fireplace, waiting for me.

"Here she is," said Emmett eagerly, darting forward to take my arm and bring me into the grouping.

Fox, disconcertingly, put a hand on my shoulder and bent to kiss my cheek. His beard bristled me, and he smelled fantastically sexy; some sort of old-fashioned leather and tobacco based scent that made my knees quiver. I didn't dare look into his face.

"How are you?" I asked in a high-pitched, too-casual tone.

"All the better for seeing you," he said. "You look gorgeous. So, Emmett, have you joined a temperance movement or are you just a terrible host?"

"Oh, sorry," he said, springing away towards the kitchen. "What'll you have?"

"Well, I did bring champagne…"

Emmett disappeared around the corner. I was missing him already. I looked down at Fox's feet. Very shiny shoes. He'd obviously come straight from the office, although his shirt was open at the neck and he'd left the jacket behind.

"I've been looking forward to this," said Fox softly.

"I didn't realise Emmett had invited you until a few hours ago," I said. "Sorry if it's all a bit ad hoc. We've been rushing around…" I flapped my hands at the half-finished living room, pointing out the three unpacked crates ranged underneath the back window.

There was a loud pop and a hissed swear word from the kitchen.

"Oh dear, perhaps he needs help…"

Fox put a hand on my forearm, precluding my escape.

"He's a grown man, Jo. He can cope."

The physical contact forced me to look at him, in an attempt to extricate myself. His eyes bore down on me, amused and intent.

"You're very nervous," he noted.

"Well," I said helplessly, wanting to flap again. "Is everything OK in there, darling?" I called into the kitchen.

Fox tightened his grip on me for a moment before releasing my arm, looking up at the ceiling with an expression of fond indulgence.

"Absolutely," said Emmett, appearing in the doorway with a glass each for Fox and me, before disappearing to fetch his own, along with the bottle. "Well, cheers." We clinked. "Here's to new homes, new careers, new beginnings, new everything."

"A new way of living," said Fox, though I wasn't sure I wanted to go that far. The old way was working pretty well for me.

"Do you know the area?" I asked politely. "Was it easy for you to find us?"

An unchallenging conversation about journeying across London and our new locale soothed us through that first glass and into dinner.

"I thought about having it outside," said Emmett, bringing in the salad bowl. "But the weather's just that little bit the wrong side of summer now. Next summer, though—there's a wrought iron furniture set left by the previous owners. I'll clean it down, paint it up and we'll have cocktails on the lawn. If I ever get around to mowing it."

"Al fresco dining, perfect," said Fox, eyeing me.

Somehow, everything he said sounded like an innuendo.

"Probably best if we all help ourselves," I said, once the shepherd's pie had made its grand entrance.

Fox smirked at me. Jesus! He was doing this on purpose.

"To the pie," I added awkwardly. "Guests first."

"So, what are your plans?" he asked, dishing up. "Workwise, I mean. Do you have anything lined up?"

"Nothing specific. I'm going to register with a few agencies tomorrow, and I might see if anything's going at any of the local borough councils. I'm not looking for anything too specialised."

"Admin work? What are your qualifications?" he asked, pretending to be interested, though it was the dullest subject imaginable.

"Speedy fingers," I said. He raised his eyebrows in a way that made heat rush to my cheeks. "Apart from that, lots of useless qualifications that have never got me anywhere, so no point mentioning them."

"I might have room for a well educated person," said Fox. "My PA is about to start maternity leave. I've been meaning to scout around the agencies for a replacement."

"That would be amazing," said Emmett.

"Oh…well…I mean…" I said at the same time.

"Don't you think?" said Emmett, noting my hesitancy.

"It would be really handy," I admitted. "Just…do you think it's risky, working together?"

"You won't be working together, strictly speaking," said Fox. "You'd be working for me. Emmett will have his own office. Your lunch hours probably won't even synchronise."

"It's got to be worth giving it a go," said Emmett.

"Jess leaves at the end of next week," said Fox. "I'll need somebody after that. What do you say?"

"Oh…well, you know. Unless I find something else in that time…OK."

"Three musketeers," said Emmett, raising his fork and clashing it with mine. "All for one and one for all."

"I really think that calls for more champagne," said Fox, joining with the clinking of tines. "But we seem to have finished the bottle."

"I could head up to the off licence," I offered, seizing the opportunity for a bit of time alone to clear my head. "There's an Oddbins just around the corner. Ten minutes there and back."

"Alone?" frowned Emmett.

"I'll go," said Fox.

"Go with him, Jo," said Emmett. "He doesn't know the area."

"Oh, no, I'm fine…"

"I don't want you going alone," said Emmett firmly. "Not after dark."

"OK, dad," I said sulkily. "I'll just finish this…"

But I'd lost my appetite for the shepherd's pie. The prospect of being alone with Fox, even for a ten minute booze run, was extremely nerve racking. I pushed the mash and mince to the side of my plate, mixing it in with the few leftover salad leaves, and waited for Fox.

The two glasses of champagne I'd consumed had left me a little light-headed, but still in reasonable control of my faculties. I wondered what I'd be like after four.

"Well, then," said Fox, laying down his knife and fork and nodding at me. "Shall we?"

"I'll go and sort out the cheesecake while you're out," said Emmett. He swapped a strange look with Fox—there was a kind of nervous excitement in it. "Not sure it's fully defrosted yet, so you don't need to hurry back."

Fox held his gaze for a fraction longer than seemed normal, then smiled and rose from his seat.

Out on the street, it was colder than I thought, and I regretted not putting a coat on.

"It's not far," I said, almost running ahead of Fox. "I spotted it while we were held up at some lights on the way here. I think we should pay for this one, though—Emmett and I, I mean. Since you're already providing us with so much."

"Slow down," said Fox, laughing. "I didn't hear any starting pistol."

Reluctantly, I waited for him to draw level with me.

"Just a bit cold," I said. "Need to keep moving."

"In that case…" He took off his scarf and wrapped it around my neck. I tensed, feeling his fingers and thumbs brush my hair. How could such a gentle gesture set my heart skittering in the way it did? "There, is that better?"

"Thanks," I said. The scarf smelled like him. I tried not to breathe it in too much. "I'm starting to get a bit too used to thanking you."

"There's no need," he said. "It's not as if I don't get

anything out of it."

I looked at him sharply. "What do you get?"

His eyes narrowed, amused but keen. "A warm feeling inside," he said.

"See, there it is," I said, pointing out the shop with some relief as we turned the corner.

Inside, I felt intensely, almost sickeningly conscious of Fox's close proximity at my shoulder as we scanned the shelves. He stood so close to me, almost touching. My body wanted to lean into his warmth and masculine firmness, my senses wanted to revel in him. Oh *God*, I was wildly attracted to him. Why did this have to happen to me?

I thought of Emmett, at home, slicing the cheesecake, sliding it on to plates. I thought of his sly smile and his long white fingers and his freckled shoulders.

"I love him," I said, surprisingly out loud.

"Of course you do," said Fox, close enough to my ear for his breath to warm it. "I know."

He reached past me for the champagne, our sleeves brushing in a crackle of pure physical electricity.

At the counter, I tried to get my card out of my purse, but he put a hand on mine, preventing me.

"No, no, I'll get this," he said, while I gave myself up to quivering lust. "It was my idea."

Back at the top of our street, Fox looked both ways before sliding an arm around my waist and pulling me flush against him. The movement was sudden and violent and made me drop the paper bag with the champagne in it on the pavement— happily, it didn't smash.

"What are you…?"

"Listen," he said. "We need to talk, don't we?"

JUSTINE ELYOT

"I can't…"

"I'm not going to make you do anything you don't want to, Jo," he said.

"Emmett…"

"You love Emmett. Emmett knows you love him. He also knows that I want you."

"He knows that?"

"He knows it, and he encourages it."

"*Encourages* it?"

"He told you, didn't he, about Suzette?"

"Yes."

"Neither of us minds sharing."

"This is mad. You think Emmett would be OK with me… and you…?"

"I don't think it," said Fox, bending his forehead to mine. "I know it. We've discussed it."

"But not with me!"

"Until now." Fox's lips were almost on mine. I could just push mine that little bit further and… "Emmett was worried about scaring you off, if it wasn't what you wanted. But you've given me just about every signal there is that you want me just as much as I want you, so I think perhaps the time has come to raise the subject."

"Emmett's just being fair-minded," I whispered. "Because he had something of yours, he feels he has to repay the debt. You aren't equal. He sees you as his mentor, his superior officer. He feels obligated to you."

"That's not how it is at all. This is how it is—Emmett loves you, you love him, I love him, he loves me, I want you, you want me. It's not complicated. It's very, very simple."

"If it was that simple…"

206

"What?"

"I don't know. I really don't…know…"

But there was something I did know, and that was how easily Fox made every inhibition slip away, stripping me nude in some kind of dance of the seven emotional veils.

I was still claiming not to know when I opened myself up to his kiss, warming myself against him as if he were a fire, our feet moving aside to accommodate each other. He was unexpectedly well built underneath his shirt, a contrast to my rangy Emmett, and I took pleasure in the difference.

His lips were not the same either, and he had a different way of kissing—harder and less voluptuous, but with such strength behind it that surrender was the only option. I couldn't have said which kiss I preferred.

Perhaps, after all, variety could be the spice of my life.

"You're sure Emmett's all right with this?" I said, gasping as he let me up for air.

"Emmett is the most admirable person I know," said Fox. "He doesn't allow room in his head for negative emotions. He doesn't get jealous, he isn't insecure, and when he loves somebody, he wants them to be happy. Do you know how incredibly rare that is?"

"Yes, and I know how lucky I am to have found him."

"He knows you'll never leave him, and he knows I'd never take you from him."

"Like with Suzette?"

"Not quite. I never thought she'd be mine for keeps, but that didn't bother me. This is different—a deeper bond. But look, I'm not going to ask you to decide now. Take as long as you need to think about it. If you decide it's not for you, nobody will hold it against you. It's completely up to you."

He pecked me once more on the lips.

"Your decision," he whispered, loosening his grip on me and bending to pick up the champagne. "Now, shall we get on?"

The walk back, short as it was, was severely impeded by my burning solar plexus and rubbery legs. How could I snap back into the Jo I had been ten minutes ago? Everything had changed. Nothing was the same.

The swagger of Fox's stride, the roll of his shoulders a few inches above mine, the lingering sense of his beard on my skin all merged into a kind of hyperreality, making my surroundings vibrate around me.

Six weeks into marriage, and I was already unfaithful, adulterous.

But was I?

Walking back into the house, I was suddenly intensely conscious that my lipstick must have been kissed off, and I put my fingers to my lips in a textbook gesture of guilty concealment.

Emmett clocked it straightaway, his eyes holding mine as Fox dropped the bag on the table and said something about having to be careful opening it, as the bottle had been accidentally dropped.

"I'll get the glasses from the kitchen," said Emmett. "Jo…"

He didn't come up with a pretext to get me in there with him, but I guess we all knew that none was needed.

Away from Fox's eyes, Emmett pulled me quickly into his arms, putting his own finger to my ruined lips.

"Are you OK?" he whispered.

I couldn't speak. I looked into his face, loving it more than I had ever done before.

"We need to talk," I said.

He nodded. "Later, yes," he said, then he kissed me fiercely. "I love you."

I felt the brim of tears.

"I love you too," I said. "So much."

He reached for the kitchen roll and handed me a wad.

"Here, save your eye make-up. The lipstick's a lost cause."

A choking little giggle sent the tears back. I dried them, picked up the empty glasses and went on my way, with a little pat to my bottom from Emmett.

We drank the second bottle sitting in the living room, me on the sofa with my feet in Emmett's lap, Fox in the armchair, watching us with an amused detachment that still somehow managed to be intense. I felt that he was making plans as he sipped and chatted about this and that—plans for me, and what he would do with me, if and when he got me.

It made me want to cling to Emmett, but at the same time, it made me want to squirm with excitement.

Just after eleven, he put down his empty glass and stood up.

"Well, since tomorrow's a working day," he said.

"Oh, yeah," said Emmett, extricating himself from my legs. "Back to the grind. Better set my alarm tonight."

"Thanks for all the champagne," I added, tottering unsteadily to my feet.

"Oh, no need," said Fox, turning his laser gaze to me. "I think there was a lot worth celebrating, don't you?"

"Mm," I said, following them to the front door.

I watched Emmett and Fox give each other manly back-slapping hugs, then got ready for my own awkward cheek-kiss or whatever I was in for.

But Fox hooked one arm around my waist and kissed me once, sweetly, on the lips before wrapping a hand around my neck and taking a longer, deeper drink of my mouth.

I stalled at first, panicking about Emmett being in the room, but I heard nothing from him but a slight moaning sound at the back of his throat, which prompted me to receive the kiss in its proper spirit, and return it with interest. Fox's hand moved down from the base of my spine, cupping my bottom as he snogged me every bit as hard as he had done out in the street earlier.

"God," I gasped, staggering back as he released me.

He leant into me, speaking into my ear.

"Just a taste," he said. "I hope you'll have an appetite for more." He took his jacket from the peg and let himself out without another word.

I couldn't look at Emmett. My eyes followed Fox's back, along the dusky street, through the puddles of streetlight until he disappeared.

"Let's go down to bed," suggested Emmett, laying a hand on my shoulder. Mutely I followed him away from the chaotic remains of the party, into our own private space.

As soon as we were in the bedroom, he pulled me into him, hard, and planted his own lips where Fox's had so recently been.

"Do you have any idea," he murmured, manhandling me on to the bed, "how fucking hot you looked, kissing Fox?"

"Do I taste of him?" I asked, marvelling at Emmett's reaction to what had happened. I had always imagined he might be the jealous type; apparently not.

"You taste of him, and champagne, and sex. What did he do to you, out there in the street?"

"We didn't have sex," I exclaimed, widening my eyes at the hunger in his gaze. "Just a bit of kissing. Which he totally initiated. I wouldn't have…"

"I told you, it's OK," he said passionately.

"You want me to have sex with another man?"

"Not *any* other man. Just him."

He'd got my skirts up by now, and he unzipped swiftly and mounted me without ceremony.

"I'm so turned on I just can't…" he muttered, thrusting in to the hilt. "And so are you."

He must have scented my arousal. The kiss with Fox had sent me into a spin of sexual longing; I needed fucking, and I needed it badly.

We rolled around on the bed, grunting and clawing, desperate to get as deep and hard inside each other as possible. I wondered what Fox would be like in bed, how things might be different with him, and the not knowing tantalised me beyond endurance.

Emmett turned me over and got into me from behind. I wondered, as his undone belt jingled with each jolt, if he was thinking of Fox doing the same, or watching us, or Emmett watching, or…

I came, and Emmett smacked my bottom hard all the way through.

"That's what you need," he growled, his own orgasm following in short order.

Cradling me afterwards, his voice all husky and sticky, he asked me if I was going to do it.

"Do what? Fuck the Fox?"

He chuckled, squeezing me tighter.

"You're attracted to him. That's obvious enough."

"Yeah," I admitted. It wasn't as if I could deny it after that steamy kiss in front of Emmett. "I am. But Emmett…why? Why are you so into the idea?"

"I think we all have enough love to go round," he said, after a pause for thought. "It's not the kind of love that gets smaller the more it's divided. It grows and expands to fill the triangle. If you see what I mean."

"What if it's a square? Or a pentagon? Or a dodecahedron?"

"I don't think it'd be the same with anyone else. My relationship with Charles is kind of unique, I think."

"Right, so if I called up Tom Hardy and asked him if he wanted to join in, the love wouldn't grow and expand that much?"

"Nice try." He jabbed me with his elbow. "But no. The elasticity of the love is dependent on the level of intimacy you have with the other person."

"You make it sound so scientific." I gave him a hard look. "But it isn't, is it?"

"Tell me what you're thinking."

"I'm thinking that this all sounds so lovely and sexy and free and, yes, I fancy Fox a lot and the thought of having you both is a fantasy come true, but introducing a third person to a close relationship has to be enormously risky. I mean, how many ménages of this kind ever work out, do you reckon?"

"The thing with Suzette worked well."

"She left in the end."

"She was never going to stay forever. And it certainly didn't hurt things between Charles and me. Besides," he said, turning on to his side and frowning at me slightly, "when you say *ménage*, that's not really what's on the table."

"No? What is then?" I was confused.

"We're not all going to live together, or even spend that much time together. It'll just be…I don't know…the odd night here and there. Just the way it was with Suzette. Charles'll have his own submissives scattered about the place, and we'll have our married life—just now and again we'll get together. I mean, if you want to. Obviously the decision's yours. Nothing happens until you…"

"I get it, I get it," I said. "That's what Fox kept saying. That everything was down to me. Trouble is, I'm not sure I want it to be."

"What do you mean?"

"If this thing fucks everything between us up," I said quietly, "I don't want the responsibility of being the person who made that decision."

"Does that mean you don't want to do it?"

I shook my head.

"No, I think I do want to do it. But I don't want to be the one with my finger on the trigger."

"You want us to…kind of…?"

"While I might *be* in control, I don't want to feel as if I am. You know how this thing works, Emmett. You know how delicate the illusion is, with dominance and submission. You and Fox both know."

"You want us to tell you what to do about it?"

"I…it's hard to explain."

"Try me."

"You say it's what you want—and I know you both *think* you want it. But…do you? Really? When you can't possibly predict what the outcome will be?"

"Pet, you know that's what Fox and I both do for a living—we predict outcomes."

"Yes, but I'm not a bunch of syntax or whatever. I'm a person. Does Fox understand that? Will he accept it if I decide not to go ahead?"

"Of course he will. I promise you, if you decide you can't go through with it, nobody will ever raise the issue again. Though, of course, you'll be free to change your mind at any time."

"But won't he resent me? Would *you* resent me? And won't that affect our dynamic—especially if I'm working in the office. I think what I'm trying to say, Em, is that I'm so happy right now. It would kill me if anything poisoned that, especially if the poison was self-administered. And *so much* could go wrong."

"There are certainly risks." Emmett nodded calmly. "Would it help you to talk them through?"

"OK. Here's one thought I had. Fox sees you as belonging to him in some way. And I've come between you, taken you away from him. He wants this as a way of neutralising me, making sure I don't have more of you than he does."

Emmett said nothing to this, just kept a level gaze trained on me.

"I mean, it makes sense," I continued, a little desperately. "All this coming into our lives and offering you a job, then me, and moving us to London and so on. He's reasserting control over you."

"That's not what's happening," said Emmett. "If I thought it was, I would have turned down the job offer. I had very little contact with Charles for quite a few years. If he didn't want to control me then, why would he now?"

"Because you're married now."

"No. It isn't about that. I think it might be about nostalgia, a little bit, because that set-up with Suzette was good. We worked so well together. The feeling of being a well-oiled machine... It was something you can't really get with many people. I think he just wants a bit of that back. The emotional and intellectual connection was so intense. And, of course, he's got the hots for you, which is entirely understandable."

"You don't think he wants to break us up?"

"God, of course not!"

"Because if I couldn't handle it and it all went wrong…what would happen then?"

"You can end it at any time. The trio thing, I mean. You can't end your marriage with me. That's not going to happen. Ever."

"You might change your mind," I said, my voice small.

"I won't. And I think you might be overthinking this. It's not meant to be a serious life-long commitment. It's about pleasure and fun. I want you to have it—we both do. It's our gift to you. If you want to accept it."

"But what will you get out of it?"

"A bloody good time, I should hope. I get to watch *and* have you at the same time."

"You could do that by taping us," I pointed out.

"Oh no, I hate watching myself. Charles has a much better body than I do. Poor bloke has to watch me instead, not the best value for him."

"Oh, stop it. You've never struck me as somebody with body insecurity issues."

"Ah, I hide it well."

I let out a deep sigh, my senses trying to stand up to my tempted curiosity.

"I want you and Fox to make the decision for me," I said at length. "And when you make it, you must remember two things. First, that I love you and want you to be happy. Second, that I trust you."

I had worked out that, even if I tried to resist their combined will, my own desires would defeat me in the end.

I was saying yes. But nobody could accuse me of it, if it ever came down to accusation.

"Are you sure?" He kissed me tenderly. "We'll do whatever you want, you know. This is a chance to live out a fantasy, even if you only do it once. And, like you've said, Charles and I both know what we're doing. You won't regret it."

"I hope not." I yawned, cuddling into him. I fell asleep wondering whether all this could possibly be real.

Chapter Nineteen

I t didn't feel real for days, even when I went into Fox's office to learn the ropes from his outgoing PA. Fox, on that occasion, was friendly and professional. There were no smouldering looks, no accidental-on-purpose touches. I even had to buy my own lunch.

It made me wonder if Emmett had told him the whole thing was off. Perhaps he had, even though we had all gone together for a check-up at the GUM clinic and emailed our clean bills of health to each other. Perhaps, after all, he had measured the outcomes and found them unacceptably risky.

But then, coming home from a Saturday afternoon spent slogging around IKEA, Emmett checked his phone messages and said, "We're going out later."

"Are we? Where?"

"Charles's place."

My skin prickled. I couldn't look at Emmett. I concentrated on moving the stack of boxes from the doorstep to the small entrance hall.

"Oh? What's the occasion?"

"No occasion," said Emmett. "Leave that alone and come downstairs. You need to shower and get changed now if we aren't going to be late."

In the shower, I tried to steady myself, but my heart was skipping around like a spring lamb. Something was going to happen tonight. *Something.* I put a hand to my crotch, wondering if I needed to spruce up down there. I hadn't found a local waxing parlour yet, and it was a tad bristly. How did one prepare for a possible threesome, and a kinky one at that? I had no idea.

Perhaps Fox was just mindfucking me and we'd end up having a perfectly civilised dinner with cocktails.

But somehow, I didn't think so.

I came out of the shower to find Emmett dressing to kill in one of his best suits.

"Is it…some kind of party?" I asked, confused.

"Put those on," he said, using the hand that wasn't wrestling with a tie to point out some clothing draped across the bed.

"*Those?*" I picked up what seemed to be one length of sheer black material. Holding it up to the wardrobe mirror, I could see that it was a halterneck dress in some kind of shiny, stretchy fabric. It was very, very short. "This isn't mine. Where has it come from?"

"Bought it the other day," said Emmett, fastening cufflinks. "It looks like nothing, but it wasn't cheap."

"You chose this?" I frowned at the bed, which contained nothing more than a pair of hold-up stockings and some strappy black heels.

"I wasn't alone."

I clenched a fist around the dress. He had gone shopping

with Fox; dress shopping, for me. It was a dizzying thought.

"Put it on, then," he said, watching me.

"OK." I put it down and went over to my underwear drawer.

"No," he said, quickly and softly. "You won't need anything underneath."

"Seriously?"

"I'm not joking, Jo. I'm telling you what to do."

And that was it—I went from half a standard young metropolitan couple to fired-up submissive in the space of that one statement.

I put on the lace-topped stockings first, then pulled the dress up my body. It was tight and I had to wriggle into it. I turned away from Emmett; I hated it when he watched me dress, although weirdly had no qualms about the reverse operation. Once it was on, it clung perfectly. The halterneck lifted my breasts in lieu of a bra and the skirt flared out just a little on the thigh. It only just covered the lace tops of the stockings, though. I would have to remain absolutely straight-spined to avoid flashing anybody.

"It's very short," I said to Emmett, checking myself in the mirror from all possible angles.

"It's meant to be," he said. He stood next to me and put one hand up inside my skirt, resting it on the bare section of upper thigh. I felt handled by an owner. I had to shut my eyes, savouring the excitement.

"And you won't let me wear any knickers?" I whispered.

"Strictly forbidden," he said, rubbing my thigh, moving his fingers over the tender inner skin. "Girls like you don't get to wear knickers in the company of gentlemen."

"Oh God," I whispered.

219

He pressed his lips to my exposed neck. "I want that collar on you," he said. "Come on, get those shoes on and let's get going. Charles is sending a cab round and it'll be here any minute."

Luckily I had sorted out my hair and make-up in the bathroom, so all I had to do was strap on the spindly shoes, clip my collar round my neck and spray on my sexiest perfume.

The taxi honked from outside the moment we reached the top of the stairs. Emmett grabbed a bottle bag from the hall table, put my coat around my shoulders and led me out.

It wasn't easy tottering down our front steps in those heels whilst simultaneously making sure the hem of my dress didn't ride any higher up my thighs, but at least the coat covered my back view.

I slid on to the back seat of the cab beside Emmett.

"You know where we're going, I think?" said Emmett through the screen.

The driver just nodded and pulled away. Unusually, he was wearing a little cap with braiding around it, like a chauffeur in a period drama.

"Nice hat," I muttered to Emmett, but he put a finger to my lips.

"From now on," he said, taking my coat from me and putting it in the far corner, "you only speak when spoken to. Is that understood?"

I turned to him, so full of questions and pleas for reassurance that not being able to voice them was almost unbearable.

"You said you trusted me," he said. "Remember?"

I nodded.

"You could have spoken then, since I asked you a question,

by the way. Never mind, you'll get the hang of it. You, my love, were the one who wanted matters taken out of your hands. Well, now they are. Well and truly. Sit back and enjoy the ride."

I was already sitting back, as it happened, and the ride was certainly memorable, if not yet quite enjoyable, due to my nerves and my constant worry that the driver might be listening in.

"Have you ever read *The Story of O*?" asked Emmett, putting a hand on my nearest leg and playing with the silky-smooth hem of my dress where it rubbed against the lacy stocking tops.

"No, I don't think I have."

"It opens with a woman in a taxi. She's on her way to be trained as a submissive. Like you, she isn't wearing underwear, and she has to lift her skirt at the back so there's nothing between her bare bottom and the seat of the cab."

I looked at him, a little wildly. Was he telling me to do this? Was I allowed to ask?

He spoke into my ear. "The cab driver has been paid not to care what we do. He's seen this kind of thing before, many times. Lift up your skirt, pet."

"I can't...are you sure?"

Emmett's answering frown was enough. Shifting awkwardly against the leather upholstery, I tugged at the hem of my dress, inching it up at the back whilst trying to keep the front level and decent. I kept my head down, my face burning hot, avoiding any chance of eye contact with the driver. It took a long time. I bet the woman in the book didn't have to contend with seatbelt laws. By the time my bare bottom made contact with the seat, the front of the dress had risen an inch or so, just enough to show the stocking tops and a sliver of skin above them.

The seat was cool and slick against my rear. Such a simple

adjustment, yet it made me feel a hundred times more submissive and sexual. Somehow this was more decadent by far than unapologetically stripping off and shagging Emmett. I wondered why, but I wasn't really up to wondering, so I abandoned the attempt and concentrated on what Emmett's hand was doing on my thigh.

"That's better," he whispered, his fingers tracing the pale line of exposed skin. If my hem rose any higher, I'd be in danger of giving the driver something rather gynaecological in his rear view mirror. "But your legs need to be spread."

"But then…"

"I didn't ask for opinions. Do it, please."

The restrictions of the seatbelt didn't allow for much, anyway, but as I parted my thighs—Emmett helping by pulling the nearest one towards him—I felt a rush of illicit arousal, a shock all over my body. I knew I would do more than this if Emmett told me to. I knew, when it came to it, there was very little I wouldn't do.

His fingers slid up to the very top of my thigh and stayed there while his other hand angled my face to his and drowned me in a kiss of headspinning passion. I wanted to move my hands towards him, to touch him, but he shook his head and broke off.

"Nuh uh," he breathed. "Only if I tell you to."

The kiss resumed, carrying us through the stop and start of the city centre traffic, blocking out the sirens and horns, keeping me secure in my little capsule of heat and sexuality. This was what I was made for—to be kissed and fondled while the whole wide world went about its business. I was Emmett's possession, and I must do what I was told, no matter what.

The cab pulled up outside a shiny apartment block by the

river, and the driver opened the door for us. I didn't dare look at him as I left, making double sure my dress had fallen back over my bottom before taking Emmett's helping hand on to the pavement. Again, he put my coat over my shoulders, and we headed for the lobby, having to ask the concierge to admit us as if we were in a luxury hotel.

I wondered what the lugubrious old gentleman made of my skimpy dress and sky-high heels. If Emmett hadn't been with me, perhaps he'd have thought I was an escort. Hell, perhaps he thought we both were! Two pretty young things on our way to visit the wealthy older gentleman.

In the lift, Emmett got my lipstick from his pocket and reapplied it carefully, his fingers beneath my chin.

"Let's get you perfect again," he said, filling in the kissed-off sections. "I don't want Charles thinking I've started without him."

I longed to say something, longed to ask for a hint of what I was in for, but I also wanted very badly to be Emmett's ideal of submission and to make this evening an amazing success, so I held my tongue.

Chapter Twenty

Fox lived at the top of the building. The door was open when the lift disgorged us, and we wandered into the kind of fantasy penthouse you only see in movies, with giant plate glass windows looking over the billion blinking lights of the city.

"It's like a film set," I said out loud, but Emmett gave me a warning look.

"What?" I whispered. "Where is he, anyway?"

Because somebody was missing from this film set. The director.

"Disobedience," he said testily. "I'll have to deal with it."

I rolled my eyes, thrown out of my earlier headspace by the new and very interesting surroundings. I was still taking in the black and white opulence of it all when Fox suddenly appeared around a corner.

"Ah, here you are," he said, smiling, looking me up and down.

I dropped my eyes swiftly and naturally to the ground, a snapshot image of Fox suited and booted like something out of a James Bond fantasy imprinted on my brain. He looked frighteningly good. I didn't want to want him, but it was too late now.

"Come over here, Jo," he invited, cordially but leaving no space for resistance. "Let me look at you properly. Emmett, the drinks tray is over there, help yourself and take a seat."

I waded through the deep pile of his carpet, worrying about the little dints my heels were making in it, until I reached him. He stood before a large square fireplace. There were photographs on the mantelpiece, and I wanted to look at them, to get an idea of who he was and where he came from, but I had no time for that once I reached him.

I continued to look down, nervous of meeting his eye. I saw shiny shoes and fine grey cloth. In the background I heard the tinkle and splash of Emmett pouring his drink, then the slight squeaking resistance of leather as he sat in one of the two armchairs on either side of the fireplace.

"Oh, you look just right," said Fox, low-voiced. "That dress was a good choice, Emmett. I said it would work her curves, didn't I?"

"It's better than the other one," said Emmett, "now you see it on her."

Fox put a hand on my hip and held it there. It felt warm and heavy and made me breathe faster.

"Look up at me," he said.

I raised my eyes with some difficulty to his. For what seemed an age we just looked at each other, watching each other's faces, hearing each other's breathing, standing on a threshold.

"Mm," he said at last, a signal of approval. "Yes. How's the scotch, Emmett?"

"Divine," said Emmett.

"It's from the Isle of Jura, a gift from a friend. I think I'll have a glass myself."

He withdrew his hand from my hip and walked away. I nearly gasped with the sense of disconnection.

"You can kneel down," Fox threw at me from over his shoulder. "That's it, like that. Eyes down. Hands behind your neck. Good. She seems to know the positions, Emmett."

"We've been through most of them," he said. "Not in a structured way, just ad hoc. I mean, we didn't do formal training or anything."

"That's not something you'd be interested in?"

"I don't think so. Every relationship's different, isn't it? I wanted a submissive partner, not a trained submissive, if you can see the distinction."

"Yes, I can," said Fox. "It's better this way, I think. More organic...spontaneous. We can make it whatever we want. Nothing to unlearn."

"Exactly," agreed Emmett.

I wondered if my opinion was ever going to be solicited, although I was in accord with them anyway. I didn't want to be trained. I wasn't a puppy.

Kneeling there, on display, being talked about, but not to, was both infuriating and arousing. I felt small and menial, and it was getting me wet.

"So, I know we've talked about this a little already," said Fox, "but tell me what sort of things you've done with her."

Oh God. I swallowed hard, pressing my thighs together.

"Most of what you'd expect," said Emmett. "Sex in all positions, oral, anal, spanking, bondage, toys, a little bit of exhibitionism..."

226

"Tell me about that."

Emmett launched into an excruciatingly detailed account of our exploits in Barcelona, on the plane and off it, with additional information about our visit to the city centre sex shop.

Fox chuckled throughout, clearly impressed with his young grasshopper.

"She's willing to experiment, I see," he said.

"Very willing. She rarely says no to anything. Do you, pet?"

I flinched, surprised at the direct address.

"No, sir," I said.

"So she's generally pretty obedient?" Fox continued.

"Generally," said Emmett. "She has her moments. Nothing a good spanking can't deal with."

"Speaking of which," said Fox, as I cringed and my stomach flipped, "how much can she take, as a rule?"

"We've built up her tolerance over the last few months. She can go pretty long and hard, with a strap or a paddle. Haven't tried the cane yet—I've been leaving that for a special occasion. But I have to say, we haven't got very far with the keeping still and quiet aspect."

"I quite like that, though," said Fox. "Nice to feel that the message is getting through. The perfectly-behaved stoics are impressive, but not so much fun."

"No," said Emmett. "I'd miss all the jumping up and down and making a fuss, if I'm honest."

"Have you ever got her to the point of safewording?"

"Now and again. She's a bit of a devil for holding out till she's practically fainting, though. You have to watch her for that."

"Tut tut. Know your limits, girl," said Fox. "Very

important."

I didn't know whether I was expected to respond to this, so I didn't.

"What about orgasm control?" Fox wanted to know. "Have you done anything like that?"

"She knows to ask permission most of the time," said Emmett. "Haven't done anything like serious orgasm denial, or orgasm on demand, though."

"Because you don't want to, or…?"

"It just hasn't come up, so to speak. I'll occasionally make her wait for her orgasm, but it makes me feel so mean." He laughed self-consciously. "Which sounds weird, I know."

"But you work on the principle that her orgasm belongs to you?"

"Oh yes. That's a given."

"And would you be prepared to have it belong to both of us? Just for the times we're together?"

"I think so," he said. "As long as we know who's granting permission in advance."

"Great." I heard Fox swallow his whisky, hard, and put down his glass. "So, shall we…?"

Emmett cleared his throat. I stiffened.

"Pet, come over to Charles, on all fours, please, then kneel in front of him."

I turned towards Fox and lowered myself on to hands and knees. The whole of London lay behind him. I wondered if anybody could see into this vast window, but most of the buildings were far enough away to guarantee sufficient privacy. I hoped.

Arriving between his feet, I raised myself up again, keeping my eyes down and my hands clasped behind my neck. He reached out and stroked my cheek with the back of his fingers, so tenderly I almost sighed.

"So pretty," he said. "Take off your dress."

My hands were already resting on the knot of my halterneck. I untied it and pulled the rest over my head. It was a bit of a struggle, the dress being so close-fitting, and I almost changed my mind halfway and pulled it over my hips, but that would have been inelegant, and I was trying my best to keep pace with the imaginary 'perfect sub' he had probably seen a thousand times.

His trained and tested lovers past would not have struggled and spent ages getting a dress off. They would do it like paid strippers. They wouldn't get hot and breathless like me, and mess up their carefully arranged hair. Oh, fuck it. It would have to do.

I threw the dress aside, mutinous and embarrassed by my poor performance. I wanted to apologise, but would that be allowed? Probably not.

I could see my bare chest heaving down below. I put my hands back behind my neck and wished I could shut my eyes.

"Hot and bothered?" teased Fox. "Perhaps a different outfit next time. Or one of us could undress you. I always like to unwrap a gift."

I dared to flick a glance up at him. He was smiling at me. I couldn't resist an upward twitch of my lip. He looked utterly enthralled by me, and I felt a surge of sweet power.

"Don't move now," he warned, reaching out and running a fingertip along my lips. He pushed it gently through their glossy barrier, making me suck on it for a moment or two before withdrawing it and stroking a line down from my cheek to my jaw. He held me steady there, pressing fingertips into the soft skin of my neck.

"I can feel your pulse," he said softly. "Racing."

Any composure I might have had was long gone. Sighing breaths poured from my parted lips. He radiated confidence and authority and I craved him beyond endurance.

"What about these then?"

His touch drifted down my neck and shoulders until he cupped a breast in each hand.

"Lovely," he said, massaging them slowly. "Nicely in proportion. Tell me who they belong to, little one."

"To Emmett, sir," I whispered.

He squeezed harder. "Just Emmett?"

"And to you, sir," I added, my scalp prickling.

"You shouldn't need reminding," he cautioned. "Never mind, we'll deal with it later on."

"I'm sorry, sir," I blurted, mortified at having displeased him so soon, and in such a cloth-headed fashion. *Obviously* he'd want me to say he owned them. Gah, what a stupid mistake.

He grazed his thumbs over my nipples, repeating the process with steady thoroughness while they hardened into helpless little bullets.

"Do you often clamp these, Emmett?" he asked.

"Sometimes. She absolutely hates it, so it's a good disciplinary tool." Emmett's voice was slightly strained. I wanted to look at his face, but I knew this wouldn't be acceptable.

"Aha, I must remember that."

My nipples felt electrically connected to my vagina by now, the latter in a state of uncomfortable wetness, my clit swollen and heavy like the clapper of a bell between my lower lips.

He pinched them lightly between thumb and forefinger. I gasped and jolted a little, but he didn't release the pressure until

I stilled.

"I've heard sore nipples are worse than a sore bottom," he remarked. "More sensitive. And they chafe against everything. But since we're on the subject of bottoms…" He patted the sides of my breasts, a regretful gesture of farewell. "Turn around and put your forehead on the floor."

I did as I was told, posing with my spine bent and my bum in the air for his inspection. He leant forward and laughed, pressing a fingertip into my tattoo.

"Oh, I like this. When you told me about the exhibitionism, you didn't mention this. Did you do it yourself, Em?"

"God, no, I wouldn't trust myself with a needle. A mate with a tattoo parlour."

"And it's permanent?"

"Oh yes."

Fox was clearly enormously turned on by this, rubbing it and stroking my cheeks with strong, grabby hands.

"How did it make you feel, little one?" he said, hands all over my arse, "baring your bottom in front of the tattooist, knowing that he knew what you were?"

"It was embarrassing, sir," I said. "But I did it for Emmett."

Fox sighed, running a finger along the crease.

"Anything for Emmett," he said. "God, you've fallen on your feet here." He delved a little further into the hot, dark place only my husband had explored before. "Nice and tight," he said approvingly, pressing at my rear opening. "And I want to see these cheeks a good solid red before too long." He gave each one a resounding smack. I could feel the shape of his hand glowing on my skin. "All right, back up again and facing me, with your legs apart."

He sat back and I obeyed his command, keenly aware of the

slick state of my pussy and upper thighs. He slid a hand, palm uppermost, over my mound and coated his fingers with my juices.

"Just as you told me, Em," he said, his eyes twinkling at me. "Soaking wet. Mm, the state of this…" He rubbed lazily at my clit, making my stomach burn and my hips tremble. Two fingertips found their way inside me. They made a slick, sucking sound as he swivelled them around.

"Oh." I couldn't hold back a little cry as he continued fingering me, his other hand back on my nipples. Pressure was building inside me faster than I could diffuse it.

"Not yet, little one," he whispered, pulling out of me and yanking me on to his lap. He wrapped me in his arms and kissed me into a starry-eyed mess. He smelled irresistible, and he felt like heaven; for a dangerous moment, I was more his than Emmett's—a mere pleading heap of naked submission.

"Are you OK?" he whispered into my ear, out of dom character for a heart-stopping moment. "Is this what you want?"

I nodded, squirming against him to emphasise the message.

"Amazing," I whispered back.

With a low chuckle, he fastened his lips to my neck, sucking at it for a moment or two before pulling away from me and tipping me back on to the floor.

"Go to Emmett," he said. "Quickly now, before I lose control of myself."

I looked back at him, a little confused, and he patted my bottom, sending me across the floor to where my husband awaited with his empty whisky tumbler held tight in his hand and a deep flush on his face.

"I want to see the two of you together," said Fox. "Like we discussed, Em."

I came to rest between Emmett's feet. He put down the tumbler and looked at me narrowly for as long as it took me to succumb to a fit of nerves. What had they discussed? What was Emmett going to do to me? And was Fox going to have a hand in it?

Emmett retrieved my hands from the back of my neck and held them between us, stooping down to me for a solemn, sealing kiss.

"I'm very proud of you," he said, his mouth still moving against mine. "But you forgot something earlier, and I'll have to address it."

My blood rushed through my veins. Fox's treatment had left me desperate for anything, but was I really ready to be spanked in front of another man?

"Come up, then," said Emmett, patting his thigh meaningfully. "This side...that's right."

I crept, very self-consciously, over his lap. Mercifully, he had me facing away from Fox—I guess my rear view was the big draw here. Emmett placed my hands in the small of my back and cautioned me to keep them there at all costs, or there'd be consequences.

I didn't like this position, which relinquished control over my body and removed one mechanism for coping with the pain, as I would be unable to grab at the nearest cushion or the cloth of Emmett's trousers and ball it into my fists. Emmett usually only enforced it when he meant me to take him very seriously.

Or he was showing off to a friend.

He lifted one knee, raising my bottom higher and making sure my thighs were just wide enough for everything to be visible to our witness. The thought of Fox looking steadily at that target area and seeing it glistening and open made me throb with guilty excitement.

"This is the first time anyone's watched her being punished?" Fox wanted to know.

"Officially," said Emmett. "We've messed about with risky situations—in front of the window, bent over a stile on a country walk, that kind of thing. But nothing like this."

"She's being very good," Fox noted. "Very docile. No fussing."

"Ha, not yet," said Emmett. "It'll come, I'm sure." He rubbed a hand over my bottom then tapped it lightly. "Are you ready, pet?"

"Yes, sir."

He began with light slaps all over my bum and upper thighs, warming me up with sensual expertise. I relaxed into the sensation, shutting my eyes, thinking hard about Fox's gaze trained on me.

"Do you know why you're being punished, pet?" asked Emmett.

"I…ah…" I tried to remember. Details were beginning to haze in my mind.

Emmett's smacks grew harder, firecrackers now, alternating cheeks.

"Hmm?" he prompted.

"I forgot that my orgasm belongs to you and to Mr Fox," I said. I wasn't sure what to call him. I settled on respectful.

"You did, that's right. You owe Mr Fox a very big apology."

"I'm very sorry, Mr Fox," I said, gasping slightly as Emmett's strokes really began to gather force. "I won't forget again."

"You'll get the chance to make a proper apology soon," said Emmett. "Don't worry."

"She colours up well," commented Fox. I heard him pouring himself another drink. He was hovering closer, just behind me. "Fuchsia pink already."

"We can put her on the balcony and use her as a beacon for incoming flights by the time I'm finished," said Emmett. "I like to get her as red as I can. It's become a persistent challenge."

Fox sniggered behind me.

"Perhaps we could have a competition sometime."

"Great idea."

Emmett was spanking at nearly full force now, and I was jolting and mewling with each resounding crack.

"You'll remember, pet," said Emmett, without breaking stride, "that you need Mr Fox's permission before you come. I think we'll be practising that a lot tonight. Do you read me?"

"Aaaoooowwww, yes sir," I wailed. I was kicking a bit, gyrating furiously in his lap, but somehow managing to keep my hands where he'd put them. He seemed to see that we were in the danger zone, because he put his free hand on my wrists, keeping me in position.

"You see what I mean about keeping still and quiet," said Emmett, panting a little now.

"She's a lively one," said Fox. "But you obviously have a seasoned spanking hand."

Emmett responded to the compliment by speeding up, peppering me so hard and fast that I felt my control slipping away and began to fake-sob.

"It hu-u-u-urts," I moaned.

"Good, so it should," said Emmett briskly. He dealt another couple of dozen or so, just to show me that I didn't get a say in these matters, and came to a halt, resting his hand on my hot backside.

"Scarlet woman," said Fox, impressed. "That's a glorious colour. Do you mind if I...?"

"Go ahead," said Emmett, and I saw a flash and heard the click of a cameraphone.

"Now then," said Emmett, running his hands up my damp inner thighs and brushing his fingers far too swiftly between them. I tensed, then made a soft moan of protest at the tease. "I'm sorry, pet, did you want something?"

I wiggled my hips hopefully.

He smacked the backs of my thighs.

"Not yet," he said. "We haven't finished with your bottom yet."

I made an incoherent sound of frustrated woe.

"You said you had a…" Emmett was talking to Fox.

"Ah, yes," he said. "I'll set it up for you."

Some kind of furniture-moving took place out of my eyeshot while Emmett continued to stroke my inner thighs, just shy of where I really wanted his touch.

He straightened his legs, sliding me off one side on to my knees, then raised me up by my upper arm, turning me to face my fate.

It was a piece of furniture clearly designed to be bent over, with a slightly curving padded top and four metal legs. Emmett led me to it and got me into the required position. My ankles were cuffed to two of the legs, spreading me wide, while my bottom was high in the air, my breasts hanging over the other side of the cushion with my hands free to cling on to a horizontal crossbar between the legs on the other side.

"Normally," said Emmett, passing a leather strap over my waist and clipping it into place, "I would cuff your hands to this bar. But we have something different in mind for today."

236

Fox came and stood beside him, then crouched down to my eye level, putting his hands over mine where they rested on the bar. He smiled reassuringly, his head on one side.

"I've seen you take a thrashing from one angle," he said. "But I want to look at your face this time."

I swallowed, panic rising up through my captive body. I saw Emmett move over to a wooden trunk in a corner of the room and raise its lid. He took out a sleek black flogger and swished it through the air before coming back to stand behind me.

OK, I told myself. Calm down. It's only a flogger. It could have been much worse—a wooden paddle or a heavy strap. Or the much-mythologised cane.

All the same, my bottom felt as tender as it ever wanted to be, especially stretched tight as it was over this contraption.

Fox brought a chair over and sat on it, in front of me, then took my hands from the crossbar and held them firmly.

"While Emmett is flogging you," he said, "I want you to keep eye contact with me, all the way through."

I gaped at him. "I'm not sure I can…do that…" I admitted. The very thought had made me seize up with horror.

"We thought you'd find that hard," said Fox. "So, if you like, I can help you." He moved one hand to cup my chin, gently but inescapably. I tried to move my head left, then right, but I was well and truly held in place. "Will that be easier for you?"

"Maybe."

Nothing was going to make this easier.

"Maybe *what?*" said Emmett sharply.

"Maybe, sir," I sighed.

"Of course, the other way," said Emmett, coming to stand beside Fox. "Is *this.*"

I yelped as he grabbed a handful of my hair, yanking my neck back.

"No, no, the first way is good, sir," I assured him. "And sir," I added, not wanting to be punished for leaving Fox out of the exchange. This threesome stuff was complicated.

"All right. Good." Emmett kissed me and returned to my rear.

Fox got my chin where he wanted it and set his gaze steadily on my face.

"You look scared," he said, stroking my cheek. "Are you scared?"

"A little, sir," I said. "Not of the flogging. Of...this."

He nodded, still stroking.

"But I think you like the fear," he said. "It heightens the sensation."

"Yes, sir."

He was right.

"Are we ready?" asked Emmett, tickling my bottom with the tips of the flogger. I tried to squirm but I was secured in all my squirmy places, helpless to defend myself.

"I think so," said Fox. His finger and thumb pressed a little harder into my jaw.

The flogger swished and landed on my sore behind with biting impact.

"Ooh," I moaned.

I shut my eyes, but Fox patted my cheek.

"If you close them, you'll get more," he said.

I opened them again and made a sad face at him. He smiled in response.

The flogging seemed to go on forever, with Emmett whipping me up into burning heat and sting, but the pain was nothing compared to the challenge of Fox's implacable gaze. I wanted desperately to hide from it, but there was nowhere to run.

Instead, I had to accept that he was watching and enjoying my humiliation, as well as adding to it with his clear appreciation. Which was crueller—the man who whipped, or the man who watched?

As my merciless husband laid stroke after stroke, I howled and whimpered, the sounds squeezed out from a captive jaw.

"You need this," said Fox, as the first tear fell. "Don't you?"

"Yes, sir," I wailed, trying hard to move my body, but restrained at every turn.

"Do you deserve it?"

"Yes, yes, I deserve it," I hissed. I was becoming something less than human, something purely submissive and sexual.

Emmett laid several evil strokes on my exposed inner thighs, then he moved between them. My clit was so swollen and wet that the whip felt good, almost orgasmic, against it.

"Oh God," I moaned. "I can't…"

Emmett went back to my bottom, which must have been as red as it could possibly be by now. It was so incredibly sore, and yet I felt nowhere near safewording. I was locked into Fox's laser stare, powerless to break out.

He rose from his chair and grabbed my hair, in the way Emmett had done, then kissed me ravishingly while Emmett finished up on my behind. My tears spilled on to his cheeks and ran down his nose while his tongue plunged inside my mouth.

I clung to his shirt, holding him near me, rapt and lost in the sensation.

Emmett laid aside his whip. Fox broke the kiss.

I lay, panting and burning, between them. I had crossed the

boundary of fear. I was in the realm of pure submissive bliss.

"Come and look at her arse," invited Emmett brokenly. "That's red for you."

"Incredible," said Fox. "Judging by the state of her down there, she's ready for a good seeing to."

"Weren't we going to…first…?"

"Yes, yes. I'm ahead of myself. Right."

Fox came back round and sat in his chair. I could see the great bulge in his suit trousers and thought it must be uncomfortable for him, but I didn't have too much sympathy to spare when my own pussy was absolutely dripping.

"Remember," he said. "Eye contact. I'll hold you in place if necessary, but I think it's time you tried to obey without help. Hold out your hands to me."

I quickly wiped my damp cheeks with the backs of them, then gave them up to Fox, who held my fingers. Once we were linked, Emmett moved in between my legs and began to touch me, slowly, teasingly, tracing out the line of my labia with his fingertips.

I sighed gently. Fox smiled, enjoying my helplessness, stroking my fingers.

"Is that good?" he whispered.

Emmett rubbed my clit and I moaned in gratitude.

"Take that as a yes," said Fox dryly.

"Yes, sir," I groaned.

The eye contact maintenance was hard; they were rolling back and sideways and all over as Emmett settled into a slow, steady rhythm. He introduced one finger, then two, then three, into my vagina, but he didn't thrust. They were there as a marker, a reminder of what I was going to get.

I was barely in need of any stimulation at all—it was a

matter of a minute, maybe two, before I felt the approach of a shattering orgasm.

I think Emmett could feel the first flutters against his seated fingers. Still stroking away at my clit, he asked me if I was close.

"Yes, yes, sir," I said.

Fox pinched my fingers, and I tried hard to focus on him, but everything was beginning to blur.

"You know what you have to do, pet," Emmett reminded me.

"I know, I know, please, sir, may I come?"

"Who are you asking?" Fox leant forward, his gaze bearing down hard on me.

"You, sir, you and…both…everyone…please…oh God."

"No," said Fox, and I let out a loud moan of despair.

"Joking," he said. "Go on then, just this once."

He dropped my fingers and cupped my lower face in both hands, keeping my eyes full on him as my climax gushed down and out of me. The enormity of the feeling was unlike anything I'd experienced before, and it precipitated me into a flurry of tears. He kissed them all away, with passion, while Emmett fell to his knees and kissed my pussy and clit. I felt cocooned in tenderness, loved and adored beyond dreams.

Fox found my lips and kissed me hard and hungrily throughout the vigorous fucking Emmett then subjected me to. Each thrust pushed me into Fox's face, and slapped up against my stinging bottom. I clung blindly to Fox's shirt, bunching it in my fists. He was my support and my strength, just as much as Emmett was now. The bond was forged.

After Emmett emptied into me, they unstrapped me from the spanking stool and carried me together to a cavernous white bathroom, in which a huge sunken tub lay already filled and foaming. They slid me into it, then undressed themselves.

"Oh God, I'm dead," I said, soaking up the delicious warmth.

They both laughed.

"I hope not," said Fox. "I haven't finished with you yet."

"So," said Emmett, a little warily. "How was it? Are you OK?"

"Apart from being dead, you mean?" I gave him a groggy smile. "I think you've blown my mind. You won't get any sense from me for some time."

He was first to climb in beside me. He wrapped his arms around me and gave me a long, heartfelt smooch.

"I love you so, so much," he said into my ear. "You know that, don't you?"

"I know. I love you too."

"You're brave and brilliant and amazing. The sexiest woman in the world."

More kisses, then Fox swung his legs over the side, and I had to turn away from Emmett to get a good look at his naked body. It was, as I suspected, Greek godlike. All the abs and pecs and what have you were present and correct, in a way I'd only really seen on screen before. He was erect, too, and I wondered when I'd have that hard, thick length inside me.

It was lovely to look at, but less lovely was the self-consciousness it induced. I was glad of the bubbles, concealing my pale softness from his view.

We slipped and slid between each other. There were lots of kisses and plenty of caresses under the guise of thorough soaping. I floated from one pair of arms to the other, sometimes sandwiched between them.

"I said she was a mermaid when we first met," said Emmett,

pinning me to the side of the tub to stop me swirling about.

"Hold her down," said Fox. "I'll wash her fishtail."

Emmett straddled me around my hips, kissing me into compliance, while Fox lifted one leg clear of the water and lathered it up, higher and higher, then the other. Eventually his hand went where I knew he had intended it to all along. He put my ankles on his shoulders and paid heavy attention to the area between my legs, massaging and exploring to his heart's content while Emmett kept me immobile.

The soap was mildly stinging on my clit, but I could barely protest, and it soon washed away. Fox's palm covered the area, flexing up and down.

"I think she's clean," he said. "Shall we get out?"

Emmett climbed off me.

"What's happening next?" I asked, watching my husband's long legs as he hauled himself out of the bath.

Fox pulled me close to him and kissed me.

"We're going to eat," he said softly, his forehead on mine. "And then I'm going to take you to bed and give you what you need while your husband watches. Does that sound like a plan?"

I nodded, my throat catching.

"Good. Because my patience is going to come to an end fairly soon. I'm actually in pain."

He rose from the water, still hard as rock, and I gave him my most sympathetic look.

"Poor man," I said teasingly.

He grabbed my arm and pulled me up with him, giving my sudsy wet bottom a loud smack.

"Trust me, my dear, it won't be me that needs sympathy soon."

Emmett was holding a towel for me, and I walked straight

243

into it, letting him wind me round and round until I was quite swaddled. He was already in a bathrobe, and he got to work on drying me while Fox knotted a towel around his waist and dealt with his unruly hair. He looked more human with it tousled somehow; younger and less perfectly composed. I wondered about his background and the formation of his character, and then I wondered if I would ever find out about it.

Chapter Twenty One

We walked into the living space in bathrobes—Emmett's a fluffy towelling number, Fox's paisley silk, mine very short and virtually transparent—to drink wine and await the takeaway delivery Fox had arranged.

What did people talk about after a kinky threesome? Apparently light conversation was in order.

"I hope Vietnamese is all right," said Fox. "There's a fantastic place just up the road; I ordered a selection of their best dishes."

"Cool," I said, and Emmett said "Great" at the same time.

We laughed awkwardly.

"Nice wine," I offered. "It's OK, you don't have to tell me the vintage or anything. It won't mean anything to me."

I think Fox cottoned on to the fact that I was teasing him for his tendency to describe the provenance and quality of everything in sight.

He raised his eyebrows at me over the rim. "Well, perhaps we'll have to educate you on that," he said.

"Do you have some kind of wine bible we can make her memorise?" asked Emmett with enthusiasm. "Tests every week. Rewards for good marks, punishment for bad ones."

Fox smiled. "Not a bad idea," he said.

Should have kept my big mouth shut. I had a feeling the pair of them were going to spend the rest of my life concocting elaborate role-plays for us to enact. The possibilities thrown up by two such depraved imaginations working in harmony hardly bore thinking about.

I was saved by the bell, and the takeaway cartons, and for the next half hour or so, the only words spoken revolved around food, drink and some light reminiscing about travel in South East Asia.

The intermission had to come to an end, though, and once the cartons were cleared away and we had drained our glasses, the atmosphere thickened and I became aware of both men's attention landing squarely on me.

"How are you now, Jo?" asked Fox.

"I'm fine," I said nervously. "Still a little bit sore, glad this chair's so comfortable. But, er, apart from that…yeah…"

Fox rose and pulled me from my chair, flush into his body. He felt alarmingly large and powerful. His erection had calmed a little during the meal, but as soon as we came together, I was aware of it growing against my thigh.

"You're afraid," he said, kissing my neck, his hand stroking my bottom through the sheer fabric of the robe.

"Nnno, not really. I'm…OK…"

"I like it," he said. "All your little hesitations and stricken glances turn me on. But you must use your safeword if you need to. Will you promise me?"

I nodded, sighing, bending my neck eagerly to meet his

ravaging lips. He squeezed my buttocks, both a reassurance and a warning.

"Good. Now get on your knees and show me how you make a man seriously hard."

His voice had changed, from gentle to uncompromising, and it flicked the switch that plunged me into subspace. It was an order. There was no way to defy it.

I knelt before him and put my hands on his thighs, but he made a sound indicating displeasure and I realised I had to keep my hands behind my back for this exercise. He unbelted his robe, letting the silk fall away from his stiffening member. He leant back on the table, needing to bend his legs a little for me to reach his tip.

I put out the tip of my tongue and drew a straight line all the way up his shaft, then I curled it round to explore the sensitive underside.

I heard his breathing deepen.

"Yes, yes," he whispered.

I continued this delicate operation for as long as I felt I could get away with it, then, just as his hand descended into my hair, I opened my mouth and admitted his swollen tip, licking lusciously all the way around it. It felt thick and it stretched my jaw as I worked my way down. I felt it growing inside me until I was sure it couldn't possibly get any bigger. Fox's hand was bunched in my hair now, giving firm encouragement to my sucking.

I took as much of him in as I could, although I didn't yet have the hang of deep-throating and had to cheat now and then by stowing him in my cheek to avoid gagging. It was difficult to do this without recourse to my hands, but I was eager to perform well and earn his praise.

"Mm, mm, yes," he murmured, apparently happy with my technique.

My eyes were teary and my jaw aching by the time he drew out. His cock stood upright in front of my face, red and wet from my devotions.

"I have other plans for this," he said, tugging lightly at my hair to get me up. "But, trust me, they involve putting it in you. Let's go to the bedroom, shall we?"

He put his hand under my elbow and steered me around the corner of the room and into a giant chamber at its end, furnished with a huge bed, a mirrored ceiling and more of the immense glass windows. My bare feet sunk into a carpet with pile as deep as the ocean. More mirrors made up the interior walls.

"I guess you like to look at yourself," I mused out loud, forgetting myself.

"What did you say?" He stopped short, staring at me. I quailed.

"Sorry, sir," I gabbled. "Just thinking aloud."

"Well, I wasn't going to spank you, but just for that, I think a little reminder is in order. Go and bend over the end of the bed, now."

Emmett came in after us and settled silently into an armchair in one corner.

I cursed myself for my idiocy, but obeying Fox's order gave me a thrill amidst the fear, so I folded myself into the required position and waited.

At least I didn't have to guess what he was doing—the mirrors saw to that.

I watched him pick up a broad-backed wooden hairbrush from the dresser and steeled myself.

248

"I think we'll go for ten, just to keep you in the right frame of mind," he said, looming over me from behind. "Count them for me."

I saw Emmett lean forward. His face was tense, almost fearful.

The first stroke fell with a satisfying splat, and a less satisfying burst of pain, on my rear.

I breathed through it, then gave him the count. "One, sir."

Nine more followed, and I was pretty sure Fox was holding a lot back, because only the last one really made me yell— usually a wooden surface of any kind can be relied upon to have me begging for mercy within seconds.

These, on the other hand, were more for ceremonial purposes, putting me in my rightful place. Fox returned the hairbrush to the dresser.

"Lesson learned?" he asked equably, returning to me.

"Yes, sir, thank you, sir."

He put his hands on my buttocks and squeezed, feeling their renewed heat.

"Any time," he said. "Now get up on to that bed and lie on your back for me."

I lay, open and ready for him, watching him shrug off the robe and run his eyes slowly, salivatingly, over my body.

"You're gorgeous," he said, kneeling on the end of the bed and taking up one of my feet, kissing it from toe tip upwards. "I hope you want me as much as I want you, Jo."

This was a change of mood, taking us out of role into a more intimate place. It felt like cheating and I squinted over at Emmett to see what he made of it, but he was enthralled, glued to us.

"Yes," I whispered. "I want you."

He caught me up in his arms and kissed me ferociously. We rolled together, mussing up the sheets and ourselves, kicking and grabbing in a damburst of passion. His size and shape were so different from Emmett's and I found wonder and excitement in each point of divergence.

He pinned me flat to the bed and had his way with my breasts, rubbing his hard length up and down my thigh in constant reminder of what was to become of me. I arched against him as he teased my nipples with his tongue, pressing my mound into his erection. My hunger for him surprised me, but I rode it through, showing him how wet I was.

"I can't...wait...any longer," he confessed in hectic bursts, pushing his fingers into my spread to make sure I was ready.

"Do it," I urged. "Do me. I need it."

"Fuck." Still holding me down, he eased slowly into me, making me feel every iota of the stretch. "You're getting it. Take it all the way...oh God, yes."

I surrendered to his penetration, knowing that this was a line crossed, a new horizon gained. Now an adulteress in legal fact, if not in spirit, I waited for shame or angst to assail me, but neither did. Emmett, in the mirror, was fumbling under his robe, his eyes intent, his cheeks highly coloured.

I had assumed that Fox, having been so aroused for such a long time, wouldn't last long, but my assumption proved unfounded. He hauled me over on to his lap, then turned me around, then twisted me this way and that. In each position, he brought me almost to the brink, saw me about to ask permission for my orgasm, then moved me again.

When I was finally allowed to come, I was straddling his hips, facing away from him, looking straight at Emmett. I ground harder and harder, feeling the sensation returning once more, ever optimistic, although I fully expected to be denied once more.

"Please, sir," I whimpered. He didn't try to change positions. I ground harder still.

"Look at Emmett," he ordered. "Ask him."

I looked straight into my husband's eyes.

"Please, sir, may I be allowed to c…" It was too late. I was there, taken over and inhabited by this dirty, illicit orgasm.

"I'd better say yes, hadn't I?" said Emmett, his eyes glassy, his fist wrapped around his cock.

He faded into a blur as my vision fell prey to my climax.

Fox pulled out briefly, rolled me on to my back and pushed back in for his final thrusts. His face lowered over mine, sweat from his hairline dripping on to me.

"You're mine now," he said, pumping vigorously. "This is the first time of many, believe me. Tell me. Tell me you're mine."

"I'm yours, sir," I vowed, then I was swallowed up in a violent kiss that only ended when he reared up, emptying into me with a shout of triumph.

As he slumped back beside me, kissing me over and over again, I heard Emmett's little moan of completion. That robe was going to need washing.

"Are you coming to join us or what?" asked Fox lazily. Emmett took off his robe and tucked himself in behind me, laying his hand on my hip and kissing the back of my neck and shoulder, while Fox kept up his work on my lips.

We twined together, the three of us, hot and sticky and smeared with each other's fluids, kissing and stroking and whispering little tokens of love until we drifted into sapped slumber.

When I woke up, Fox was in the bathroom and I was alone with Emmett.

"Em," I whispered, prodding him awake.

"Whassat? Eh?" He propped himself up, shaking the sleep out of his eyes, then cuddled back into me. "Look at you," he yawned. "You look totally fucked."

"I am," I said, "by two men. Are you really OK with it, Em? I have to ask."

"I have to admit," he said slowly, after a pause. "I was thinking there might be some grinning and bearing involved at times. But there wasn't. It was all incredibly, incredibly erotic and hot and arousing, and it just made me love you even more. What about you?"

"It was amazing," I said. "Both of you."

Fox returned to the room and I whispered into Emmett's ear, "Especially you."

"Ah, you're awake," said Fox. He sat himself down between us and kissed us each on the lips. "Anyone for another go?"

Menagerie

Chapter Twenty Two

We have a signal, the three of us—me, Emmett and Fox —and when the signal is given, the dynamic between us shifts and I am no longer Jo, the normal human being. I become in that instant Jo the submissive.

The signal works like this. The rule is that all three of us have to be up for it, or it's null and void. Usually, Fox messages Emmett, or vice versa, and gets his consent, then one of them messages me with a question mark.

If I message an exclamation mark, the game is on. If, for whatever reason, I'm not in the mood, I message an ampersand. Not sure why I chose that, but ampersands have come to represent tiredness and stress by association in my world, and I don't much like looking at them now.

On the whole, though, the exclamations outnumber the ampersands by quite a significant margin.

It was an exclamation mark on that day, a few months into our arrangement, when we found out about the Big Deal.

I was sitting at my desk, just outside the foxhole, as we

called Fox's big impress-the-clients office (when he wanted to actually work, he usually came out and joined me and Emmett), going through the online diary. Emmett was opposite me, wearing earphones, working very intently on something. His phone bleeped. He looked at it, looked at me, and smiled.

I was getting to know what this meant and, sure enough, a minute or so later, my own phone furnished me with a question mark.

"I thought he was out," I said, looking at Emmett. "At lunch with those bigshots."

"He's on his way back," said Emmett. "He'll be here any minute. So…?"

I made a face at him and texted the exclamation.

This was my cue to head to the ladies', which was shared with the whole floor in this big complex of small City concerns. I hoped, as ever, that the facilities wouldn't be heaving with women from the corporate law start-up across the hall, who seemed to virtually live in there, applying lipstick and swapping insider tips on potential new client leads.

For once, it was empty, and I slipped into a stall, kicked off my heels and began the awkward business of unsnapping suspenders and easing off my knickers. Once this was done, and the knickers stowed in my handbag, I performed the even more awkward business of removing my bra.

We had done this at work only a handful of times, and I was still extremely nervous of crossing the landing in this underwear-free state. Nobody would know about the knickers, but my nipples made unmissable dents in my heavy cotton shirt that, in my imagination, were probably visible from the furthest ends of the floor.

My exit from the toilets coincided with Fox stepping out of

the lift.

"Jo," he said, beaming.

He took a quick look around to make sure we weren't observed, then put his arm around my shoulder, steering me back to our office. His hand slid quickly down over my shoulder, fingers testing my breasts to make sure they weren't covered. My nipples hardened quickly at his touch, and I looked up into his face.

"Your lunch went well, then, sir?" I said.

"Really well. I'll tell you all about it later."

It had been a reasonable assumption. Fox rarely suggested this kind of thing unless he had pulled off some kind of major coup—it seemed to be his way of celebrating. If you're thinking our working life was one long orgy, you'd be mistaken. Sometimes weeks would pass without any of these text messages —although we still met up regularly to play at weekends, when we were all free.

It made office life interesting. Quite often I would sit at my desk, reminiscing or fantasising about some swoon-inducingly hot scene, and long for my phone to buzz. But Fox and Emmett both loved their work and tended to forget about much else while they were absorbed in it, so I spent more time reminding them to eat or go home than I did taking off my knickers.

We entered the office. Emmett started to shut down his machine.

"Be right with you," he said, as Fox and I moved through into the foxhole, which—unlike our space—had privacy blinds, although the exterior windows still looked out on to the skyscraping landscape of corporate London.

Fox pushed me against his enormous desk and began kissing me hungrily, unbuttoning the top of my shirt as he did so. I could taste traces of red wine and spearmint gum. Emmett came in to find Fox's tongue down my throat and his hand inside my shirt, kneading at my breasts.

"Can you believe this slut, Marlow?" he panted, as Emmett came closer. "She doesn't wear a bra to the office."

"I think she likes everyone to see her nipples," said Emmett. "Every man in town's had a good look at those by now."

Fox unbuttoned my shirt further, pulling it apart to reveal my breasts.

"Why don't you wear a bra?" he asked me.

"Because I'm not allowed, sir," I replied.

Fox played with my breasts and nipples, pinching and stroking with scientific interest.

"You're not allowed? You're forbidden to wear a bra? By whom?"

"By my owner, sir, and by my master."

"Two men?" Fox grinned at me. We often played this game. He liked to hear me state my position in explicit terms.

"Yes, sir. My owner is my husband, and my master is his friend. They are both in charge of me, sir."

"In charge of you? In charge of *these*?" Fox pushed them together, his thumbs pushing down firmly on my nipples.

"Among other things, sir."

"What other things? Show me."

I hiked up my skirt, unveiling first my stocking tops, then my suspender elastics, then my newly-shaved pussy.

"All of this, sir," I said, as he dropped on to his knees to investigate.

Emmett climbed on to the desk and arranged himself behind me, so that I sat between his legs. He began kissing my neck and fondling my breasts, as Fox parted my lower lips and breathed gently on what he found there.

"So you're forbidden to wear knickers too?" he said, massaging my lips slowly, drawing soaked sounds from what lay within. "Why is that?"

"In case either of my masters wants to use me, sir."

"You have to be available?"

"Constantly, sir."

Fox pushed his face into my open wetness and began to devour me. I moaned and leaned back into Emmett, who caught my mouth in a kiss that mimicked Fox's activities below. Every part of me was open and available, and ready to be taken by them. As ever, when I found myself in this kind of situation, I imagined someone from security or building services barging in on us and seeing what I was, what these men had made me.

As Fox's tongue lavished my clit and pussy with attention, and Emmett pinched my nipples and explored my throat, I pictured the intruder, slack-jawed, then moving his hand to the hard bulge in his crotch… It would end with me ordered to suck him dry while Emmett and/or Fox fucked me from behind, or whipped me, or whatever. The fantasies varied according to my mood.

Doubly stimulated as I was, it wasn't long before I felt a certain swelling sensation in the pit of my stomach. I grabbed Emmett's face and tried to push us apart, making anxious noises in my throat as a signal. He understood and broke the kiss, just in time for me to gasp, "Please, sir, may I come?"

Fox wasn't in a position to give permission, and I don't know what I'd have done if Emmett had said no. He'd been giving me lessons in the art of orgasm denial, but apparently I was a slow learner.

He gave me the nod just in time. I shimmied and shook on

the end of Fox's tongue, pouring my essence into him. He lapped it up, and kept lapping, while I made helpless mewing noises and tried to kick my legs out of his confining grasp.

He finished only when *he* had had enough. I knew that by now.

"Better," he growled, finally licking his fill. "Got the taste of that foul wine out of my mouth at last. I thought that place was supposed to be in the Good Wine Guide, for Christ's sake."

He stepped back, wiping his lower face. Emmett took advantage of having control of the desk now, leaning back and turning me around to straddle him while he unzipped his blue suit trousers.

Once his erection had sprung out of its confines, he guided me forward, my tight skirt rucked around my waist, and had me impale myself. He grabbed my bare bottom and pulled my cheeks apart, easing his passage into my tightness. I groaned, thinking of Fox looking directly at the target thus revealed. We had not quite managed double penetration with two cocks yet— somehow the angles were very hard to get right—but we certainly hadn't given up.

Keeping one hand on my bottom, Emmett moved the other to my breasts, which jiggled madly in their strange position, hanging out of my half-unbuttoned shirt. He moved his hips slowly and slyly, making me work harder.

We'd been at this for a couple of minutes when I felt the first sound smack on my bum. Fox stood behind us. He pushed my spine down, so that my arse was raised high and my nipples grazed Emmett's silk tie and shirt, and spanked me hard and steadily through the fucking.

"You look incredible," he informed me. "That gorgeous arse, framed by those suspenders, working away while you're skewered on his cock. I can see you going up and down on it, while your backside gets redder and redder."

I couldn't answer; Emmett was kissing me like a madman. The smacks might have been hard or they might not—I was beyond the point of caring. They added their own signature to a dirty stew of sensation that was fast bringing me to the point of a second orgasm.

Before I got there, Fox finished spanking me and got something out of a drawer. The next thing I felt was his lubricated finger, pushing and wriggling its way into my tightest spot while Emmett and I ground together like machinery, making fast, slapping sounds on the desk.

I begged to come, and Fox said no.

Tears gathered in the corners of my eyes.

"But I *need* to," I wheedled.

"You'll wait until you get permission," he said calmly, then he removed his finger and replaced it with the hard, smooth tip of a silicone butt plug—one of the larger ones, if I wasn't mistaken.

"Oh God," I half-wept. "Please."

"Behave," he said sternly, giving me another salutary smack on an already very warm bottom. Emmett, apparently aware of what was going on, slowed down and let me concentrate on what Fox was doing.

"Go on," he said, "let it inside you. That's what you really need, pet."

"But it's so…" I gasped and wiggled my bottom, knowing I couldn't escape, but trying anyway, "…big. Aaahhhh."

Fox pushed firmly and decisively, then held it where it hurt the most until he knew my submission was absolutely won.

"Do you need it?" he asked me. "Beg me for it, Jo."

"Please put it all the way in, sir," I implored. "I need to feel it."

He made me take every inch of that beast, then he started spanking me again.

"Oh God, I *have* to come, please, please, please, sirrrr...."

Both Fox and Emmett gave simultaneous consent—Emmett, I gathered, teetering on his own edge—and there was a giant rocking wave of orgasm, from Emmett to me, from me to Emmett, with Fox holding my hips and pushing his hard trousered cock against the plug in my arse.

After that there was a lot of coming down to earth, and awkward climbing about on the desk, and wiping down of surfaces to be done. I collapsed on to Fox's expensive ergonomic wheelie-chair, skirt still hiked up, tits still out, while Emmett tried to tackle a stain on his suit trousers.

Meanwhile, Fox had a problem.

"Oh, sir," I said, although it was still a struggle to move my lips.

"This isn't over yet," he said, his eyes dropping, a little apologetically, to his crotch.

"D'you want me to...?"

"She's knackered," said Emmett. "Why don't I?"

There was a complicated conjunction of eye contacts. You'd need a diagram to work it out, so I won't attempt to describe it.

I sat forward, awaiting Fox's response. I had to be honest; I wasn't really up to giving the kind of long, lavish, deep-throated blowjob he preferred at this moment. And, to be even more honest, I kind of liked the idea of watching Emmett do it.

"What do you think, Jo?" asked Fox. "Are you too tired?"

"I'd need a while to get myself into the groove," I admitted. "Right now, I just want to chill with a glass of water."

"Be my guest," said Fox, indicating the water cooler. "But I was really wondering about the other aspects of the situation."

"Oh, about Emmett?" I said, heading for the cooler. "No, that's fine, carry on."

Emmett, aiming a tissue at the wastebasket and scoring, turned to catch my eye.

"Are you sure?" he said. I wondered if he wanted me to save him.

"Do you…I mean…do you want to discuss it in private?"

"Do you?"

"Not especially. I mean, like I said, I'm fine with it."

"But are you really? Or are you just trying to be cool? Honestly, all I want is for everyone to be happy."

"I'll be happy once I've got rid of this fucking erection," interposed Fox, for whom this exchange must have been frustration itself. "I really don't care who does the honours, but at this rate I might as well go and sort myself out."

"Em, put him out of his misery, will you?" I said, returning to the chair. "Unless, I mean, you know. Unless you'd rather not."

"Oh, for God's sake," huffed Emmett. "Charles, how do you want me?"

Fox smiled, a little painfully.

"How about on your knees?" he said, unzipping with dramatic deliberation and perching himself on the edge of the desk.

Emmett shot me a rueful grin and a wink, then stepped forward and dropped down in front of Fox. I eased the wheeled chair a little to the side, aiming for a decent view of them in profile.

Fox's trousers fell gently to his ankles, revealing his well-muscled legs and the scimitar-curve of his cock, which was now an angry purplish red, desperate for some attention.

Emmett put his hands up to it and began to work on squeezing and teasing, stroking his long white fingers up and down the shaft, picking various points at which to exert pressure.

I watched in fascination, hoping to pick up some tips. After all, a man wouldn't have to try and guess what might feel good. A man would *know*.

"You've done this before," accused Fox softly, his breath coming fast.

"I actually haven't," said Emmett. "I've sometimes thought about it, though. How I'd do it…"

"Do it," echoed Fox. "Shut up and do it."

I let out a long breath as Emmett closed his full lips over the tip of Fox's cock. He bobbed gently up and down, his cheeks hollowing as he worked, his vivid hair making the scene look like some beautifully composed piece of erotic art.

Fox threw back his head and put a hand in Emmett's hair, the way he did with me. Of course, there was less to get hold of, but it looked hot and I wished I could take a photograph.

Emmett sucked and played with Fox, while Fox began to piston his hips, slowly at first, then harder for the full face-fuck effect. I heard Emmett make gagging noises and I felt for him. I was never keen on that part myself.

"Swallow it, boy," growled Fox, clearly in his final throes, but Emmett disengaged at the crucial moment.

"Ew, no, I'd rather not," he said, getting a good spurt of semen on his ear and in his hair for his delicacy. "Oh my God, Charles, be careful."

But Fox was clearly beyond such strictures. He leant way

back on the desk, his neck at full tilt, eyes closed, cock twitching into a slow detumescence.

Emmett turned a woebegone face to me. I tried to look sympathetic, but my grin refused to narrow. I handed him a tissue.

"So now you know," I said teasingly. "You should have swallowed. It's not that bad."

"I think I'll take your word for it," he said, dabbing at his hair. "I thought I was going to, but at the last minute, I just couldn't face it."

"Don't give up your day sexuality," muttered Fox, still half-supine on the desk. "Although, the rest of it was bloody good, I have to say."

"I've got a future on the Soho meat rack if this doesn't work out, is that what you're saying?"

"You're pretty enough," I told him. "Prettier than me, half the time."

"I think I'll pass. Thanks for the experience, though. I can chalk that one up."

Fox sat up. "You seriously haven't done that before?"

Emmett shook his head, laughing. "Why, have you?"

"Sure," said Fox. "At school. Boys' school. Boarding. Nothing more needs to be said."

"But you aren't gay," I said.

"No, I was curious. And if you gave one, you got one, so that was the incentive. I can't say I loved having some rugger bugger's sweaty post-match tackle in my face, but it was the price you had to pay."

"You'd think they'd wait until after they showered," I said, grimacing.

"Half the time it was *in* the shower," he said. "Anyway,

enough of my adolescent sexual experimentations. Make yourselves decent. I'm taking you both out."

Fox took us to a South American place that did incredible cocktails and strongly-flavoured barbecued meat dishes. Lively dance music carried us along on its party wave. Fox, I could tell, was high from his business deal and the sex, and when Fox was in that mood, Emmett always lit up along with him.

"So go on, then," said Emmett, once we were established in a booth. "Spill. What's your news?"

"Well." Fox took time to look at each of us, coveting these last few minutes of having a secret. "Our friends have agreed to invest in us to the tune of fifty million US dollars."

Emmett coughed with shocked laughter.

"Fifty *million*?"

"Fifty million bucks," repeated Fox. "I think we'll be moving to bigger premises, hiring more staff. FoxWeb is *go*."

"That's amazing," I breathed. "Absolutely amazing."

"It's not bad, is it?" Fox grinned cheesily. "For a start." He banged his cocktail glass down on the table. "So I've decided we need to celebrate."

"I thought that was what we just did," said Emmett.

"That was good, but we can do that any time," he said. "I'm booking us a week away."

"Wow. Where?" I sat up, running my finger around the salty rim of my glass and licking it off.

"Somewhere we can do whatever we want," he said. "A beach house, in the south of France, near Cap d'Antibes. The season will just be starting there. Temperatures in the mid-twenties, sun every day, a pool, a terrace, a chef and a maid on call. What do you think?"

"Sounds awful," I said, laughing. "Count me out."

"Oh, I don't want to do that," said Fox, holding me in an unbreakable green gaze. "It just wouldn't be the same without you, sweetness."

Chapter Twenty Three

B ougainvillea, that was what it was called. The purple and pink flowers that wreathed the villa's white walls and hung over the open patio doors reminded you that you had definitely left the UK. I stood in the centre of the terrace and took a three hundred and sixty degree view of our holiday home, from the striped awning over the outdoor dining table to the pool to the lawn to the azure sea, far below, glittering between the bays and cliffs.

"It's perfect," I said, looking at Emmett beside me. "Isn't it?"

"Yeah," he said. He put his arm around me, but his teeth were teasing his lower lip, in the way they did when he wasn't quite sure about what he was saying.

"You don't think?"

"No, I do. It's everything I... OK, don't think I'm complaining, but this would have been such a good place for a honeymoon. If we'd had one."

"Oh!" I slipped my arm around his waist. I understood what

he was saying. "We can still have one. Let's start looking at brochures when we get home."

"Yeah," he said, but more warmly this time. "We'll do that."

Fox, who had been helping the cab driver with the luggage, appeared in the patio doorway with a bottle of champagne in hand.

"Look what the owners have left in the fridge," he said. "Shall I get glasses?"

We sat at the canopied table, sipping champagne in the fragrant smoke of a citronella candle, warding off the bugs that gathered in the slow fall of dusk.

"To the investment bankers of Hong Kong, and to us," said Fox, as we clinked our glasses together. "FoxWeb has brought us together, and I hope it will hold us for a good, long time."

Nothing kinky happened that night. We simply relaxed on the terrace, enjoying the stunning bouillabaisse the hired chef made, and drinking what had been left in the wine rack.

We went to bed early. Emmett and I had rather drunken, clumsy, giggly sex while Fox watched a movie and worked on his laptop in the living room. I wondered if he could hear us and, if so, was he jealous?

Was he jealous of us? Could that be possible? Emmett had once mentioned a short-lived marriage, but that was years ago and Fox seemed to have been perennially single, albeit far from celibate, ever since. I sometimes wondered if Emmett knew him as well as he thought he did.

The next afternoon we took a picnic to the beach. Nothing was said, but all three of us tingled with the anticipation of an interesting evening ahead. Fox and Emmett competed in various sea-related activities, while I lay and read and occasionally swam.

But when we returned to the villa, it quickly became clear

that all was not well with Emmett. His entire upper half was a shiny tight red and he was confused and wobbly.

"Oh God, he's got sunstroke, I think," I said in a panic, leading him into the shadiest part of the villa. "What do we do? Oh God, I *told* him to cover his head and drink lots of water."

"It's my fault," said Fox. "I made him spend all that time in the sea. Get him into bed and make him drink something. I'll see about calling a doctor."

"I can speak a bit of French, if you want me to…"

"I lived in Switzerland, Jo, I can handle it."

"Oh, of course. I forgot."

I stayed with Emmett, making him sip iced water, while Fox poured fluent French down the phone.

The doctor prescribed nothing more than rest and plenty of fluids, so once I'd forced some melon and more iced water into him and laid a cold flannel on his forehead, there was little else to be done. He was uncomfortable but exhausted, and drifted quickly into sleep.

"Not like you to be so careless," I whispered, kissing his scarlet cheek.

I stayed there, sitting by his side, watching his sandy eyelashes flutter beneath his reddened eyelids, wishing him well again. I could hear Fox moving about in the living room, and I was nervous of joining him, for reasons I couldn't properly articulate.

Perhaps I could just get into bed beside Emmett…but it wasn't even six yet.

Fox's footsteps moved inexorably towards the bedroom. I didn't look up when he pushed the door further open and stood against the door jamb.

"He's asleep," he said softly.

I nodded, flicking a glance over to Fox. He had changed into an open-necked shirt and long linen shorts. His skin was golden, his brown hair a little bleached from the sun. He looked good.

"Best thing for him," he said. "I don't think he needs nursing, Jo."

"I don't mind," I whispered back. "I'll sit here and read my book for a while, I think."

Fox gave me a long, unnerving look.

"OK," he said. "The chef'll have dinner ready for eight."

"Fine," I said, looking at Emmett. "See you later."

I put my book down at half past seven. Emmett was still sleeping, snoring gently and apparently at peace. I went into the ensuite, showered, and changed into a candy-striped maxi dress with a halter neck. I thought a lot about what underwear to put on, but in the end I went for simple white cotton briefs and a strapless bra. These were not for show.

Definitely not.

The chef greeted me with a smile as I went past the kitchen. It looked like steak. Emmett would be sorry to miss it.

Fox was outside, under the awning, browsing an international edition of the *Financial Times* and sipping at something with a lot of shrubbery in it.

"Jo," he said, brightening as I stepped outside. He raised the glass. "Do you want one? Mint julep. Franco makes them perfectly."

"That sounds good." Fox grabbed an empty glass and poured another from a jug.

One cocktail and one glass of wine, I vowed to myself silently. *No more than that.*

"Franco?" I said, coming to sit opposite Fox. "He's not

French?"

"Yes, he's French. Italian parent or two, I think. We're not far from Italy here."

"No, I guess not."

"How's the patient?" His cheek dinted a little, a suppressed smile.

"Far away in the land of nod," I said. I took a sip and gasped a little. There was a hefty dose of bourbon in there.

"Poor boy," said Fox. "He needs to be careful with that colouring. Red hair and strong sun are a bit of a fatal combination."

"He's usually so careful," I said. "I can't get him outside from May to October without three layers of sunblock and a sombrero."

Fox laughed.

"Well, not usually a sombrero, but he's very careful," I amended. "The holiday spirit must have gone to his head. But he did put on quite a lot of sunblock, I thought…"

"He'll be OK in a day or so." Fox dismissed the conversation. "He'll just need to make sure he spends more time under a sunshade. Anyway." He leant into me, his eyes fixing mine. "How are you?"

"I'm…y'know…fine. Unwinding. That was all a bit stressful for a while back there."

"Unwind away," said Fox. "Perhaps we should give the hot tub a whirl later. Might work away some of the tensions."

"Oh, I don't know," I said.

"You're nervous," said Fox, making heat flood into my cheeks. "You're always nervous when you're alone with me. Why is that? I thought things had moved on."

I fidgeted with my mint sprigs.

"Obviously they have," I said. "And you're a great boss and a great friend and a great…" I looked at him under my eyelashes. "…You know…"

"Fuck?" he suggested.

I shot a look at the house. The chef was sizzling away out of earshot.

"If you want to put it that way. But I still don't feel I really know you, Charles." I dared a look at him. He was thoughtful, intent. "And I also don't know what you really want. That's what makes me nervous, when I'm alone around you."

"Emmett must have talked to you about me," he said.

"Emmett knows you in a different way." I paused. It was hard to explain. "When you met, it was as mentor and protégé. When *we* met, it was…well, the footing was different. The dynamic…everything. I don't know if I'm putting this very well…"

"The relationship is different."

"The relationship is *weird*. I'm getting to know you in the wrong order. It shouldn't start with kinky sex and then move to dinner table talk. I just don't know how to think about you… how to feel about you…"

"You feel what you feel," he said. "But I take your point."

We shut up for a moment as Franco brought the plates to the table. As I'd thought, steak. With prawns and an amazing salad and about fifty choices of dressing. A bottle of red and another of white joined the food, with iced water in a jug.

"OK," said Fox, once Franco was out of the way, helping himself to Emmett's portion in the kitchen. "What about a Q and A? You ask. I answer."

I thought about this as I poured myself a glass of white wine.

"You were talking about going to boarding school as a boy," I said. "Are you from a wealthy family?"

"Not really. I grew up on a farm. The school wasn't Eton or Harrow or anything like that. Just a country boarding school. I think they let girls in now. Too late for me, alas."

"I really can't picture you on a farm. You're so…polished."

He laughed.

"You wouldn't recognise me. I spent my schooldays on the rugby pitch and my holidays in the pig pen."

I narrowed my eyes.

"Nope, sorry, really can't picture it. What happened?"

"I left school at sixteen with a handful of pretty low-grade qualifications. My dad found me an apprenticeship with a friend of his who ran his own IT company—and this was thirty-odd years ago, so we're talking giant hardware and green digital lettering. I found I took to it. In the meantime, I was resitting some of my O Levels at the local FE college, at which point the penny finally dropped that I was mildly dyslexic."

"They didn't work that one out at your boarding school?"

"They did not. Well, they didn't have a special needs department back then. You could be clever, average, or thick. I was thick."

"But you so aren't. God. That's terrible."

He shrugged. "Once I had my diagnosis, everything changed. I got some intensive tuition, got my qualifications, but what was much better, I finally knew who I was."

"It must have been awful, thinking you were just…"

"Yeah. I mean, this was the late eighties, nobody really talked about self-esteem much back then. But let's say mine wasn't the highest, until I found out why my brain didn't work like the other kids' did."

"It must have been such a revelation."

"It gave me something I had never felt I had. Control. And I found I liked it. *God,* I really liked it."

He sat back, shutting his eyes in reminiscence.

His story had done something I hadn't expected; it had touched me. The thought of this strong, confident man sitting at a classroom desk trying desperately to decipher paragraphs of text his friends read with ease was strangely devastating.

"Do you think that's why…?" I started delicately, popping a prawn into my mouth.

His eyes snapped open and he grinned wickedly.

"The dom stuff? Oh, I don't know. I was into chasing girls and tying them to trees from a pretty young age. But, without wanting to get too psychoanalytical about it all, perhaps that was a reaction to a feeling of powerlessness in other areas of life."

"You didn't think of just staying on the farm and working there?"

"I have an older brother. The farm is his birthright, apparently. I'm happy with things the way they are, anyway. I can't say it's worked out badly."

"No, you can't say that." I looked around at the glorious evening. Crickets chirped in the trees and shrubbery; the azure sea was pocked with yacht sails.

"That's why I'm drawn to people like Emmett," he said. "Very clever people, for whom it's all been effortless all the way through. I've learned a lot from him."

"Have you?" I felt a little glow of wifely pride.

"Oh yes. Our skill sets are different. I'm more on the technical and practical side, while he can do things with numbers and programming languages that will always be beyond me. I'm a big-picture strategist, he's a detail-orientated perfectionist. That's what makes us such a good partnership."

"Yes," I said. "You are a good partnership. I sometimes feel…"

His expression flicked from openly expansive to utterly concentrated on me in the second it took to utter the words.

"You sometimes feel…?" he echoed. "Jo?"

"Like a bit of a spare part. A hanger-on. A latecomer. The third party who'll never quite get all the in jokes."

"Oh, Jo. Emmett and I barely had any contact while I was in Switzerland."

"No, but you were biding your time. You always meant to come back."

"Did I? You know more than I do about it then."

"I know that you came scurrying back as soon as you heard he was getting married."

There was a silence, and the steak churned in my stomach.

"You think I'm jealous of you?" he said.

"I think it made you realise how much you missed him."

"OK," he said slowly. "That's a fair comment. I probably wouldn't have left the Swiss office when I did if it hadn't been for that. It made me rethink things."

"I don't think you're jealous of me," I said. "That wasn't what I meant to imply. I'm sorry if I did."

"Thanks," he said. "It's not you I'm jealous of, no. It's Emmett."

I swallowed. Digesting any more steak was looking like an increasingly unlikely proposition.

"Why are you…?"

"He's got what I never managed to find," said Fox, quiet but intent.

"You mean…?"

"He told me about the way you met," said Fox. "I've never known that kind of spontaneous magnetic attraction. I've never met anyone at a business conference or a training session. Don't get me wrong, I've had women who were very interested, but it was always a one night thing. We were never right for each other, in one way or another. When I meet women, it's through contacts in the BDSM scene. I've got close to some of them, but I can't seem to… I don't even know what I'm saying any more. You shouldn't listen to me."

"You just haven't found The One?" I suggested, making air quotes as I said it.

He levelled his gaze.

"I wouldn't say that."

I pushed my chair back.

"I'll just go and check on Emmett…"

"No, don't run away from me." His voice hardened into its most commanding register. "This might be the only chance we get this week to talk one on one. Tell me, Jo. Tell me how you feel."

"It's complicated."

We both smiled weakly at the modern cliché.

"All right," I continued, but I was going to need more wine if we were doing truth or dare, especially as truth more or less *was* dare. I poured myself another glass. "I've felt so many different things, and combinations of things, at different times, that I don't feel up to teasing out all the strands. But I guess there are a few that stand out."

His eyes remained fixed on me. He wasn't going to give me any wriggle room.

"First of all," I said, "there was, as we've already mentioned, some jealousy. Your relationship with Emmett is older than mine. You knew him before I did, and I'm jealous of *everyone* who knew Emmett before I did…like, how *dare* they get their hands on him before me?" I laughed self-consciously. "And your relationship was close. You got to mould him, to make him who he is. I got the fully-formed model, which I'm fine with really, but all the same, there's a little part of me that will always wish we'd met younger."

"That's normal," said Fox. "I think most couples feel something similar, unless they were childhood sweethearts. Does the jealousy affect how you feel about me now?"

"No, I've mostly moved on from that. Just a twinge now and again, if he's telling some story about the past. Another thing…is fear…or more like threat. When you turned up at the wedding I felt incredibly threatened by you."

"Threatened in what way?"

"In several ways. First, that you had come to take Emmett away from me. You have such a powerful influence over him that I felt I needed your approval, or he might start to look at me differently. To be good enough for Emmett, I had to be good enough for you. If you really pushed the point, you could even have stopped him loving me. Perhaps that's paranoia, but it was a very strong feeling, for quite a long time after you came back."

"That's paranoia," said Fox. "Nothing I could do or say would stop Emmett loving you. The boy's got it bad. Besides, I *do* approve of you. I hope I've made that more than clear."

"I get that you approve of my body," I said.

"It's much more than that."

"That's the other threat," I said. "The other threat is all mixed up in my mind and it's hard to say out loud. I'm not sure I even can."

"I'm sure you can. You're being very lucid."

"You're…well…you're obviously…I find you attractive." I wasn't sure why this was so hard to say, when the fact I enjoyed regular threesome sessions with him had made this abundantly clear.

"And that's a threat?"

"It is a threat because…despite everything…I still feel very *wrong* about it. Like I should only have eyes for Emmett."

"Cultural conditioning," said Fox. "Everyone's supposed to be looking for The One." He copied my air quotes. "And nobody is supposed to look outside that tight pair-bond, once it's formed. Although in practice, everyone does. Just not everyone acts on it."

"There's a difference between admiring a man's tight butt as he walks down the street in front of you, and actively pursuing a man because you can't get him out of your mind."

"And is that how you feel? That you can't get me out of your mind?"

I looked into my wine. The answer wasn't there.

I nodded reluctantly.

"Oh, Jo," he said, and there was such warmth in it that I wanted to be in his arms immediately. "I know how that feels."

"Do you? Really?" I risked a look up at him. His eyes shone like green glass.

"I don't think you can do some of the things we do with each other without getting, well, *involved*. Kink is such a bonding activity. The level of trust, the intensity of it. Sometimes you get a bond you don't necessarily want or need. But it's real and it can't be wished away."

"I've tried wishing it away," I sighed. "Can confirm it doesn't work."

"So can I."

He put down his glass and rose from the table. I panicked slightly, wondering what he had in mind. He took the seat beside me and faced me diagonally so that our knees touched, taking my hands and resting them in his lap.

"Jo, I sometimes wonder to myself how things could have been different, if I'd met you before Emmett did," he said.

I caught a breath. "You do?"

"Quite a lot actually. And I try to tell myself our little trio would be the same, but to be honest I'm not sure it would. I'm not sure I could share you with Emmett, if I had you."

I couldn't speak. I was busy falling through space.

"Which makes me a selfish man," he continued, "and less worthy of you than Emmett. He isn't a possessive bastard like me. He puts you first and himself second. Congratulations on picking the right man."

"I didn't pick him," I whispered. "I didn't know you then."

He shut his eyes tight.

"I know," he said painfully. "Believe me...I know..."

"Charles," I said, squeezing his fingers, "if you'd met me before Emmett did, you'd probably have ignored me. I'm just a regular office drone. I'm averagely good-looking. I don't stand out in a crowd. You wouldn't have given me a second look."

"You're far from average," he said with a sad smile. "But you're probably right. What attracted me to you was the fact that Emmett was attracted to you—and I know Emmett has excellent taste. I'm not an 'eyes meet across a crowded room' type of guy. It takes me a long time to get interested in somebody."

"So any friend of Emmett is a friend of yours, huh?"

He nodded, his eyes crinkling at the sides.

"And any lover of Emmett…" I added.

He shut his eyes again, smiling fully now.

"Emmett is like sexual litmus paper," I pursued. "And I'm just the right pH for you both."

"Now you're getting silly," he warned. "But you see what I mean."

"But any wife of Emmett can't be a wife of yours. Because that would be illegal."

"We could always move to Utah."

I snorted. "I think that's more sister wives than brother husbands."

He bent his head, chuckling gently, and lifted my fingertips to his lips.

"I know I can never have you to myself," he said, after leaving them there for a moment. "I know I've missed that boat. But would it be so bad, just for one night…"

Oh God. This was so hard. I wanted nothing more than to yield and fall into the hot tub with him, doing everything it was possible to do with a man until dawn.

"Only if Emmett knew," I said, trying to pull my hands away and failing. "And didn't mind. We can't exactly ask him now. It wouldn't be fair anyway…and I don't want to ask him. I don't want him to have to deal with the idea of me wanting something that doesn't include him…oh God. I can't do it. I just can't. Please don't ask me again."

I managed to wrench my fingers away from him and stood up abruptly, marching across the lawn to the garden wall. This was the problem I had with flouncing off. I never quite knew where I was flouncing to, which spoiled the effect. I had to march right back again, past Charles—who watched me with a thoughtful air—and towards the swimming pool.

Somebody had left a pair of flip-flops by the poolside. I saw them too late, tripped over one of them and fell, flailing, right into the water with a massive plunging splash.

I was only in the shallow end, and there was no danger of drowning, but I was confused and panicky, my maxi dress ballooning up around me like a sodden parachute. Within seconds, Charles was in the pool with me, pulling me into him, steering me to the ladder.

We sat down on the tiled poolside, gasping and laughing at the shock of it. Charles's arm was still around me, holding me at his side.

"Should've pulled the cover over," said Charles. "Oh, look at you, you're dripping."

His forehead pressed against mine and our noses touched. We were laughing, then we were kissing, upright at first, then lying down, pulling and tearing at each other's wet clothes, twisting and writhing together, feeding and devouring.

My dress clung to me as if glued to my skin, and my hair was plastered to my face as I rolled on top of him, and then he rolled on top of me.

He peeled off his shirt and unhaltered my halterneck. My bra was see-through now, showing the hard buds of my nipples.

"Jo," he whispered, palming them as he kissed my neck, "whatever happens isn't your fault. I made you do it. I'm making you do it. OK?"

I came to my senses, suddenly and swiftly.

"No, it's not OK. I'll still feel guilty forever, and maybe Emmett will never forgive either of us. I can't risk him. Not for you, not for anyone."

He drew away and rolled on to his back, moaning in a kind of spiritual agony.

"I'm sorry," I said, and there were tears in my eyes. "You can have as much of me as you want while he's in the room. But never without him. I'm sorry, and I love you, but…that's it."

I got up and fled, back into the villa. I hid in the ensuite for an hour, then climbed into bed next to Emmett. I lay and watched him sleep until long past midnight, when I heard Fox come in and turn off all the lights. I stiffened for a while, thinking he might come in, but he didn't.

What were you supposed to do when you loved two men?

Chapter Twenty Four

The sun was up when I opened my eyes, and Emmett was awake, covering himself in medicated moisturiser.

"Oh, babe," I said, with a sympathetic half-laugh. He really was very sunburnt. "How are you this morning?"

"I think I'll live," he said. "I'm not going anywhere near the fucking sun ever again, though. Shade all the way from now on. Seriously, I can barely move."

"Oh, hon. Let me do your back and shoulders."

He moved, with much ouching and hissing, on to his stomach and I got to work on soothing his tortured skin.

"I'm so sorry, pet," he said, into the pillow.

"Sorry? You don't have to apologise to me. I'm not the one in pain."

"No, but you've come here expecting a glamorous decadent week of full-on kinky threesome sex, and here I am, a beached lobster."

"I don't care about the kinky threesome sex. I care about you."

"And I care about you, sweet pea," he said, moving his head so that our eyes met. "*And* I care about Charles. This isn't what either of you signed up for."

"And neither did you," I said uneasily.

"No, but this is all my own stupid fault. I was so busy water skiing and kitesurfing that I skipped the sun cream for too long. Nobody else to blame there."

"I don't mind. Charles doesn't mind. You'll be OK in a day or two anyway."

"I'll be a peeling wreck. Very attractive."

"You're always attractive to me. Red, white or green with purple spots. I love you, Em, I really love you."

There was a little break in my voice and concern filled his eyes.

"Darling, are you all right? Hey? What's wrong?"

Wincing, he reached out to touch my face.

"Last night," I said haltingly.

"What happened last night? Did you have a row with Charles?"

"No, well, kind of. He wanted…Oh God, I feel like I'm going to ruin everything telling you this…and nothing happened anyway…"

"He wanted to take you to bed?" Emmett deduced, saving me from having to say it myself.

"Well…yes. I didn't do it, Emmett. I wouldn't do anything behind your back." *Well, not as much as that*, I thought, remembering our guilty poolside grapple.

"I bet he wasn't happy about that."

Emmett's voice was toneless, his face without expression. I wished he'd swear or rage or cry or something.

"No, not really," I said with a pathetic little laugh. "Em,

285

what are we going to do? He really seems to…like me."

"Well, what do you expect?" Emmett smiled, his forehead creasing. "Of course he would. You're lovely. Do you like him?"

"Do I? Well, I do like him. Yes. Not as much as I like you. Never that much."

"But enough to want to spend time with him? Maybe alone?"

"I'd always rather you were there," I said.

"But if that's not possible?"

I chewed my lip. "I *was* tempted," I confessed. "He's very attractive and I've grown to really like him…care about him… you know."

"Are you in love with him?"

"Oh, Emmett, don't! I don't *know*. It's not what I feel for you…but it is a strong feeling, OK? Oh God, this is torture."

"Hey, calm down. It's all right, pet. Come and lie down with me a minute."

I did as he asked. Being so close to him was automatically soothing. If I was near him, everything was always all right.

"That's better," he whispered, kissing my cheek, which was about all he could reach without painful readjustment of his position. I turned my face so we could kiss properly.

"I'm sorry." It came out as an exhausted sigh.

"Jo, ssh. You're getting all het up about something that really isn't a problem."

"Am I?"

He kissed me again.

"Yes. Look, I knew this would happen."

"What? You did?"

"When Charles turned up at the wedding, I saw right away that there was a vibe between you. I mean, you didn't even see it yourself—you were so disturbed by him. It was the disturbance that made me see it."

"Oh, you and your all-seeing eye."

"You know it's what brought us together, so don't knock it, eh?"

"No." I smiled, remembering.

"I thought, I bet she falls for him. And obviously I had to ask myself how I'd feel about that. The answer was: horrible if it all happened behind my back, but probably OK if it didn't. So I, well, I kind of engineered this—the threesome arrangement and all that."

"It was your idea? I thought Charles…?"

"You thought he was calling in his debt, after sharing his submissive with me? Well, I made it look like that. But it's hardly the same thing. Suzette was a well-known scene player who was always going to move on eventually. You're my *wife*. The love of my life. All that."

"I know," I said. I'd always been slightly uncomfortable with the unevenness of the exchange. "But, Emmett, if you didn't want any of this, you know that would have been fine with me. I wouldn't have had a secret affair with him. You do know that, don't you?"

"Yeah, of course I do, sweet pea," he said. "But you'd be thinking about it, and fantasising about it, and torturing yourself. I'd never know if you were picturing his face during sex. I really didn't want that. I thought my solution—though it seems bizarre and extreme—was the least painful for all of us."

"Oh God, Emmett, you're so…" I didn't have words for it. What was he so? Noble? Self-sacrificing? Bloody weird?

"Listen, I don't want you to think I'm in agony when I see him with you. I'm not. I actually really like watching you together. I get a kick out of seeing how hard he's fallen for you —it's a kind of validation. And I know that neither he nor you would actually ever want to hurt me. So that's a nice little power trip in its way. In reality, I have everything under my control."

"My God. And Fox thought it was the other way around. You are a Machiavellian genius, sir."

"I am," he said modestly. "But I do sometimes think about the two or three percent chance of the pair of you going off together and leaving me alone."

"Two or three percent chance? You've done a calculation?"

"Well, yeah," he said, a little sheepishly. "There were so many variables. But I thought those were definitely odds worth taking a punt on."

"You never cease to utterly amaze me," I said, kissing him. "Never. And, by the way, you need to update that spreadsheet. Scratch out two or three percent and replace it with zero."

"Oh, love." He kissed me back. "I'm glad we've had this talk. I think it was needed."

"Everything's going to be fine," I said. "But what about Fox? What should we do about him? If anything?"

"I'll tell you what I think you should do," said Emmett.

"What?"

"Go into his bedroom right now and fuck him senseless."

"What? Are you serious?"

"Totally. But I want you to film it for me, so I can watch it tonight. It'll get me in the mood for the outrageously kinky threesome I plan to be fit for by the end of the week."

"You are actually serious!"

"Yes. Don't you want to?"

"I…could…be persuaded, I suppose." I laughed, a bit shrilly. We were through the looking glass now.

"Then let me persuade you. Go in there, totally naked, and get him to tie you up and use you. I'll be able to hear everything if you leave the door a little bit open. It'll take the edge off my invalid boredom. Go on, Jo. I'm begging you."

"Oh God. Totally naked?"

"Or in some sexy, skimpy thing. Whatever. Just indulge me in this."

We kissed again, a kiss that conferred whatever the kissing equivalent of Dutch courage is, and I went to the bathroom to freshen up. I dabbed some of my muskiest shimmery perfume oil on my pulse points, put on a long diaphanous robe to pretend I wasn't naked, although in reality everything was clearly visible, and came out of the ensuite to display myself to Emmett.

"Perfect," he sighed. "You can wear that again when I'm back to normal."

"I promise I will," I said.

"Now go."

In the corridor between the bedroom doors, I was attacked by shyness. The open door of our bedroom was so inviting, so comforting...I could just go back and hide out with Emmett for the rest of the day.

My nerves got the better of me, and I took refuge in the kitchen, using the assembly of a fruit salad and the brewing of coffee as displacement activities. But when this was done, I could delay no longer.

I put the fruit and coffee on a tray and knocked at Fox's door.

Confused mumbling from the other side betrayed his sudden waking.

I opened the door.

"Maid service," I said brightly, walking carefully across the various rugs dotting the tiled floor.

I put the tray down on the bedside table and smiled nervously at him.

He had shot up into a sitting position, his eyes switching from sleepy to glittery in the time it had taken me to approach.

"What's this?" he demanded, reaching out for me. "Come here."

I stepped within range; he pulled me unceremoniously on to the bed beside him and pinned me to the mattress in an urgent, hot-breathed kiss.

"What are you playing at, minx?" he murmured, once I was well and truly tangled in him and the bedsheets. "Blowing hot and cold."

"I take it you prefer hot?" I panted.

"Scalding," he said. "What do you think you're doing, coming in here in that obscene dressing gown? You know what you're asking for, don't you?"

I nodded. "I'm begging for it," I said.

"Christ." He ground into me, his tongue snaking down my throat in another intense kiss. "You can't do this to me." He shut his eyes and groaned, his hand on his forehead. "And I can't do this to Emmett."

"Can't you?"

He shook his head, flopping on to his back beside me.

"I drank the best part of a bottle of cognac after you left me last night," he confessed. "I think I'm only alive now because I drank two jugs of water before sleeping. And I decided, after my sixth glass, or it might have been my seventh, that I was going to let you go, and have another crack at finding someone of my own. I have too much love and respect for the pair of you to…"

"It's all right," I said. "Emmett knows. This is his idea."

He turned to his side, examining my face as if for traces of deceit or trickery.

"Emmett wants you to come to me?"

"I promise. He made me keep the doors open so he could listen in. I think he feels sorry for us having to keep our hands off each other while he lies there in his bed of sunburnt pain."

"Jo, if you're not telling the truth, I swear…"

"I'm telling the truth. You can go in and ask him if you want."

He ran his fingertips down the side of my face, stopping to put his thumb over my lips. I kissed it.

"I'm going to take your word for it," he said softly. "But I feel like hell at the moment, so I'm going to go and take a shower first." He slid the gown off my shoulders, so the silky fabric fluttered against my nipples on its way down. "And you're going to wait for me…" He took the cord and began to wrap it around one wrist, raising my arm to secure it to the top right bedpost. "…right here…"

He repeated the action with my other wrist. The cord was long enough to stretch along the top of the headboard, keeping my arms up and tethered tight. I looked up at him as he bound me, thrilling at the set of his jaw and the strength of his body.

"You should have drunk that coffee first," he teased, parting my knees and planting himself between them as he rested on his heels, surveying my helpless state. He reached over and took a cup, sipping from it greedily.

"You're going to keep your legs spread while you wait," he told me, replacing the cup and pushing my legs wider. "And you're going to concentrate really, really hard on this." He prised my lower lips apart with his thumbs and bent to blow very gently on my exposed clit. "You're going to think about how much you want it to be touched and played with, and you're going to use the power of your mind to get yourself as wet as you possibly can. This…" he flicked it delicately, "…is all of you, all of your body and mind, the very centre of everything, for as long as I take to get in and out of the shower. All right? I know you won't disappoint me. I'm going to expect you to be ready."

He patted the flat of his hand between my straining thighs, kissed the tip of my nose and disappeared into the ensuite.

I sat, legs apart, wrists bound, nipples stiff, eyes shut, listening to the heavy splash of water on tile until I was giddy with desperation for his return.

Held in this undignified position, open and waiting for him to come and fuck me however he wanted, I felt my lower stomach flutter and roll while my clit grew fatter and my juices multiplied.

I just hoped Emmett wouldn't go back to sleep while he waited for the real action to begin.

Fox came out of the shower looking thoroughly revived, his eyes keen as blades, flashing in my direction. He stood at the foot of the bed, his silky dressing gown open just enough to show me the fine definition of his pectoral muscles, his hair seal-dark with damp and swept back from his forehead.

My mouth dried as he looked me over. I wanted very strongly to close my legs, but Emmett had trained me well, and I maintained the required pose.

"What have you been thinking about, while I was showering?" he asked, perching himself on the end of the bed.

"What you said," I replied. "Thinking about getting ready for you."

"Are you ready?" he asked. "If I touch you, what will I find?"

I shut my eyes. He put his hands on my ankles and nudged them just a fraction further apart, so that my thigh muscles felt the burn of it.

"Look at me, Jo, and tell me."

I looked straight at him. It burned worse than my thighs; I felt the heat of it all the way through my body.

"I'm wet," I told him. "And I need you to touch me… please…"

Arranging himself so that he knelt between my knees, he bent forward and took one breast into his mouth, flicking his tongue over my nipple until it was teased into maximum hardness, then repeating the process on the other side.

I whimpered and struggled a little in my bonds, needing that attention transferred lower, silently praying for him to take his hands off my thighs and let his fingers creep inwards.

"You belong to me," he said, pressing his forehead to mine. "Don't you?"

"Yes," I said.

"Yes what?" He gave my inner thigh a light slap.

"Yes, sir."

"I'm going to take what's mine. I told you to be ready. Are you really ready?"

He dipped his fingers in, testing me. I moaned and squirmed on his fingers.

"Oh yes, you're ready," he confirmed. "You don't need a lot of foreplay, do you? Just the thought of getting filled up is enough for you." He grabbed my hips and lined himself up, swiftly and steadily, pulling his dressing gown cord with one hand to unveil his own readiness. "I have to admit," he said, sinking into me in one long plunge, "it's working for me right now as well. There. Is that what you wanted?"

"Mm, yes, sir." My words were swallowed into an indecent kiss.

I half-lay, half-sat there, tied up and impaled on his thick, hard cock, taking his probing tongue into my mouth, feeling his rough stubbly beard prick my cheek, having my bottom squeezed hard by his big hands, and the rich mix of sensations had me close to coming already.

He began to thrust, each forward motion knocking the headboard against the wall. I wrapped my legs around his hips and held on for dear life, having no other means to control any part of this fuck. I could only lie there and take what he gave me.

If Emmett had fallen back to sleep, he would be awake now. The headboard banged against the wall while Fox grunted and I cried out, louder and louder with each new attack of friction. His hands were everywhere, all over me, squeezing and pinching, spreading my bum cheeks so that he could explore between them with an inescapable finger.

These explorations, coupled with an angle of penetration that sparked up every nerve ending from my clit to my g-spot, brought me quickly to a howling orgasm. He continued to power into me, riding me through it, making the animal most of his opportunity until he too fell over the edge with a growl and filled me with long, generous spurts.

He untied me with trembling fingers and we both fell, panting and spent, into each other's arms.

"Christ," he said hoarsely. "Sorry. No finesse there. I just had to have you like that…some kind of madness."

"Don't apologise," I said. "It was incredible. So elemental.

Everyone needs that from time to time."

"Elemental, yeah," he said, stroking my soaking face. "Good one. I'll take the next one a bit slower." He kissed my mouth, slowly and sensually. "I take it you're up for a next one?"

"I've got all day."

"Excellent."

We lay there, stunned by sex, until the sweat grew cold then dried on our bodies.

He pulled himself up into a sitting position and reached for the fruit salad bowl.

"This'll sort you out," he said, taking a slice of peach and pushing it between my lips. A peach had never been more ambrosial.

I struggled into a sitting position, wincing at the ache in my thighs and shoulders, and let him feed me chunks of melon, grape halves, little bursting pomegranate seeds, until my thirst was slaked. He kissed the juices from my chin and the side of my mouth, then made me lie down again, arranging the remaining fruits in a pile around my belly button.

I hissed with the cold of it, but soon relaxed into giggles as he distributed slices and chunks around my breasts and thighs and between my legs, scooping them up with his mouth and licking the residual juices clean with his tongue. Grape halves were moulded around my nipples, while peaches found their way into the crevices between my thighs, to be nibbled away at until my peach-tasting clit took their place in his mouth.

"You're ruining these sheets," I said, as another mess of fruit pulp slid down my thigh and mingled with the wet patch that had already leaked out of me.

"Do you care? You won't be washing them." He put the empty fruit bowl back on the nightstand, unbound me and knelt before me, his hand wrapped around his semi-erect cock. "But you can help me with this. Come on. Get me hard again. I want you as many times as I humanly can today."

I sucked him into full tumescence and we took a slow, luxurious ride through all the laziest positions the karma sutra had to offer. We lay on our sides, his hand on my hip, rocking me through my next orgasm before turning me around and cramming himself into me from behind.

We dozed, then fucked again, then dozed again until the sun was noon-high in the sky and the sound of Franco clattering in the kitchen preparing lunch awoke us properly.

"Better take a break," whispered Fox. "Do you want a shower? I'll go in and talk to Franco for a minute."

I showered off the accumulation of stickiness, some of it from the fruit, most of it from Fox and I, and went in to see Emmett, still in my diaphanous gown and nothing else.

He was out of bed, sitting in a cane rocking chair messing about with his tablet.

"Did you hear us?" I asked nervously, my back to the wall.

"Couldn't really not," he said, looking up with a half-smile. "I thought you were going to batter your way through that wall at one point. And you're such a screamer."

"I am not!"

"I'm going to record you one day." He launched into an impression of me climaxing which had me indignant and amused at the same time.

"That's *such* an exaggeration. Anyway, Franco's here, so you'd better keep it down."

"And you'd better keep your bits covered." He paused, putting his tablet in his lap. "So…how was it?"

I went over to sit at his feet, laying my head against his

shins. He reached down to ruffle my wet hair.

"I won't lie, it was lovely," I said. "Fox is very…intense. And very athletic."

"He's a serious gym bunny. Does that make it better for you?"

"No, not better. And don't ask me to compare you, because I won't. It's just different, that's all."

"But good?"

"Mm. Good." I thought about Fox's cats' eyes on me as I came again and again on his cock, and shivered a little. He possessed me with those eyes, as surely as if he'd chained me up and stamped his initials on me. "And he almost sent me away."

"Seriously?"

"He said he didn't want to hurt you. Wouldn't touch me until I told him you approved."

"Well, that's a bonus," said Emmett thoughtfully. "That's really interesting."

"You thought he wouldn't care?"

"I know he's a man who gets his way. Always. Without fail."

Bare footsteps on the tiles outside hushed us. Fox put his head around the door.

"Grub's up," he said. "Franco's gone for now, so no need to worry about our state of undress. Emmett, do you feel up to eating under the arbour?"

"Sure," said Emmett. "A bit stiff but I think I can make it outside. Jo?"

I helped him to his feet and walked beside him as he made his slow, pained way out through the villa and on to the shaded patio.

Chapter Twenty Five

A giant bowl of fennel and melon salad awaited us as we made our way to the table, together with bread and some grilled fish.

Charles lounged in his silky dressing gown, Emmett in a light white cotton-waffle robe. I was still virtually naked. At least I was clean. Charles still looked as if he'd done several rounds in a hot tumble dryer. I wondered what Franco made of it all, if anything.

"Look at the state of you," I said, reaching out to tweak a lock of unruly hair over Fox's forehead. "What must Franco think?"

"Franco is paid enough not to think anything," said Fox. He made a sympathetic face as Emmett oohed and aahed his way into a chair. "Why? Do you care what he thinks? Do you want me to invite him to fuck you as well?"

I huffed and glowered at him, but he enjoyed my humiliation and the thought of having this power over me, and simply grinned back.

"Emmett, your wife is a dream come true," he said.

"I know," said Emmett.

"I want to thank you for your generosity. Seriously. Thank you."

"I want to thank you," said Emmett, "for refusing the gift until you knew I gave it."

They clinked glasses of iced water while I poured one for myself.

"But Emmett," said Fox, flicking a glance my way, "do you think our little one here should be sitting at the table on the same level as her masters?"

Emmett sucked in a breath, and so did I. The ice clinked in my glass over a thrilled silence.

"That's a very good point," he said. "Perhaps we're allowing her a little too much in the way of equality."

"It's affecting her attitude," said Fox.

"She's definitely less respectful here than at home," said Emmett. "I'll leave you to deal with her. I trust your judgement."

"Thank you," said Fox. He looked at me and his eyes were hard. "Put your cushion here and kneel on it," he commanded, pointing at the floor beside his feet.

It was on the tip of my tongue to moan *Do I have to?* I'd been looking forward to a long, lazy, sunny lunch and now I was going to have to serve. I'd been fucked three times already and I had that feeling of having been lightly punched in the crotch, thanks to the vigour of Fox's style and the impressive breadth of his cock.

But I did as I was told and put myself at Fox's feet with my head bowed.

"Stay there," he said, rising to go inside the villa.

299

"I'm hungry," I muttered to Emmett.

He tutted at me. "Behave yourself," he said. "You know how to. Just because we're on holiday doesn't mean you can get away with any nonsense."

"He's relentless, though," I whispered, then I shut up quickly as Fox reappeared, accompanied by a familiar jingling.

Emmett laughed. "Good thing nobody checked your suitcase at customs," he said.

"I always come equipped," he said. "Just as well I did, or this one would be getting away with all kinds. Hands behind your back."

This last was addressed to me. I obeyed quickly, and my reward was a thick leather collar wrapped around my neck, over the one I always wore for Emmett. It had a number of D rings at the back, and Fox had me clasp my hands behind my neck so he could cuff and attach my wrists to these.

"We'll add to these after lunch, I think," he said, reseating himself beside me. "I need to eat first."

In this position, my face only just reached over the table top. I had to kneel there and watch as Fox and Emmett helped themselves to the food. Once their plates were full, Fox turned his attention to me again.

"Oh dear, did you want something?" he teased.

"I'm rather hungry, sir," I said. "It's been a very physically taxing morning."

Laughing, he took a forkful of fish and fed me with it.

"Thank you, sir," I said sweetly.

This was the right move. He gave me bread then, and more fish, and plenty of salad, interspersed with sips of iced water.

"We can't have our pet fainting away," he said. "Can we, Em?"

"Absolutely not." He winked at me. "From what I heard, she was put through her paces this morning."

Fox trailed a leaf of lettuce across my lips.

"What did you hear?" he asked idly.

"A lot of noise," said Emmett. "How did you use her?"

Fox replaced the lettuce with his finger, making me suck some olive oil off the tip.

"I wasn't very adventurous, to be honest," he said. "It was all pretty vanilla."

"Not like you," said Emmett.

"No. But sometimes it's nice to take a break from the kink. A short break. I think I'm probably ready to move on to wilder shores now."

He dipped his fingers into a shallow dish of oil and balsamic dressing, drew aside my robe and circled one of my nipples with it, slowly, so that I felt an immediate weakness in my thighs and solar plexus.

"So, just regular fucking then?" Emmett asked, watching Fox's fingers at my nipples as if his eyes were magnetised to them.

"Regular fucking. Lots of positions. Bit of oral. Lots of fingering. All on the bed. How many times did you come, pet?"

"Three...no, four, sir." His finger went round and round. When all the oil was transferred to my nipple, he dipped it again and moved to its neighbour.

"You're so blasé about orgasms that you can lose count of them?" Fox's eyes narrowed. He gave my nipple a little pinch. I could do nothing to protect myself against his cruel fingers.

"No, sir, no, I just..."

"Perhaps we should deny you any more?" he suggested, circling again.

Despite its exhausted state, my clit was back in full bloom, everything tingling where it had been deadened by overuse.

"What do you think, Emmett? Does she deserve to come, if she finds the coming so unmemorable?"

"Perhaps not."

I wanted to pout at him, but I knew that would be a grave mistake. My nipples were glistening and silky now, Fox's finger gliding without resistance from one to the other.

"I think these are ready now," he said, reaching into his dressing gown pocket and bringing out something that made my stomach drop. I almost voiced a protest, but that would certainly have increased my sentence.

Fox affixed a jingling crystal-drop nipple clamp to each of my slippery nipples; sadly the lubrication made no difference to their tight hold on my poor swollen buds. Once they were there, they were there to stay.

I managed not to whimper, but Emmett smiled at the variety of pained expressions crossing my face.

"She absolutely hates being clamped," he said.

"I know," said Fox, flicking each crystal drop in turn so that they swayed and tinkled. "That's why it's so good for her. Hmm, pet?"

"Yes, sir," I sighed, and they both laughed.

He took my captive upper arm and guided me expertly bottom-up over his lap. My nipple clamps drooped over the side of his thigh as he prised my legs apart to give Emmett an eyeful of my charms—an enhanced eyeful, once he had lifted the flimsy gown and arranged it around my hips.

"So, we were talking about her attitude," he said, patting my upturned buttocks in a menacing kind of way. "And it struck me that a lesson might be in order, just to get her submission back on an even keel. Would you agree?"

"I think I would," said Emmett. "Quite a sharp lesson, too. She's been a cheeky little trollop ever since we touched down in Nice." He paused. "I can see she's had a busy morning from here."

Fox snickered, pulling apart my labia to give Emmett the full range of incriminating evidence.

"Red and sore," said Emmett. "Like something else is going to be soon, I hope."

"I can help you with that," said Fox, and I yelped as his hand fell heavily on my defenceless bum.

He spanked me steadily, his palm covering both cheeks and a good portion of my upper thighs until I glowed with stinging warmth.

"That's the warm-up," he said, to my dismay, because the pleasurable early stage had ended on about the sixth stroke and I was feeling the discomfort build.

He reached for something on the table. Glancing sideways, I saw him take a wooden serving spoon from the salad bowl. It was heavy with a large, flattish end and was damp with salad dressing. I was pretty sure it would sting like a motherfucker and I tensed accordingly.

"Ten strokes," Fox warned me. "Count them."

The first one landed with an almighty splat. The dressing was cold at the same time as the stroke burned, which was an interesting new sensation. I might have taken some time to appreciate it if it hadn't hurt so bloody much.

I cried out and kicked before uttering a sulky "One, sir."

Halfway through, Fox paused to ask me whether this was having any effect on my attitude.

"Yes, sir," I said, hearing it wheedle out pathetically.

"A little more respectful?" he asked, running his hands between my thighs, testing me for wetness and finding copious amounts.

"Super-respectful, sir," I assured him, wriggling to get his touch exactly where I wanted it. He withdrew it at once.

"Didn't I say you weren't allowed any more orgasms today?" he reminded me sternly.

I thought better of voicing protest. I still had five to go with that salad-tossing fiend and I didn't want any additions.

"No more," he said, rubbing and teasing my clit. "Not a single one." He pushed two fingers inside me and used his thumb to keep up the pressure on my swelling bud. "Not until we're both satisfied with your behaviour."

"Oh God," I gasped, feeling my arousal build to titanic proportions. It wouldn't take much to tip me over the edge now, with my bottom so hot and sore and my nipples throbbing from the clamps and the whole humiliating, exciting thrill of my position.

"If you come now," said Fox, still teasing my soaking pussy, "I'll have you cut a switch and I'll wear it out on you, once I've finished paddling you."

That was enough to sober me up. They'd switched me once before, on a woodland walk out in the sticks, and I was in no hurry at all to repeat the experience. I tensed down below and thought hard about the research I'd been doing for Fox into stock market flotation.

He noted the change in me and was moved to mercy. Well, not really mercy, given that he was about to smack me with a large wooden implement again, but what passed for it in Fox's world.

The last five strokes burnt down to deep tissue, leaving their crimson imprints on my oil-streaked cheeks. I imagined they'd be there for some time to come.

I yelped and spluttered through them, while Emmett made remarks about how good I looked with a properly spanked bottom and how they should make it a daily ritual.

"I'm game if you are," said Fox. "I'm not so sure about our little pet here, though. What do you say to daily spankings?"

"Whatever you think best, sir," I said, not wanting to jinx myself.

He laughed and rubbed a big palm over my throbbing cheeks.

"Lesson learned, I'd say. Emmett, can you move?"

"Just about."

"Can you pass me that bottle of oil?"

I felt Fox shift to take delivery, my tummy tight at the thought of what he might have in mind. Fox was erect again, his hard length bruising my pubic triangle.

The bottle was the type with a curved silver nozzle at the top. Fox pulled my cheeks apart and placed the cold metal between them, just above my tight pucker.

What he had in mind was becoming clearer.

Oil glugged out and washed its way into the spread crack, dripping on to my thighs and into my pussy lips.

Fox put down the bottle and massaged it slowly and firmly into every cranny, finally introducing his finger into my lubricated back passage.

"You're going to fuck her arse?" said Emmett.

"Mm hmm, and you're going to help me, if you can. So nice and tight, she's obviously been doing her exercises."

It was true. Emmett and Fox made me work those muscles daily, to keep myself in peak condition for their cocks. Once

Fox had prepared me, he pulled out his fingers and had me stand up and face Emmett, which I did with both sets of cheeks aflame. The nipple clamps tinkled as I moved, reminding me of the dull, dragging pain up there.

Fox moved the chair so it faced Emmett and sat back down in it, so that his gown fell open to free his hard cock.

Then he put his hands around my waist and drew me back down, into an almost-sitting position. But before my cheeks could reach the seat, they were diverted so that Fox's cock tip slipped between them and found the greasy pucker they sought. He pulled me back, slowly, slowly, whispering encouragement, until I was taking the first thick inch inside my yielding passage.

To do this with Emmett watching, his eyes glazed, his mouth slightly open, set off an incredible mix of emotions and sensations. Fox made me impale myself the rest of the way, moving his hands up to my breasts, flicking at the dangling clamps.

This made me move faster, and I shut my eyes through the moment of acute pain and sat down hard until my sore cheeks rested on his thighs and I was crammed full.

"Well done," he said, cupping my breasts and giving them a squeeze. "Emmett, take a picture, would you?"

Emmett snapped us enthusiastically. My legs were open, resting on top of Fox's, so he got quite a view.

"Now, if you can, I'd like you to grab the dildo from the side table and put it inside her."

Emmett rose slowly from his chair, took the large silicone fake cock, and came to kneel—again with exquisite carefulness —in front of us. Before following Fox's direction, he kissed my clit, very gently but enough to make me moan with need for more.

I wasn't going to get more, though. Instead, the cold, smooth dildo penetrated me, moving up inside me until I felt it nudge Fox's cock, the two heads separated by just a small partition.

"Perfect," said Fox. "How does that feel, pet?"

"Very full," I wailed. I knew I was going to come, no matter what, and then I would be punished again.

"Now, I want you to tuck your legs either side of mine…so your knees are up and your feet flat on the seat…can you manage? Keep your thighs wide…like that."

Moving from legs out to bent was a tricky manoeuvre without dislodging either of the foreign bodies in my channels, but I managed it somehow, with the handy help of Fox and Emmett.

"There now…" Fox's breath came in shorter bursts. "Emmett, can you keep hold of the end of the dildo and give it a bit of a jiggle now and then?"

"I think so," said Emmett, who now leaned against the table to the side of us, his hand at the base of the dildo. He gave it an experimental twist and thrust and I responded with a shuddering moan.

"Good, so now…I think…this position will work…" Fox took hold of my hips and performed a motion that was half withdrawal and half pushing me forward. I felt the rude in-and-out of his cock in my bottom, echoed by Emmett's fidgeting with the dildo. It was hard work and required every ounce of muscular strength I possessed, but the overpowering sensations it conferred were worth it.

Both Fox and I worked together, shoving and thrusting, pushing back and sliding out, while Emmett manned the dildo as best he could between our machinations. The nipple clamps rattled and swung in perfect rhythm, until Fox reached up and removed them, causing me to yelp as the feeling flooded back into my numbed buds.

"Don't you dare come," he whispered into my ear, which—as he must have known—switched me straight away into my highest gear of arousal.

"Oh…no…" I panted. Emmett moved his thumb to my clit and began to strum. "Please…don't make me…don't make me…"

Fox pounded between my cheeks, the chair squeaking and skipping all over the patio. Emmett leant down and kissed me, sucking my tongue into his mouth while he kept the dildo in cruel motion.

I was utterly beaten. Nothing could stop me coming now. My vision whited out and I howled into Emmett's mouth while my orgasm stripped out every mechanism of control in my body and mind and left me helpless in its thrall.

"Oh, excuse me, I am so sorry."

Franco stood, eyes on stalks, at the patio door, saucepan in hand, apparently looking for somebody to discuss the evening meal with.

He disappeared into the depths of the kitchen, and I lay my broken head back on Fox's shoulder and hid my face inside his gown.

"Oops," said Emmett with a self-conscious chuckle, kissing my forehead.

"It's OK," whispered Fox, his lips all over my neck. Had he come? I couldn't be sure. I think he might have done, but I was so swept away in my own climax that nothing else had registered. "Emmett, can you go in and talk to him about dinner? I need to finish up here."

Emmett nodded, his cheeks pink with more than sunburn, and followed the startled chef into his lair. Fox managed to half-stand, with me still attached, and put me on my knees on the cushion that still lay at his feet. He continued to fuck my boneless, exhausted body for another minute or so while the world around me turned pink and black and starry, until he came inside me and the pair of us lurched on to the sun-warmed tiles and lay there, spooned and immobile, panting and sticky.

"Poor Franco," I said, when my lips would frame words again.

"Don't you worry about Franco," said Fox with a weary chuckle. "He was chosen for more than his culinary skills. His broad mind, for one thing."

"Really?"

"Met him on a fetish website."

"Ah."

He stroked my hair and peeked over my shoulder, ready to take my unsuspecting mouth with his. The kiss was both dirty and sweet and took us through the softening and removal of his cock from my back passage.

"I'm sorry I came," I said, breaking off, running my fingers through his beard.

"Well, don't worry about that for now," he said. "We can save that for another day, I think."

"Mm. Good. Charles?"

"Mm?"

"I think I love you."

I felt his chest heave against me, heard the grateful exhalation.

"You know how I feel about you," he said.

"What are we going to do? How is this going to work?"

"Well." He laid my head beside his, on the cushion, looking into me. "I haven't been here before, Jo, so I don't know. But I do know that we'll *make* it work—you and me and Emmett—because we love each other. So don't worry or overthink it too much, love. If it's meant to work, it'll work."

Emmett came back out, smiling benevolently down at us.

"You've still got that dildo up you," he remarked to me.

"Never mind," I sighed. "How was Franco?"

"Turned on, if you ask me. I told him we'd go out with him and his dom one night—I hope that was OK?"

"He's submissive?" I sat up groggily, blinking in the heavy sunlight.

"Yeah, and gay, but maybe we could sort out some kind of scene together. I don't know. Up to you."

"A night out's fine," I said. "Let's just go with the flow as far as anything else is concerned."

I put my arms out, begging Emmett to come and join us on the tiled floor.

"That might be painful," he said warily, but he managed to kneel and then sprawl beside me, positioning himself so that I lay snug between him and Fox.

"Are you OK, Joe?" said Fox sleepily.

"I'm fine," I said, but he laughed.

"No, I was talking to Emmett. Sorry. Old nickname."

"You called him Joe?"

"He once described himself to me as 'an ordinary Joe', which I found funny, because he's very far from that. So I kept calling him it…for a while anyway. I got the company to list it as his middle name at one point."

"Oh my God," I said. "Emmett J Marlow. Is that the J?"

"Busted at last," said Emmett.

"I was desperate to hear you say your full name in the wedding vows, but you never did…because it isn't your real full name. You know, that was the first thing I ever said to him. Asked him what the J stood for on his name card. Well…wow."

"I brought you together," said Charles. "Two ordinary Joes, who will never, ever be ordinary."

"You can say that again," said Emmett, then, after a pause, "These tiles are killing me. Shall we just all pile into a bed? And forget about having separate rooms?"

We rose, with much complaining and staggering, to our feet and proceeded through the villa, half-naked, very clearly post-coital, past a pot-clanging Franco, into the room formerly designated as mine and Emmett's.

It belonged to all of us now.

The future was in triplicate.

ABOUT THE AUTHOR

Justine Elyot is the author of best selling erotic novels *On Demand* and *The Business of Pleasure*, as well as enough short stories to fill several anthologies.

She can often be found moaning about stuff on Twitter. @JustineElyot

OTHER SINFUL PRESS TITLES

Lightning Source UK Ltd.
Milton Keynes UK
UKHW042327311018
331570UK00001B/13/P